THE
GIRL WHO
COULD FLY

THE
GIRL WHO
COULD FLY

victoria forester

SCHOLASTIC INC.

New York Toronto London Auckland
Sydney Mexico City New Delhi Hong Kong

ISBN 978-0-545-24392-6

12 11 10 9 8 7 6 5 4 3 2 1   10 11 12 13 14 15/0

Printed in the U.S.A.   40

First Scholastic printing, January 2010

To be nobody but yourself in a world which is doing its best,
night and day, to make you everybody else
means to fight the hardest battle which any human
being can fight; and never stop fighting.

e e cummings

CHAPTER ONE

PIPER DECIDED to jump off of the roof. It wasn't a rash decision on her part.

This was her plan—climb to the top of the roof, pick up speed by running from one end all the way to the other. Jump off.

Finally, and most importantly, don't fall.

She didn't make plans in the event that she did fall, because if you jump off of the roof of your house and land on your head, you really don't need any plans from that point on. Even Piper knew that.

So that's what she did. She jumped clean off of her roof.

But before we get to what happens next, you'll probably need to know a thing or two about a thing or two.

Piper lived with her ma and pa on a farm. It wasn't much of a farm to be sure, just an old clapboard house and a bank barn that leaned dangerously to the left. For longer than anyone could remember, the McClouds had lived in Lowland County on those same twenty rocky acres of land. Piper's grandpa and great-grandpa and great-great-grandpa, and so on and so on, all breathed their first, last, and everything in between right in the same house where Piper was born, and because of that, the McClouds never planned to live anywhere else. Betty McCloud felt that folks ought to stay in one place and not move around too much so that the Almighty knew where to find them if He needed to.

"If the good Lord wanted things to keep changing all the time, then the sun wouldn't rise up the same way every blessed morning." Betty was a plain, no-nonsense, solidly round woman who believed in only two things: the Good Book and something that she called "providence," as in—

"I told Millie Mae not to fool with that newfangled gardening hoe. Can't say I'm surprised them black beetles is eating clear through her tomatoes now. It's providence, I tell you. Providence."

Unlike Millie Mae, Betty McCloud never tempted providence.

Joe McCloud, a lanky man with sun-weathered skin the color of browned autumn leaves, never said a word about providence, but then he never said much about anything. If pressed with a question, he'd likely ponder it for a long stretch before finding the words to answer in his measured way, "Well, that's just the way things is." And the way things was, was plenty good enough for Joe McCloud.

So it was in this manner that Betty and Joe quietly went about the business of tending to their land, as the seasons and years passed them by, one no different from the next. And never was it heard to be said in Lowland County that a McCloud didn't do things as they were supposed to be done. That is, until someone said precisely that.

"No, I ain't. It's not the way of things." Betty McCloud argued with Doc Bell when he announced that she was pregnant. After all, Betty had celebrated no less than twenty-five barren years of marriage and was no longer considered a young woman.

Four months later Betty McCloud birthed a baby girl.

That baby girl was named Piper. Piper McCloud.

News of Piper's birth traveled with great speed through the remote fields of Lowland County, where cows outnumbered people by a ratio of ninety-three to one.

"It's not the way of things," Millie Mae hotly declared to the ladies' Tuesday afternoon sewing circle, each one of whom immediately pressed her ears more closely inward. "Fancy a woman Betty McCloud's age prancing around with a newborn baby! A first-time mother at that. It ain't right!"

Many of the ladies nodded in agreement. Dire predictions soon followed that the child was sure to grow up queer in such circumstances, and without a sibling to boot.

For the first time in her life Betty McCloud was tempting providence. And she knew it. She certainly didn't need the whispers of local gossip to inform her of the fact. In an attempt to restore balance and appease providence, Betty and Joe set about the business of strictly rearing Piper in the prescribed way that McClouds were raised. Which is to say, without a lot of fuss and nonsense and a solid portion of hard farmwork thrown in for good measure. They were simple and honest farmers and they didn't hold with any fancy child-rearing notions that some city folks got into their heads.

Much to their relief, Piper was what every other baby was. At first. It was only when Piper reached the age when most babies were learning to crawl that her development took an entirely different turn.

It was a Thursday afternoon like any other that Betty set about changing Piper's diaper on the kitchen table, no differently than she'd done a hundred times before. When Betty turned away for just one moment, Piper rolled, quick as a flash, off of the edge of the table. Now any other baby would have immediately fallen to the floor and screamed itself silly. Not Piper. To Betty's astonishment, Piper simply *floated* in the air next to the table.

"Lord save us," Betty choked, her hand clutching the terrified swallow inside her chest. Piper giggled and bobbed up and down in the air.

Betty quickly scooped Piper into her arms and held tightly on to her from that moment on. The word *providence* flashed through Betty's mind. *This is what you get when you don't do things as they should be done,* the left side of her head said to the right.

As time passed, and despite Betty's sincere prayers, the situation got worse, not better. Piper was discovered bobbing about the parlor ceiling and either wouldn't or couldn't return to the ground. Joe was dispatched out to the shed to fetch the ladder. Several weeks later in the wee hours of the night, Joe discovered Piper sleep-floating several feet above her crib. Then there was that particularly gusty day when Piper suddenly took to floating and was swept up in a wind that carried her three full fields before she became snared in the branches of a tree and Joe was able to fetch her down.

When Piper reached the age of five and was still known to unexpectedly float across a room, Betty finally felt that the time had come to broach the matter.

"Seems like she ain't normal is all I'm sayin'," Betty helplessly offered to Doc Bell.

"How's that?" Doc Bell questioned. Doc Bell had seen generations come and go and all manner of things happen to them in Lowland County. He'd seen the youngest Smith boy cough up a screwdriver and a whole package of two-inch nails. He'd been there when Clara Cassie Mareken's head turned all of the way around and then back again. Doc Bell had even seen a grown man talk backwards after he was bumped on the head by a hay baler. The little girl dangling her legs off of his examining table had ten fingers and ten toes, was no taller or smaller, no smarter or dumber, no thinner or fatter than a child her age should be. She was, in short, like every other child in the farming community of Lowland.

"Well, Mr. McCloud and I, we've been noticing that she's . . ." stammered Betty, not sure exactly how to describe her condition, ". . . well, she's a might high-spirited."

Doc Bell chuckled and turned away to wash his hands. "A child her age should have plenty of energy to spare, but it isn't anything you need worry yourselves about. Give her plenty of exercise and lots of fresh air. Nothing wrong with her, she's as normal as you or I."

When Doc Bell turned back around, he discovered that Piper had somehow managed to hoist herself five feet into the air, where she was dangling on the light fixture that hung from the ceiling. There she began to swing back and forth. For the briefest of moments, Doc Bell looked into Betty's alarmed face and the notion that Piper McCloud might indeed be more than high-spirited crossed his mind. Doc Bell was a man of science, though, and so he naturally let the matter go.

"You've got a little monkey on your hands, Mrs. McCloud." Doc Bell chuckled.

And upon that medical recommendation and with great relief, Betty decided to let the child be. All the same, she felt it wise to homeschool Piper until such time that her high spirits, however normal they might be, were . . . well, less high.

By her ninth birthday Piper had long nut-brown hair that was fixed into two braids, bright blue eyes (which she liked), more freckles than the sky had stars (which she hated), and her most constant companion was loneliness, as well as some other feeling she couldn't quite place a name to.

"Ever think something's not right but you can't get at it, Pa?" Perched atop a fence, Piper watched Joe as he fixed a loose blade on the plough.

Joe shrugged uncertainly.

"It's like I got an itch right in here," Piper continued, pointing to her midsection just below her ribs, "but I can't get at it and it just keeps scratching at me and scratching at me, but on the inside. You reckon maybe there's something that'll make it stop itching so?"

Joe shrugged again. He often felt dizzy when Piper talked to him. It wasn't that the words she used were so different—heck, Piper talked like everyone else in Lowland County. It was the ideas that the child got into her head. She asked questions he wouldn't have thought up in a million years and couldn't begin to figure an answer to.

"I told Ma about it the other day and she figured it was caused by all the fool ideas I had in my head." Piper continued, heedless of her father's inability to respond. "I didn't think my ideas were fool but Ma says that I'd do better to keep quiet, keep my feet on the ground, and to mind my own business. She says it's wrong to be frittering away my hours asking questions when there's work to be done. But I don't see how a question can be wrong. Can you, Pa? Ma says the Bible sets out what's right and wrong so we don't have to bother ourselves with it none but it seems to me that it ain't so matter-of-fact. Like when you kilt that old cow last week and I didn't want to eat it 'cause he was my favorite and so gentle besides. Ma said I was sinful to waste food. But I said that maybe we shouldn't go about killing and eating cows when they was so peaceful-like. Ma said that was foolishness and that God put the cows here just so as we can eat 'em. But that don't seem like such a good deal for the cows to me. Preacher told us not more than four Sundays ago that God loves all his creatures, but it ain't loving to my way of thinking to create a thing just for it to be food. Them cows ain't never done nothing to us. Which got me to thinking that maybe we got it wrong and they got a purpose we don't know nothing about. Maybe it's a secret. So I started watching the cows, quiet-like so they wouldn't notice, aiming to see if I couldn't guess that purpose. And I think I knows it now, Pa. I do. Wanna hear?"

Joe drew his forearm across his brow to steady the dizziness. Somehow this conversation had spiraled out of control and he was about to learn the secret destiny of cows, a revelation that Joe McCloud was not ready for. Not ready by a long shot. Had he known how to stop Piper from continuing, he would have. Alas, all he could do was stand helplessly rooted to the spot as Piper continued.

Which, of course, Piper did.

"It was the way they was flicking their tails to ward off the flies that gave it away." Piper leaned in toward Joe and lowered her voice secretively lest the chickens catch wind of her words. "You see, all of them was doing it but one. The black heifer with the brown eyes was just standing real still, looking off to the next field over where the sheep was grazing. The flies were buzzing around her just the same as the others but her tail stayed dead still. So I got to watching that cow and every day she did the same thing until I realized what she was looking at."

"What?" Joe asked, breathlessly unaware that he posed the question.

"The place where her calf done died on her not more than six months 'fore. Remember?"

Joe nodded. Indeed he did remember. It had been a difficult birth and the weakened calf had only lived a few hours before it passed on.

"She's mourning him something terrible and it seems to me that if a cow can feel so for its young'un, then it's probably got feelings about all sorts of things. Feelings we don't know nothing about. And then I got to thinking that if each of them cows got feelings, then they can have a purpose no different from us folks. Which got me thinking about our purpose. And I realized that a person should get a handle on their purpose in this life if they aim to do something about it. You know what I mean, Pa?" Piper looked into her father's face and found only lines of confusion.

"Piper McCloud!!!" Betty squawked as she emerged from the henhouse to find Joe, once again, standing like a fool listening to the child.

Joe sheepishly got back to working on the plough while Piper scrambled from the fence.

"But I was just telling Pa how . . ."

"I couldn't care less about your fool ideas and stories.

When there's work to be done I expect you to do it. Now git."

Several days later in the heat of the afternoon, Piper escaped to the biggest oak tree on the farm and climbed halfway up it to enjoy the breeze that rustled through the leaves there. The itch inside her was acting up and wouldn't give her any peace, and so she rolled over on the branch and held her stomach. From her position, she could spy a robin landing on her nearby nest, where she began feeding a fat worm to her babies. Watching the robin, Piper let her mind wander.

Maybe other kids my age have the same itch. Piper considered. *Maybe if I could talk to 'em they'd tell me how to get at it.* Fat chance that was ever going to happen, what with her stuck out on the farm and all. *I never get to go nowheres or do nothing,* Piper thought to herself. *Only two places I've ever been is church and Doc Bell's.*

"Why can't I go to school like them Miller kids?" Piper had asked her mother a thousand times. Each morning Piper watched them from the hayloft walking to school. She'd have given her front teeth to go with them.

"You do your schoolwork just as well here, that's why." Betty, as always, was plain and to the point.

All of a sudden Piper was roused from her thoughts

11

by an unexpected drama that was unfolding on the branch before her very eyes. The mother robin was nudging one of her babies toward the edge of the nest. The little fellow was hardly bigger than Piper's thumb and had a smattering of feathers poking out of him. Using her beak, the robin gave her baby a good shove that pushed him clear out of the nest, over the branch, and into the air. To Piper's horror, the baby robin dropped like a stone in a flurry of wing flapping. But then, just as he was about to hit the ground, he managed to pump his wings so hard that he stopped falling and started slowly, very slowly, rising. Right then and there that little bird learned to fly, and Piper saw the whole thing.

"Holy moly," Piper breathed and shook her head in wonder. It was the darndest thing she'd ever seen. Then the mother robin did it again and her second baby was born into flight. By the time the third baby was being readied for takeoff, Piper was struck by a lightning of an idea.

Piper sat bolt upright on the branch, almost falling off of it completely. Grabbing hold with both hands, she steadied her body while her mind raced like a jackrabbit.

From the moment she was born, Piper had floated. It came naturally to her, like breathing. Because she'd always done it, she didn't think it was such a big deal. One minute she'd be sitting on the rug in front of the fire and the next she'd be bobbing up to the ceiling. It happened all of the time and it was fun. The problem with floating was that you never knew where it would take you, which wasn't all bad, but sometimes a person likes to have a bit more direction in their life than to be at the whim of any strong breeze. There's a big difference between floating and flying. Clouds float. Balloons float. But birds fly.

Maybe Ma and Pa just forgot to push me like them baby birds, Piper considered, knowing full well that she was going to have to take matters into her own hands. *It's high time I got to flying too.*

Not wanting to waste any time, Piper quickly shimmied down the tree trunk and immediately set about formulating a plan.

The very next morning Piper woke up before the rooster crowed. The sky was just beginning to glow in the east as she eased her way out of bed. Pushing open her window, she was able to slide across the ledge until her feet hit the shingles. From there it was hard work to crawl up to the ridgepole. She stayed on her hands and knees and moved slowly.

The roof was slick with dew. Just one wrong move and quick as a flash she'd slide right off. She kicked her long, white nightgown away to stop it from tripping up her feet.

It was when Piper had climbed to the very top of the roof and was balancing on the ridgepole that she realized exactly how scared she was. To be precise, she was terrified. All of a sudden Piper knew that there was a big difference between planning something and actually doing it. The roof was steep and high, and below it the ground was as hard as a rock. If things went wrong, she was going to get hurt, and hurt badly. Piper's breath caught in her throat and for a moment she couldn't breathe at all.

Her thoughts came fast and furious then. *What if I can't fly? What if I smack the ground with my head? Maybe my brains will spill out all over the place and then I ain't never gonna leave the farm and make a friend. Maybe it's best I hightail it back to bed and forget the whole notion.*

Now perhaps it was because Piper didn't yet believe in a right way or a wrong way of doing things, and so for her, all things were still possible. Or maybe it's because the itch deep inside Piper that no one, least of all herself, could get at was itching so much it was going to drive her crazy. Or it could have been the same reason that Piper was able to float—which is to say, no one really knows. Whatever reason it was, Piper stayed on that roof and didn't go back to bed. Instead she raised her arms up at her sides like an airplane and placed one foot in front of the other. With fear, courage, and anticipation all mixing together in her stomach, she began to walk the ridgepole of her house.

Just below where Piper walked, Betty McCloud woke

with a start. She had heard something, that much was certain.

"Mr. McCloud," she hissed. Joe didn't stir.

"Mr. McCloud!" This time Betty punctuated her words with a sharply placed elbow to Joe's ribs and his eyes flew open. "There's someone on our rouf!"

"What's that?" Joe mumbled, half awake.

"The rouf! Someone's on our rouf!" Betty pointed upward and Joe heard a scuffling sound above his head.

With each step Piper took, she picked up speed, until she was running down the ridgepole and fast approaching the place where there was only sky and no roof left.

"Like the birds I will fly." Piper imagined the baby robins.

And then there was only one step left to take. Piper took it, thrusting herself with abandon into the morning air.

It was the cows grazing in the field that were the only ones to see Piper's trajectory. What they saw was a small girl in a long, white nightgown jumping off of the roof and into the sky.

For one blissful moment she hung in the air, like an angel.

Then, just as quickly, the moment passed and that same young girl fell headfirst, like a freight train, toward the ground below.

The cows had never seen a human do such a thing

before and they watched in moo-less astonishment. Not much ever changed on the farm and even cows can do with a bit of excitement.

Just as Piper approached the first bedroom window, it flew open and Joe, his twelve-gauge shotgun in hand, poked his head out. Joe was completely prepared to deal with a mischievous raccoon or that sassy brown squirrel trying to nest in the roof again. He was even ready to tangle with one of the pesky Carlton boys out rabble-rousing. A young girl hurtling through the air in an attempt to fly, however, was completely outside Joe McCloud's repertoire of possible eventualities.

"Ahhhhhhh!" Piper screamed as she screwed her eyes tightly shut.

"What the . . . ???"

Joe's eyes bulged at the sight of Piper plummeting at him. He threw himself backwards to avoid a head-on collision and ended up tripping on Betty, who was lurking fearfully behind him. His long legs tangled around themselves and he was sent sprawling onto the bedroom floor, which was a good thing too, because he placed himself in the perfect spot to cushion Betty's fall a moment later. So positioned, they did not see Piper falling past their window.

In three seconds Piper was going to hit the ground headfirst. It was going to hurt . . . a lot.

Now, three seconds isn't a long time. You can count to three faster than you can read this. Try it. See.

The largest of the cows, the one with a black patch across its right eye, let out a *moooo* in spite of himself. If it was possible to understand cow mooing, it's quite likely he was trying to warn Piper.

Piper's eyes were squeezed shut and her face twisted in certain anticipation of the coming impact.

She was not more than a heartbeat away from eating dirt when the miraculous happened. Like a plane in an air show, Piper grazed the ground in a death-defying loop that changed her course by a hundred and eighty degrees and turned her face from the ground to the sky. She sailed upward with the unexpected thrust and precision of an F-22 Raptor.

With her eyes clenched shut, Piper continued to brace for an impact that never came.

"Cockle-doodle-doo," the rooster crowed.

It wasn't until Piper was touching the blue and gold of the rising sun—and the mist of a cloud doused her face with a fine, cool tickle—that she allowed herself a tiny peek through her right eye. The vision she caught out of it was so surprising and strange that she closed it tightly again. She tried the view from her other eye and it proved to only mirror her first glimpse. Slowly, very slowly, she opened both eyes.

Oh, but what a world she saw!

The green fields rolled out in every direction and glistening streams cut through some of them. The clouds disappeared into mist the closer she flew toward them and the breeze lifted her higher.

Piper dipped and dived, twirled and whirled in a sky that was every color from white to blue to orange to pink.

"Wheeeeee," Piper gleefully screamed.

"I can FLY," she called out to the morning sun. "I CAN FLY!"

In the farmhouse below, Joe and Betty unsteadily rose to their feet. Gripping the edge of the windowsill, they peered out and caught their first glimpse of a little girl in a white nightgown flying through the air.

And at long last there was no doubt in either of their minds that their daughter, Piper McCloud, did not do things as they had always been done.

For once Betty could think of nothing to say. Instead, she watched Piper fly back and forth until the world began to spin and black dots appeared before her eyes, and she sank down to the floor in a dead faint.

CHAPTER TWO

I F THE good Lord wanted folks to fly, then he'd have gone and given 'em wings. That's what." Betty paced back and forth in the parlor like a wet hen with a bad case of lice. Dazed and sick with worry, Joe merely shook his head or nodded in agreement to whatever it was she said.

Piper had fantasized about her parents being jubilant. In reality, she'd have been satisfied with happy. At that moment she was even willing to settle for not mad. "But . . . din't ya see? *I. CAN. FLY.*" She emphasized each word, just in case there was confusion on anyone's part as to what had just transpired.

"That flying ain't normal. It ain't natural. Lord above, if the new minister were to see ya, there's no tellin' the things he'd preach at us."

"But—"

"And when Millie Mae gets to gossiping about

this . . . heaven protect us! You don't see other youngens gadding about in the sky, do ya?"

"But I don't gets to see no other youngens 'cause you won't let me," Piper argued, finally getting a word in.

"Watch your lip, little missy. I din't raise a child to sass me back," Betty warned. "And I kin tell ya they don't fly. And neither should you. It's just plain wrong."

"But—"

"It ain't the way of things." Betty clutched her night-clothes about her, fuming. "You listenin' to me, Piper McCloud?"

"But Ma . . ." Joy was busting out of the place inside Piper that not more than a day before had been a terrible itch. "Maybe there's a reason for it. Something special. Like the way you says the Lord works in mysterious ways and—"

"Don't you take the Lord's name in vain."

"But I—"

"Piper, my mind's made up and there ain't no changing it or arguing around it. There ain't no earthly cause for a youngen to be meddling about up in the sky. I'm putting my foot down." Betty wagged her index figure at Piper in utter seriousness. "No more flying and that's all there is to it. Ya hear?"

"But—" Piper was promptly silenced by the grim determination in Betty's eyes. *This is just plum crazy,*

Piper fumed inwardly. They might as well have asked her to stop breathing air as to expect her to turn her back on the wonders of flying. The fact of the matter is, the minute you get a mouthful of blue sky dancing across your taste buds there's no keeping you from it. No matter how much trouble you'll be getting yourself into.

Betty and Joe accepted Piper's stunned silence as agreement. "Sure as anything you'd get attacked by some rabid bird. It ain't no place for a youngen up there." Betty sniffed, considering the matter closed.

And so Piper meekly nodded her head and let her folks believe what they wanted. First chance she got, though, she rushed off to the back field where no one would see her. Shaking with anticipation, she scrambled atop a boulder jutting from the side of the hill and threw herself off it and . . . landed on her backside. HARD.

"Owwww."

Getting up, she dusted herself off and did it again. Wouldn't you know it but it happened a second time. Piper couldn't have been stuck tighter to the ground than if her feet had been glued to it. Not that she let that stop her from trying for one single minute.

Piper jumped. And fell. And jumped. And fell. That was how Piper spent her first day of practice.

It was discouraging to say the least, but it taught Piper

a valuable lesson—flying doesn't come easy, even if you're a natural-born floater. Raw talent only gets you so far in this old world and the rest is a whole lot of practice, persistence, and perspiration. She got lucky on her first jump. Beginner's luck. But from there on out, Piper fought tooth and nail to get herself back up into the sky and to be a real, honest-to-goodness flier.

Days and weeks passed by and Piper continued to practice every single day with little or no success. She often wished that she had someone to teach her instead of having to figure it all out herself. Each mistake cost her a bruise or a bump, and her body was fast becoming a black-and-blue testament to her many trials and errors.

Lesson one, as Piper soon discovered, was: Never think about the ground. Ever. The second she even considered the possibility that she might fall, she fell and some part of her body was hitting some part of the earth. The sky was her goal, and she trained her mind to think of nothing else.

As soon as Piper mastered the whole thinking part, she was able to get back up into the sky, and that was when she stumbled across lesson two: You can fly without having to actually jump off of anything. The first step in achieving this, as Piper learned, was to stand perfectly still and close her eyes. Then with all her might, she'd think:

I'm as light as a cloud, as free as a bird.
I'm part of the sky and I can fly.

(But the trick to it was that she'd think that and *nothing else* and then hold the thought for a long, long time. Try it, it's a lot harder than you might think.)

Then her whole body would get relaxed and this tingling sensation would start pumping right out of her heart and spread like wildfire through every place in her body, until she was almost burning up with all of the tingling, and that was when her feet would rise up off of the ground and she'd be flying.

Two weeks after she started practicing, Piper was finally able to get into the sky and stay there. It happened on a Tuesday.

Piper was hot from standing in the field under a blistering sun and focusing with every ounce of her being. "Dang it all," she muttered after a third failed attempt at lifting off.

Taking her position again, she stood very, very still and thought only one thought with all of her might. Tingling began to fill her body. And then she thought the thought harder—*I'm part of the sky and I can fly*. The tingling grew and grew and that was when her feet left the ground. *I'm as light as a cloud, as free as a bird*. She rose higher and higher. The farther she went, the lighter she felt, and still she clung to the thought. At forty feet into the air, higher than she'd ever gone, she stopped.

"I'm a flier," she whispered and felt a strong sense of relief and pride. It felt so natural to be in a sky full of clouds and have birds flying past. Like a homecoming. She also noticed that flying up high made all of the things she left behind on the ground seem not as important. They were so small, after all, and the sky was so big.

Swooping over the summer crops of corn, wheat, oats, and barley, she dipped down low and picked stalks as she passed. Over Clothespin Creek she watched the fish swimming way deep down at the bottom, something you can't see when your feet are stuck in soil. And there was so much more for her to see, but before she knew it, it was the dinner hour and time to land.

From that moment on, the sky was no longer the limit. In the days that followed, Piper got to see the world for the first time, or at least the world of Lowland County. She saw Mr. Stanovislak selling white lightning from a still hidden in the woods, Jessie Jake kissing Beth Belle (his best friend's girl) behind his cowshed, and old maid Gertie Gun dramatically reading dime-store romance novels aloud in her pumpkin patch.

She saw other things too: a young fawn delicately taking its first drink from a clear stream; a big brown bear scratching his back against a rock so rigorously that the rock actually rolled away and down a hill; and at the top of an oak tree, the biggest beehive she'd ever seen. Five nasty stings later, she decided not to fly by that particular oak tree again.

Unwittingly, Piper was also responsible for the religious conversion of old man Jessup. While working on his roof, he caught a fleeting glimpse of Piper flying past and instantly mistook her for an angel sent by his recently departed wife. Without delay, the old man, who'd sworn never to set foot in church again, got down on his knees, confessed all of his sins, and, to the astonishment of all, didn't miss church once from that day on. The new minister thanked God. Piper thanked her lucky stars that old man Jessup wasn't wearing his glasses.

Piper was very careful not to fritter away all of her time sightseeing. She considered herself a serious flier, not a tourist, and set an ambitious learning schedule, which included landing practice, ascent and descent, velocity control, and hovering. Unfortunately, Piper was not a particularly fast learner and there was much more error than trial to her flying.

"Piper, you ain't yerself these days." Betty abruptly passed a bowl of string beans to Piper, rousing her from her exhaustion. It had been a hard day of flying and Piper had yet to touch her dinner. Looking up, she noticed that both her ma and pa were watching her with concern.

"Ever since that morning when we catch you . . . well, since *it* happened, it's like you been walking 'bout the place like you was whipped. If you ain't at your studies or your chores, you're off somewheres that we can't find you and you're getting so thin you'll fade right away 'fore our very eyes." Betty couldn't help but notice of late that the child wasn't herself anymore, and was shocked to find the house empty and too quiet without Piper's endless questions and unexpected floating. It was like the spark had gone right out of Piper, and Betty feared her spirit had been crushed.

"I'm sorry, Ma." Truth be told, it took up Piper's energy learning how to fly, and her body hurt from the bruises that had piled up on top of her bruises. Most nights she'd fall asleep at the dinner table before she even touched her food.

"Your pa and I got to talking some," Betty continued, "and seeing how you ain't as high-spirited as you was and it's getting so we can hardly recognize you, we was figuring it was high time we all attended the Fourth of

July picnic. We reckoned it'd be just the thing to raise your spirits up some."

"A picnic?" Piper was more shocked than a turkey on Thanksgiving. "I get to go to the picnic next week too, Ma? You mean with all the other kids?"

"Well, don't get all out of control on me now. But you can, if you continue to behave yourself like the good Lord would want."

Piper almost shot up off of the ground like a rocket and did pinwheels in the air while yelling, "Yeee-hawww" at the top of her lungs like a crazed chicken (but didn't) and from that moment on battled a frenzied ecstasy inside her chest.

For the next week Piper thought nonstop about the picnic. *P-I-C-N-I-C,* she spelled it in her mind. Or sometimes she'd do it backwards, *C-I-N-C-I-P.* When she wasn't thinking about it, she was peppering her mother with questions.

"Will there be other youngens at the picnic?"

"Likely so."

"Think they'll wanna play with me?"

"Don't see why not."

"Reckon we can stay for the fireworks?"

"For pity's sakes, hold your tongue, child."

Which Piper sincerely tried to do, but failed miserably at.

CHAPTER THREE

"WILL YOU be my friend, Piper?" Sally Sue asked hopefully.

And Piper smiled.

It was the perfect end to a perfect picnic. They'd shared ice cream and Sally Sue had told Piper her worst secret (that she'd snuck her mother's lip rouge and wore it to school) and Piper had told Sally Sue her biggest dream (to fly around the world). Sally Sue had shown Piper how to do a jig and they'd danced under the trees and giggled until their stomachs hurt. When the fireworks came, they lay on the cool grass and watched them explode in the night sky. And that was when Sally Sue became Piper's friend. Later they would become best friends, would be maids of honor at each other's weddings. They'd live next door to each other and their children would play together. Best friends for life. That's how it was going to be.

At least, that is how Piper imagined it being. Over and over again in great detail until her imagined picnic fantasy seemed a concrete reality.

And then at long last, there was finally no more need for the fantasy because in reality Piper stood between Betty and Joe on the lawn of the First Baptist Church, where right before her very eyes was every single soul currently alive in the entire county of Lowland. All ninety-seven of them. It was nothing short of overwhelming to Piper to see such a throng of people amassed in one place.

Picnic tables groaned with peach cobbler, cherry pie, fresh berries, mountains of corn on the cob, ham, and fried chicken, and the barbecue was going strong with ribs. Fourth of July banners and balloons decorated trees and tables alike. Kids bobbed for apples, men threw horseshoes, the new minister and his wife enjoyed the banjo and fiddle played by the Straitharn boys, and women drank lemonade and fanned themselves under the trees. There wasn't a place that Piper could set her eyes where something or other wasn't happening.

"Mind what I says now. Keep your feet—"

"Keep my feet on the ground. I know. I know," Piper absentmindedly repeated, distracted by all of the picnic sights. "You've told me and told me, Ma." Just then Piper spied three girls eating ice cream and her heart skipped a beat. Already the picnic was everything she imagined it was going to be.

For her own part, Betty was drenched in a nervous sweat. Standing on the edge of the lawn on the verge of the picnic, Betty suddenly wasn't sure it was such a good idea. Having spent Piper's entire life keeping her away from folks, Betty had learned to never leave anything to chance. On Sundays she would see to it that they arrived moments before the church service began and would sit in the back pew with Piper firmly wedged between her and Joe. The moment the service was over, Betty made sure that they were the first out the door. Birthday party invites extended to Piper were politely but firmly refused, and any other social events were simply out of the question as far as Betty was concerned. Even when visits to Doc Bell were needed, Betty insisted upon the first appointment of the day so that the waiting room was empty. It was no wonder that it took all of Betty's willpower not to hurry the child back to the farm when faced with the full throttle of peopled activity before her. Maybe she'd jumped the gun and rushed things. Maybe the child wasn't ready.

Joe's lips were twitching nervously as though he wanted to say something but couldn't quite figure out how to translate the thought into sound. When he saw Millie Mae Miller spy them from across the way and practically sprint at Piper, he almost bolted to intercept her. Joe couldn't abide Millie Mae and her gossipy mean-spirited ways. Sure as anything she'd be spreading rumors about Piper before you could say "jackrabbit stew."

"Can I have some ice cream, Ma?" Piper noticed a blond girl with big brown eyes heading for the line of children waiting for ice cream.

"Watch your dress," cautioned Betty, who also saw Millie Mae's pointed attention and was relieved that Piper was escaping her scrutiny.

Moments later Millie Mae trotted up, clearly disappointed that Piper had already moved on. "Weren't that your Piper?" She looked after the child with an intense curiosity that bordered on mania. Millie Mae held the unofficial office of town gossip in Lowland County, and it was a position she took very seriously. Nothing went on in the county that she didn't know about, and relate in vivid detail and at great length to anyone who might be the least bit interested, and even to those who weren't at all interested but were unlucky enough to be cornered by her and unable to get away without being rude. If Betty's greatest fears could be contained in two words, those two words would be *Millie Mae*.

"You keep that child all to yourself too much, Betty. It ain't good for her. It's high time she was out and about," Millie Mae sniffed.

"Didn't see fit to take her out before. Ain't no one worth her time meeting anyways," Betty spat reproachfully.

Joe was careful to hide his smile as the full meaning of Betty's jab hit Millie Mae.

"That so?" Millie Mae cut back. "I heard tell it's 'cause she ain't like other youngens." In truth, the only person who had ever actually said that about Piper was Millie Mae herself.

"That's a fat lie, if I ever heard one. Only a fool would say such a thing. The child's as normal as you or I. Just go ask Doc Bell." Betty was incensed.

"I reckon I'll make up my own mind on that account. Thank ya kindly."

With that, Millie Mae stalked away, her head full of steam. Millie Mae Miller hadn't risen to the post of town gossip for no good reason, and in her gossiping bones she knew that there was something not right about Piper McCloud. May the good Lord help her, today she was going to get to the bottom of it.

Piper got into the line for ice cream behind a girl just about her age. As Piper well knew, that girl's name was Sally Sue Miller. After long years of jealously watching Sally Sue's daily journey to and from school from her perch in the hayloft, Piper was finally standing a foot away from her. As if by some miracle, Sally Sue, who was

32

all but overcome by desire for a creamy cold treat on such a hot afternoon, breathlessly turned to Piper and exclaimed, "My favorite ice cream's strawberry! What's yours?"

"Strawberry." Piper was thrilled that they already had so much in common. "Ever wonder why they call them *straw*berries? I mean, they don't look nothing like straw. They're red."

Sally Sue had never had such a thought but now that she did consider it, she had to admit that it was mighty strange. "Huh, you're right about that."

"Maybe they should call them blush berries. Or rosy-berries."

"Or red berries."

"Or scrumptious berries."

"I ain't never renamed something before."

"Ever wonder what it'd be like to eat nothing but ice cream all the time?" Piper had. "I'd have lamb-chop ice cream for dinner with a side of corn ice cream."

Sally Sue giggled. "I'd have bacon-and-egg ice cream for breakfast."

"Castor-oil ice cream when you're sick." Piper imagined. "And ice-cream toothpaste before bed."

"Ice-cream sandwiches at school." Sally Sue allowed room for Piper to stand next to her in the line. "My name's Sally Sue. What's yours?"

Everything was going exactly as she hoped it would. Piper beamed. "I'm Piper. Piper McCloud."

Suddenly Sally Sue took a step back. "Piper McCloud? I heard my mama talk about you. She says you ain't right in the head."

Piper gasped, outraged. "There ain't nothing wrong with my head!"

Sally Sue looked at Piper's head closely and, indeed, could see nothing wrong with it. She shrugged.

"My mama says there is and she ain't never been wrong before." Sally Sue pointed to where Millie Mae stood watching them and Piper instantly recognized her.

"I can tell you, she's wrong now," Piper insisted. How dare she say such things about her! It was so darned unfair, it made her want to holler. Instead she said, "And your mama shouldn't go around kicking dogs."

Sally Sue's mouth flew open and she blushed deeply. "My mama ain't never kicked no dog."

"Has too." Piper had seen it as plain as day when she'd flown over their house not more than a week ago.

"Has not. And how would you know anyways?" Sally Sue challenged, placing her hands on her hips.

" 'Cause I saw her with my own eyes. That's how. She was right back of your house smoking a pipe and the dog barked and she kicked its bee-hind so hard it yapped." Piper triumphed.

It was a short-lived victory because Sally Sue's eyes began to swim in tears of shame. "You don't know us, how come you know these things?" she whispered and took another step away.

Before Piper could answer, Rory Ray, Sally Sue's oldest brother, came barreling down on them. "Sally Sue, quit your crying or Ma'll pack us all up home." Rory Ray was quickly flanked by the four other brothers.

As an only girl with five older brothers, Sally Sue's life was a torment and the stress was showing. Even her mother had to admit she was a terrible crybaby. "I ain't crying," she wailed.

"You is too. I'll whop you if you start your blubbering."

"It's her fault." Sally Sue nodded at Piper.

"Hey, ugly, d'ya make my sister cry?" Rory Ray redirected his wrath at Piper.

"Uh—uh." Piper didn't know how to answer. She hadn't imagined any scenarios like this when she visualized the picnic.

Sally Sue sniffled loudly.

"Shut your piehole, Sally Sue," Rory Ray barked at her. "Ma's looking this way." The five brothers gathered around Sally Sue, whose face was red, her eyes bulging with unshed tears and her lower lip quivering. She couldn't trust herself to speak so she just pointed at Piper.

Rory Ray shoved Piper to the ground, where she landed in a swirl of dust. Hand-me-down farm boots surrounded her at every turn.

"Leave my sister be, you freak."

"Hey, ain't you the kid who's got something wrong in the head?" One of the brothers kicked dirt in Piper's face.

Piper coughed, choking on the dirt.

"Stupid or no, you'll leave her be. Ya hear, freak?"

"C'mon, Rory Ray. I wanna get me some ice cream," one of the brothers pleaded.

Rory Ray grabbed Sally Sue and dragged her in front of all of the boys in the line, leaving Piper on the ground.

Piper sat in the dirt for a long moment, devastated. In the course of only a handful of minutes, she had found and then lost her best friend. It was a terrible and bitter blow and while the dust swirled around her, Piper mourned the birthday parties, graduations, weddings, and shared birth announcements that were never to be. When the dirt settled, Piper looked up to find Millie Mae Miller's eyes fixed firmly upon her, a sneer twisting at her lips.

Piper hated Millie Mae for laughing at her and telling stories that weren't true. How dare folks judge her when they didn't even know her at all! It wasn't right. Piper's keen sense of justice was tweaked and she immediately resolved to show them exactly how wrong they all were.

Getting to her feet, Piper quickly dusted herself off. Holding her head high, she jutted her chin out and marched right over to a group of kids playing with a ball. If folks thought there was something wrong with her head, then she was going to show them different. All they needed was a chance to get to know her better. By the end of the picnic, she was going to see to it that Millie Mae Miller ate every single one of those ugly words she went around saying. And if Millie Mae got a bellyache from their bitter taste, Piper wouldn't feel sorry for her neither.

Alas, despite Piper's Herculean efforts, late afternoon arrived to find Millie Mae no closer to eating her words and Piper no nearer to securing a friend. Bo Bo and Candy Sue, the sun-kissed Hassifer twins, initially took a shine to Piper but her funny ideas became a distraction from their unabated chatter about, and flirtation with, the many strapping young farm boys who caught their eye. When Piper was unwilling to join them on a trek into the nearby bushes along with the sweaty Stubing brothers, she was quickly discarded.

If Piper had been able to overlook the fact that Jessie Jean Jenkin's chief pleasure was stripping the wings off of struggling flies and then feeding them to her pet spider, Beelzebub, she might have taken Jessie Jean up on the offer of pricking their fingers and becoming blood sisters. Sadly, for Jessie Jean, Piper could not. Then, of course, a lot of the other kids recognized Piper's face from church. Despite the fact that they'd never said more than one word to her, or she to them, Piper's reputation, courtesy of Millie Mae Miller, had preceded her, and not a single Christian soul among them was willing to give her the benefit of the doubt.

While unwilling to admit defeat, Piper realized that things were definitely not going the way she had planned, which was precisely when a baseball game was called to order, providing Piper with a perfect public opportunity to redeem herself and show her true worth. Gathering in the open field next to the picnic, along with the other small fry of Lowland County, Piper watched with fascination as pushing and pulling and shouting kids chaotically organized themselves into teams.

Junie Jane, a tough girl who'd whack any kid who called her a girl, quickly declared herself the captain of one team while Rory Ray took the other. The selection process promptly followed.

"Billy Bob," Rory Ray called out. Billy Bob, a strapping boy who could slug the ball to the moon, lumbered out of the waiting group and took his place behind Rory Ray. The other children jostled to be noticed, Piper among them.

"Piggy Pooh," Junie Jane called out.

"Lizzie Lee," Rory Ray countered.

"Sally Sue," Junie Jane returned.

With a sinking heart, Piper watched as, one by one, everyone else was chosen until she and Timmie Todd remained. Timmie Todd had just turned six and was small for his age. He also had a nasty reputation among the other children for picking his nose and eating it, not to mention the fact that he bathed no more than once a week. Standing next to Timmie Todd, Piper felt humiliated.

Then, as though that were not enough, Rory Ray agonized choosing between the two of them.

"Oh, alright already, I'll take Timmie Todd." Rory Ray kicked the dirt when he said it. Piper was officially the last to be chosen, and her mortification was complete. Or so she thought.

"I don't want her on my team. She's not right in the head," Junie Jane bickered, introducing Piper to the deepest reaches of humiliation.

"If I'm stuck with that," Rory Ray balked, pointing at Timmie Todd, "then you hafta get stuck with her. Fair's fair."

"Ah, beans," Junie Jane spat, but Piper finally had a team.

Bathed in the late afternoon sun, the whole community gathered on the side of the hill to watch and cheer the children's baseball efforts. Betty and Joe McCloud couldn't take their eyes off of Piper. They had seen her attempts to make a friend, and each time she was turned down flat, their hearts got a little heavier.

"Play ball," shouted Junie Jane, and the game began.

BAM! Billy Bob hit the ball hard and straight for the outfield . . . straight for Piper. With her glove held high in the air, Piper reached up, on her very, very tiptoes. She stretched as far as she could, careful not to let her feet leave the ground. Despite her every effort, the ball went right over her head and hit the grass ten feet behind her. She scrambled for it, but her feet clumsily caught on each other, and moments later, she was facedown in the dirt.

"Aw jeeez." Junie Jane spat out her gum in disgust.

Betty and Joe sighed, but Millie Mae Miller nodded at several ladies as though Piper's performance only confirmed her point.

As bad as things seemed for Piper, they somehow managed to get even worse the more the game progressed. Facing Rory Ray, an ace pitcher known for a mean spitball, Piper held the baseball bat aloft, ready to do battle. Half the game was already over and her team needed this base. Their hopes weighed heavily upon Piper's ball-hitting abilities. Rory Ray wound up and threw the ball with all of his might; Piper gave it everything she had and . . .

"You're outta there," Rory Ray called gleefully.

A collective moan rose from her teammates.

At the bottom of the ninth, with two bases loaded and two outs, Billy Bob covered the plate, confidently prepared to hit the home run that would win the game.

Junie Jane, a fighter to the end, called a time-out and gathered Piper and Jimmy Joe to her side.

"Billy Bob's gonna hit hard and far. McCloud, you're on the bench. You'll take McCloud's place on the field, Jimmy Joe." Junie Jane knew that Jimmy Joe could catch a fly in his bare hand on a moonless night. Besides, Piper hadn't caught or hit anything the whole game.

Jimmy Joe reached for the glove in Piper's hand, but Piper held firmly to it.

"I can catch it, Junie Jane," she pleaded.

"You couldn't catch a cold if you lived in Antarctica without a winter coat."

"Could too." Piper was reduced to begging. "Gimme a chance, Junie Jane, I won't let you down. Cross my heart, stick a pin in my eye, and hope to die if I lie." Piper did as many of the arm motions as she could while holding the glove.

"Gimme it." Jimmy Joe pulled roughly on the glove, but still Piper held firm.

Junie Jane was not a soft girl. She didn't coo over puppies, she hated the color pink, and unlike every other girl in school, she hadn't once wished that Rory Ray would kiss her. In spite of herself, she suddenly felt empathy for Piper McCloud. Had things been different, if there hadn't been something wrong with Piper's head, Junie Jane probably would have given her a shot. As it was, Junie Jane wasn't going to blow the game for some retard.

"Give it over." June Jane yanked the baseball glove out of Piper's hands so hard that Piper fell to the ground.

"Y're on the bench, McCloud," Junie Jane yelled as she ran back to the pitcher's mound, her mind already on the next play.

For the second time that day, Piper found herself in the dirt, her humiliation laid out for all of Lowland County to see. Millie Mae Miller was smiling in triumph while pretending to be sympathetic. (Which was not an easy expression to pull off.) Kids were smirking in her direction.

On the side of the hill, Piper saw Betty and Joe, and they looked like they'd been shot clean through the heart. Their features carried the unmistakable look of pity, which drove Piper to feel a deep shame of herself. Why hadn't she been able to catch or hit a ball? Why wasn't she able to make a friend? What a terrible thing it was to have your own ma and pa looking at you as though you were nothing. And Piper felt like nothing.

Burning up, Piper dragged herself out of the dirt and walked away from the game and everyone there. She didn't know where she was going and she didn't care if she ever got there.

On the mound, Junie Jane spat on the ball, wound up, and sent it speeding toward Billy Bob. Billy Bob leaned into it, thrusting his huge shoulders forward. All the eyes in Lowland County rested on him, waiting and urging him on. Their breath stuck in their throats and they couldn't move as the small white ball spun through the air toward the big boy holding an old wooden bat. Billy Bob swung hard and—*CRACK!*

The bat splintered in half with the force of Billy Bob's swing. The ball exploded like a rocket into the air. But to the surprise of all gathered, particularly to Junie Jane, the ball didn't go into the right outfield and the waiting hands of Jimmy Joe as planned. Instead, Billy Bob proved he had more smarts than anyone, including his mama, gave him credit for, and sent that ball into the left outfield, where Gomer Gun was sleepily picking dirty wax out of his abnormally large ears.

Parents, grandparents, great-grandparents, and the minister too got to their feet and followed the ball with keen eyes as it rose higher and higher and then even higher into the air.

Billy Bob caught a freight train to first base, which

instantly ignited his team into unabashed jubilation, while forcing the opposing players into fits of panic.

"Catch that ball, Gomer Gun," Junie Jane hollered.

"Run, Billy Bob," the other team was shouting with all their might. Gomer Gun shook himself into semi-consciousness and ambled his lanky frame into a position that might somehow catch the ball.

"Go, Gomer. Go, Gomer," shouted his team.

Several fathers whistled softly and shook their heads in wonder as the ball continued to climb in the sky. Underneath it, Gomer Gun futilely jumped into the air and swung his arm about, like he was trying to snatch crab apples off of a high branch. It was no use. That ball had grown wings and was reaching for loftier spheres. Gomer Gun's arms came to rest fruitlessly at his sides as he too stood and watched the ball ascending to the celestial realm.

"Awwwwww," Junie Jane spat. "Dawgone it all." She threw her glove down in a very unsportsman-like way and muttered things that would have gotten her a hide-tanning had any parent been within earshot. As the ball sailed away, the entire team deflated and kicked the dirt or took off their ball caps and sighed deeply.

Meanwhile Rory Ray's team was ascending to a fever pitch of excitement as Billy Bob, now complacent with victory, began Sunday-strolling the remaining bases.

In the stir, all but Betty and Joe forgot Piper's retreating form. It was Betty who saw Piper pause as the ball headed her way, high in the air. And it was Betty who saw Piper looking up at the ball with a curious intensity that immediately sent Betty to her feet. With eyes wide and hand reaching for her heart, Betty whispered, "Dear Lord, no."

Piper's entire body was tingling before she could even think straight. There wasn't a doubt in her mind what she was going to do. She was going to catch that ball and show them all.

Let's see a retard do this, you old bat, she thought at Millie Mae spitefully. Less than a second later, Piper's feet lifted off of the ground and she launched upward into the air.

"Holy cow." Jimmy Joe stopped short. "Look!" He was the first, besides Betty and Joe, to see Piper flying. He watched her, rooted to the spot as the color drained from his face. Seeing his reaction, several kids turned to look, and soon expressions of bewildered wonder and confusion spread like wildfire across the field.

Like an arrow shooting through the air, Piper chased after the ball. She made certain that she held her form—arms and legs straight and steady. She hadn't yet practiced retrieval techniques, and chasing a ball through the air is harder than it looks. Once she got her altitude right, she picked up velocity and sped after it.

"You can do it," she cheered herself along as she closed the gap.

The tips of her fingers flirted with the leather of the ball. Lunging to snatch it she missed, then wobbled dangerously on the verge of completely losing control. Adjusting her right arm, she held firm, got her legs back into position, and darted at the ball with all her might. With one final lunge, the spinning orb rested in her victorious hand.

Piper immediately stopped in midflight and looked at the ball in shock. "I did it," she whispered, glad and excited and thrilled all at the same time.

Suddenly Piper became so swept up in her victory that she shot up and performed a triple spiral backflip. When she was finished, she held the ball high above her head in a pose befitting a pro baseball player in the throes of the World Series and yelled, "YIPPPPEEEEEE!!!!!!"

The silence that followed her joyful shout was deafening. Even in the sky, Piper suddenly became aware that absolutely no one else was cheering or celebrating. Peering downward, the image of slack-jawed children and amazed farmers greeted her.

Piper waited but it never came. No one cheered. None of the kids asked her to play. Sally Sue did not run over and apologize or beg for friendship. Instead, parents' blank stares quickly turned to concern and soon they were grabbing the hands of their children and walking— make that dashing—away from Piper as though she were a contagious disease.

"This is the work of the devil," one woman was heard to say darkly to another.

Another farmer shook his head. "She's given all them youngens bad notions."

When Piper's feet hit the ground, Betty and Joe snatched her away without a word. During the entire journey home, not a single syllable was uttered between all three of them. It wasn't until Piper had been placed in a kitchen chair back at the farm that Betty let loose her fury.

"What in the name of blazes was you doing, Piper McCloud?"

"But, Ma, I caught the ball." Piper held up the ball as evidence. Sometimes it seemed to Piper that her ma and pa missed the point entirely. When all was said and done, it had been a very hard, very confusing day all around for Piper. Nothing had gone as she had hoped and yet, despite everything, she had at last prevailed and achieved a certain victory by catching that baseball. Surely, she should be getting credit for that. "Wasn't that what the game was all about and what everyone was cheering for? Din't I do it?"

"You was flying! I told you and told you. . . ."

"But, Ma, you said there wasn't any use for flying, but there is. See?" Piper held up the ball a second time, because it was a fact. "And I thought up more uses besides. Like fixin' the barn roof or . . ."

"PIPER McCLOUD!"

"But, Ma, if you'd just try flying, I know you'd like it. And I could show you how. It's not difficult and I already learned a bunch of hard lessons so you wouldn't have to get 'em so painful like I did and—"

"There won't be any more flying 'round these parts. And I never wanna talk about it or see you up in that sky again. And I mean it this time." Betty stamped her foot. "GO TO YOUR ROOM, Piper McCloud!"

CHAPTER FOUR

LOWLAND COUNTY was immobilized by a pandemic of gossip fever, and as the town's official gossip, Millie Mae was suddenly a person of great importance. Folks who in the past had turned tail at the mere sight of her were suddenly inventing excuses to pay her a visit. Years of persistent practice had prepared Millie Mae well for the sudden spike in demand for her services and she hit the ground running. By evening time, her rendition of the events at the baseball game had morphed from a five-minute breathless account to an elaborate dissertation that stretched more than one hour and thirty-three minutes, including vivid descriptions, a blow-by-blow report, and a short demonstration.

Like a wildfire in a hot dry summer, the news blazed outward and jumped the county line so that before long, New York, Tokyo, London, and every city besides wanted to know about the mysterious girl who could fly. Millie

Mae worked overtime and was happy to oblige the ever-increasing number of inquiries that came her way from all corners of the globe. From ten o'clock that night to six o'clock the following morning, Millie Mae was booked solid and talked nonstop, loving every precious minute. She told everything she knew and saw, and even a bit more besides.

While the McClouds slept, people they'd never met in far-off places they didn't even know existed were reading detailed accounts about Piper and the baseball game. Headlines with bold exclamation marks shouted out:

FLYING GIRL CATCHES FLY BALL!!!

FIRST HUMAN FLIGHT DOCUMENTED

PEOPLE FLOCK TO LOWLAND COUNTY TO CATCH GLIMPSE OF FIRST FLYING GIRL!!

From Moscow to Saigon to Sydney to Athens and every place in between, breakfast conversation was dominated by one single subject—the girl who could fly.

At dawn the following morning, a stampede of reporters had materialized with the morning sun, as if by magic, and set up camp on the McCloud farm. Cameramen, large news trucks, newspaper reporters, and photographers quietly trained their lenses and eyes on the farmhouse where they waited to catch and record their first glimpse of Piper McCloud.

50

Oblivious to the events of the outside world and the activities taking place on the other side of her very window, Piper slept deeply beneath her quilt. It had taken her a long time to get to sleep the night before, especially as she knew that morning would bring a punishment from Betty for her disobedience. In her confused and exhausted state, Piper had somehow reasoned that if she didn't go to sleep, the following day would be unable to dawn and the punishment could be avoided. After everything that had happened at the picnic and the baseball game, though, Piper was bone-tired and was relentlessly dogged by her need for sleep.

Lying in bed, she was successfully able to keep herself awake by fretting herself silly. *I've really cooked my goose now. Ma and Pa ain't never gonna let me off the farm again.* Not that it mattered anyway. *None of them kids want to be my friend. Sure as anything they don't now.* No doubt her ma and pa were going to be watching her like a hawk from that point on too. *I reckon I can forget about getting any flying time tomorrow or for many tomorrows after that.* Piper sighed. If there was one thing she hated more than anything, it was wasting a perfectly good sky. Everything was starting to feel utterly hopeless, especially as Piper knew that had she to do it all over again, she wouldn't have done anything differently. *What's so gosh darned wrong with flying, anyway? Everyone's got something they do better than everyone else.* It wasn't fair from Piper's perspective that folks were so riled up about it.

I'm just gonna change their minds, is all, Piper firmly and silently resolved. *They just don't understand but soon as I give 'em half a chance they'll come 'round.* As soon as Piper settled the issue in her mind, she fell under the spell of her dreams and spent the night passing through blue skies dotted by fluffy white clouds. She would have slept most of the morning away had an anxious world not had other plans in store for her.

"Piper McCloud?" A voice sounded in her small room just after sunrise.

"Ummmm." Piper turned over, half awake.

"Piper, wake up!"

Piper showed no signs of complying, when suddenly the blankets on her bed were whisked to the floor, causing her to wake with a start. Sitting bolt upright in her bed, she looked about, but the room was completely empty. *Great, now I'm imagining things.* As if she didn't have enough problems as it was.

"Piper?" the voice said again.

This time, Piper knew it wasn't her imagination. It was a male voice and it sounded like it was coming from the corner by the door. But who? Or what? She squinted her eyes and looked everywhere, but the room was empty.

"Who's there?"

"Don't be afraid."

Piper screamed, leapt out of bed, and backed away from the corner of the room where the voice was coming from.

"I'm here to help you," the voice said.

While that might have been true, Piper wasn't about to take any chances. Without turning her back to the voice, she quickly pulled open her curtains, allowing light to stream in. The morning sun hit the corner of the room and, by squinting her eyes just so, Piper was definitely able to see *something* against the door, but what exactly was it? It looked like an outline of a man or a wavy bit of air. But all the same, there was actually *nothing* there.

"Look in the window." An eager voice shouted from the farmyard below. "It's Piper McCloud!"

For the second time that morning, Piper jumped out of her skin, turned on a dime, and caught her first glimpse of . . . something different.

Piper's eyes, already opened wide, somehow grew wider to take in the fact that every available place on the farm was crowded with people! Lots and lots of people and all different kinds of them too. And not only people but news trucks and equipment!

A man with several cameras around his neck was pointing up at Piper with great excitement. "That's her! It's Piper McCloud!!!"

People with cameras were materializing out of nowhere and a battalion of high-powered, high-tech flashbulbs took aim and held in their crosshairs the figure of a little girl peeping out of a window. They fired at will. Piper's startled eyes took a direct hit and she was thrown backward, clutching her scorched cornea.

"Owwww." Piper stumbled blindly, falling to the floor.

"Piper? That you making all that noise in there?" Betty entered Piper's room a moment later, feeling a strange gust of air brushing past her. (This was to be the least strange thing that happened to her that morning.) To her astonishment, she discovered Piper curled up by the bed, holding her eyes. Bright lights, brighter than Betty had ever thought possible, were throbbing nonstop from outside the window, and then a crane-like contraption rose up into the air, upon which sat a man crouched behind a huge camera.

"Heavens to Betsy!"

"Ma, my eyes is burning up."

Snapping out of it, Betty lunged forward, scooping Piper up. "Mr. McCloud," she screeched, "Mr. McCloud, we're bein' attacked."

Joe went from a dead sleep to a dead run. He entered the hall clothed in his long underwear and his twelve-gauge.

"They's everywhere," Betty said as she bustled Piper into the corner of the hallway. "Went and blinded our Piper with some terrible lights and they're tryin' to take over the place."

Joe bounded down the stairs. He headed straight for the doors and double-locked all of them and then propped chairs up against them just to be certain.

By late morning the siege was still going on and showed no signs of abating. Two windows had been broken, the hens had lost over half of their feathers, and the number of reporters had grown exponentially. Betty, Joe, and Piper remained huddled in the upstairs hallway like frightened prey. Thankfully, Piper's vision had almost completely returned, except when she looked too far right or left, and then it hurt like heck. Outside the house, the noise grew and grew. More trucks. More people. More shouting.

"Mrs. McCloud! How long has your daughter flown for?"

"Mr. McCloud, did you teach her to fly?"

"Will Piper come out and fly for us?"

And on and on they persisted until Piper thought she'd lose her mind. Suddenly the outside world was downright frightening, and what's more, it was making her ma and pa scared, which in turn made Piper feel terrible. She wracked her brains for a solution.

"Ma, maybe I should go talk to 'em some and then they'd let us be."

"You'll do no such thing." Betty held on to Piper firmly. "They's strangers. Every single last one of 'em, and there's no telling what they'll get up to. No sir, you ain't going nowheres."

"But, Ma, what if they never let us alone? What then?"

"The good Lord will watch over us and protect us, child. That's what."

As it turned out, Betty was partially right. Someone was indeed about to protect them, but their orders came from a slightly lower realm.

Deployment of the Containment, Security, and First Contact units commenced at oh-two hundred. Ten hours later, a line of twenty unmarked black SUVs and two transport trucks sped toward Lowland County in strict formation. They dominated the roads, pushed smaller vehicles onto the shoulder, and held to their course, undeterred by the collateral damage of crossing animals or loose livestock.

Agent A. Agent (yes, his last name by some strange cosmic joke was actually Agent—and, no, he didn't become an agent because his last name was already Agent) approved and scrupulously supervised every move. He was a humorless man of indeterminate age who stood ramrod straight and held a steady body-fat count of less than three percent. His men made jokes that he was more cyborg than human. Had Agent Agent overheard these jokes, he would have taken them as a compliment.

When they arrived at ground zero (also known as the McCloud farm), the situation was about as bad as any they'd ever documented. Media and general onlookers had flocked to the scene and were posing what Agent Agent considered a threat to their target (also known as Piper McCloud).

"Raising alert status to code red, Alpha Team and Omega Team on standby for immediate deployment."

The convoy roared up to the house and, in record time, fifty agents, equipped with every conceivable piece of technology, achieved predetermined targets. Security forces rounded up media and civilians alike and escorted them from the premises while containment crews confiscated all tapes, pictures, and evidence.

"Area four B secure."

"Area seven L secure."

"All containment protocols complete."

In T-minus five minutes, Agent Agent stood in the epicenter of the completely deserted farmyard, meticulously monitoring every detail of his men's movements. He was a perfectionist who left nothing to chance and was careful to ensure all safety protocols were in place (you could never be too careful when establishing first contact) and all eventualities had been accounted for (he had to expect the unexpected at all times) before calling in his next order:

"Air unit, you are clear to land."

"Roger that, team leader."

High above the farm, a massive helicopter dropped out of the clouds. It was bigger than even the largest military helicopters and the force of its blades was devastating.

"What's that sound?" Piper called over the din from the huddle in the hallway.

Betty didn't answer because she was too busy praying. Joe didn't answer because his mouth had gone completely dry. And then more terrible than all the noise and the shaking was the ominous silence that soon followed when the mighty beast outside had settled itself in the dirt.

In the farmyard, Agent Agent smartly opened the helicopter door as one dainty leather pump, followed by its twin, stepped down onto the dusty McCloud soil.

They belonged to Dr. Letitia Hellion.

Reed thin, she was as delicate as a prima ballerina combined with the aura of a majestic fairy queen. She wore an elegantly tailored black suit beneath which peeked a crisp white linen shirt made from the finest cloth. Her hair was coiled into a lovely twist at the nape of her neck and its jet-black sheen set off deep green eyes and the purest, whitest skin. Anyone who was fortunate enough to have the opportunity to set eyes on Dr. Letitia Hellion swore she was the most exquisitely beautiful woman that they had ever seen.

She walked with such grace toward the house that it might have appeared that her feet didn't touch the ground at all. Agent Agent and the two other agents who flanked her movements appeared like Neanderthal apes in contrast.

Knock! Knock! Knock!

Dr. Hellion, Agent Agent, and more than fifty security, containment, and science personnel waited patiently for their knock on the McCloud door to be answered. In the upstairs hallway Joe, Betty, and Piper didn't move.

"Mr. and Mrs. McCloud?" Dr. Hellion called up in a clear, refined voice. "My name is Dr. Letitia Hellion and I am a representative of and for the government of the United States of America. Please open your door."

All doubt existing in Betty's and Joe's minds was immediately dispatched. The McClouds were law-abiding folk, and if the government of the United States saw fit to pay them a visit, far be it from them to refuse their country's call. Before Piper knew what was what, she found herself standing between her ma and pa in the yard before Dr. Hellion, who produced an official-looking identification card and introduced herself.

Shyly studying the beautiful stranger from behind her mother, Piper suddenly felt like a little planet being pulled into orbit around Letitia Hellion's steady and powerful gravitational force. Her white skin, dark hair, and flashing eyes all pulsated with a confidence that was magnetic and inescapable.

"My men have secured the area and are maintaining the strictest surveillance to ensure your safety and protection," Dr. Hellion said, indicating where all the agents were posted at key points about the farm. "I am the director of an institute that specializes in providing assistance to people, much like yourselves, who find themselves in . . . well, shall we say, difficult situations." Dr. Hellion considered Piper with intense green eyes. "I understand you have a child who likes to fly."

Betty instinctively put an arm on Piper's shoulder. "Our Piper's a good girl. I ain't saying that we don't got our problems with her, but she didn't never hurt no one."

"No, of course not. I understand. We've encountered many people, just like you, whose circumstances are . . . unique. It's nothing to be concerned about. We know exactly what to do." Dr. Hellion's manner was warm and reassuring and the tension in Betty's jaw lessened. "Right now Agent Agent has a few questions that he'd like to ask you. Would you mind if he spoke with you for a moment in private?"

Agent Agent stepped forward and guided Betty and Joe to the porch, leaving Piper alone with Dr. Hellion. Piper found herself tongue-tied and mesmerized as the full force of Letitia Hellion's attention shone on her.

"It seems like you've been having quite a morning." Dr. Hellion smiled. Piper nodded. "I don't suppose you are used to getting so many unexpected visitors?"

"No, we sure don't," Piper agreed.

"Perhaps you also had something strange or unexplainable happen to you this morning? Like hearing a voice but not seeing anyone there?"

Piper's mouth flew open. *How did she know?*

The expression on Piper's face confirmed Dr. Hellion's suspicion. "Perhaps we'll speak more about that later. But for right now, Piper, why don't you tell me about your flying?" Dr. Hellion spoke about flying as though commenting on the weather.

"Well . . ." After all the trouble, Piper didn't know if she should answer. Letitia Hellion instantly saw the confusion in Piper's face and bent down so that she was eye level with her. Placing her hand on Piper's small shoulder, she held her wavering blue eyes in the strength of her green ones.

"I know that you don't know me very well yet, Piper, but I hope one day you'll think of me as a friend. If you let me, I could be someone who could really help you."

Dr. Hellion paused, seeing the lines of confusion and uncertainty that crossed Piper's forehead. "Maybe you are thinking right now, *She doesn't understand. No one understands what it's like to be so different. To be constantly hiding who you really are and lying about it too.* I also know, though, that you don't like lying. It doesn't make you feel very good."

Piper was struck dumb. That was exactly how she felt! How did Dr. Hellion know?

"You are also wondering what you can possibly do about it. And the truth is that you don't really know what to do, or who to turn to, and you are starting to have moments when things feel completely hopeless."

Piper realized her knees were trembling. "Wh–what do I do?"

"That's a very good question, Piper. And I can help you answer it. But first I need to see how far along you are with your flying—if you've progressed to inverted loops or maybe even reverse propulsion."

"You mean fly backward?" Piper hadn't even thought of trying that yet.

"It's a very advanced skill and I wouldn't expect that you would have reached that level yet."

"I've floated ever since I was born but I only just got at the flying. I'd appreciate a few lessons. Then again . . . some folks 'round these parts don't take to it much."

Piper glanced over to where her ma and pa were talking with Agent Agent.

"I understand. It's not easy to do what you do. There are consequences." Dr. Hellion nodded solemnly and Piper knew she did understand and, what's more, felt understood.

"I've met many others, just like you. Once I have assessed your flying skills we can sit down and decide exactly where you'd like to go with it."

"You mean you want me to fly? Now? Here?"

"Yes. Can you do that for me?"

Piper looked about as though expecting to get in trouble for merely considering the idea of flying. "You're sure it won't cause no trouble?"

"You have my word." Dr. Hellion gave her word firmly. Getting to her feet, she stepped away to give Piper room. "Please take your time. Whenever you feel ready. Talk me through it if you'd like."

Piper was well aware of the many eyes that were watching her, not to mention Betty, who was closely minding her from the porch.

"Well, if you're sure." Piper took a deep breath and turned so that she couldn't see her parents' faces. It sure made a change to have someone actually taking an interest in her flying, and she suddenly felt excitement welling up inside of her.

"See," she explained to Dr. Hellion and the men closest

to her, "any of you could do it, if you put your mind to it. All you have to do is stand still and think about the sky." Piper silently repeated her special words and a rush of tingling swept through her body. A moment later her feet left the ground. "Next thing you know, you'll be in the air. Simple as that."

Piper flew.

Everyone looked up.

All of the men present had seen many unexplained and classified phenomena. For them, the extraordinary had become routine. It was precisely why they had been subjected to a painstaking selection process, exhaustive training, and ongoing assessments. And yet even so, those same men unwittingly let expressions of wonder and awe slip across their hardened features and let gasps escape their weary lips as they watched Piper fly.

No question, Piper McCloud was special, even among the special.

Once in the air, Piper decided to keep it simple. Turning a few spins, she followed them with a quick loop-the-loop and finished with a pirouette.

Dr. Hellion's breath fell away. "Dear God, she really can fly."

CHAPTER FIVE

"PIPER, THERE are others . . . like you. And a place where you will belong." Dr. Hellion spoke quietly and Piper leaned forward to drink in every single word.

"No fooling?"

True to her word, Dr. Hellion had seen to it that Piper didn't get into any trouble once she landed. Afterward, Dr. Hellion went into the house with Betty and Joe and stayed there a long time before calling Piper in to speak with her privately. In no time at all Piper felt like Dr. Hellion was an old trusted friend.

"The only trouble with flying is that it gets lonely up in the sky when you're the only one," she told Dr. Hellion confidentially. "I was thinking that maybe I could teach others to fly and then everyone could do it. I mean, it's not so hard once you get the hang of it." Once she got started talking about flying, Piper couldn't stop.

Dr. Hellion listened carefully to every single word. "Is that what you'd like?"

"More than anything. That and learning to fly better because I wanna fly clear around the world." Piper's face lit up at the thought of it. "Then I can see everything and maybe there are other fliers out there that no one knows nothing 'bout. Maybe I could find 'em. Or at least meet a lot of interesting people in far-off places."

"Sounds like you have it all figured out."

Piper shrugged. "It seems to me that it don't hurt none to get yourself a dream and a plan. 'Cause if you don't, then you'll never go nowhere."

"I couldn't agree more. Well, Piper, it's good that you've told me all of this because your mother and father and I have just been sitting here discussing your future and I suggested to them that it might be in your interest to come with me for a while."

"With you? Where?"

"My institute. It specializes in assisting special needs children, like yourself, in learning skills so that they can fulfill their dreams."

"You mean I'd get to go to school?"

"Like I was telling your parents, we'll teach you everything you need to know."

"I'd sure like to fly better." Piper couldn't wait to get some good flying lessons.

"There is also one other thing you should know, Piper. What happened to you this morning in your room—that voice you heard. Well, I don't want to go into too much detail and I certainly don't want to scare you, but unless you have protection, there are those out there who have an interest in getting to you. Unfortunately, they have great means at their disposal. At the institute, we can see to it that you are safe."

A shiver went up and down Piper's spine. "Why would they wanna get at me?"

"It's very complicated, and frankly, it's not something I'd like you to worry about. When I spoke with your parents, they told me that the final decision to go to the institute or not would be left up to you. Based on your circumstances, I think it would be a wise decision, on your part."

Without hesitation, indeed without even thinking, Piper wholeheartedly agreed with Dr. Hellion, who happily got to her feet. "So it's settled."

Like a whirlwind, Piper rushed up to her room to tell Betty, who was in the middle of pulling clothes out of Piper's drawers. "Dr. Hellion says she'll teach me everything I'll need to know, Ma. Ain't that great?" Piper blurted out. "And I'm gonna go to her institute."

"I figured as much." Betty nodded, and Piper suddenly noticed an unmistakable look of great concern on her mother's careworn face.

Betty and Joe were simple country folks at their wits' end. They loved their child with all of their hearts and didn't want her going away for even one second. All the same, protecting Piper from the likes of what had happened earlier that morning was now a heavy consideration. Dr. Hellion promised to keep their Piper out of harm's way. She also patiently pointed out that Piper's special needs required an individually crafted learning program specifically designed for her abilities. Had the McClouds given any thought to how they were going to address that? No? Well, Dr. Hellion was an expert with exceptional children. Her facility was created for just such occurrences and would gather any resources necessary to see to it that Piper had all she needed. No expense would be spared.

While it was true that the McClouds were sticklers for their routine, they were not unkind people. They would have cut off their right arms before knowingly hurting Piper in any way. And so with the greatest reluctance and against their best instincts, they were letting their only child be taken from them.

Betty had already packed Piper's warmest sweater, woolen gloves, and socks. Everything Piper owned was all neatly arranged in an old carpetbag that was light to carry, even to Piper's arms. Seeing her clothes all packed up jolted Piper out of her euphoria and stopped her short in her tracks.

"Ma, what are you doing with all my clothes?"

"Fancy institute or not, I'm figuring you'll need a stitch or two to cover yourself with." Betty pushed Piper's long underwear into the bag.

"But . . ." Piper didn't understand. "Why are you packin' 'em all up?"

"You'll have to leave with Dr. Hellion and you won't be able to live here anymore."

"What?" Piper's confusion grew. "But that ain't right! Why can't I walk to the institute like I see them Miller youngens walk to school every day?" It didn't occur to Piper that it would ever be otherwise.

"Dr. Hellion's institute is real far, Piper. Too far to walk to and too far to come home from, even on holidays."

All at once, Piper came to realize that there were greater implications to what had seemed like a common-sense decision. She sank down on her bed. "No!"

"Now, now, child. Don't get yourself into a state. Like you says, Dr. Hellion's got everything all figured out."

Piper noticed that her mother's hands were shaking as she folded the only handkerchief the McClouds had ever owned. Made with a delicate linen and embroidered with tiny bluebirds, the handkerchief had been carefully passed down through the generations. Betty had only ever used it once and that was on her wedding day.

Neatly folding it and placing it in the old bag, Betty was now quietly bestowing it on Piper. The simple gesture woke Piper up to the finality of leaving her parents and the farm.

"But I didn't know." Piper wrung her hands. What was she going to do now? She wanted to go to Dr. Hellion's institute but not if it meant leaving her home and her ma and pa. Suddenly a simple decision had become very complicated and Piper couldn't figure her way to an answer that didn't include disappointment and regret. How had she gotten herself into such a muddle?

"You'll be safe, and they'll give you special schooling." Betty could see Piper's mounting concern and tried to reassure her. "You'll get to meet other youngens, maybe make some friends."

Piper shook her head. "I don't reckon I'll go now."

Betty sniffed, turned away quickly, and gathered up a hairbrush. "Ain't nothing in this life comes easy to any of us, child. Every road you walk down's got a price. Sooner you learn that the better. Don't matter the direction you go, there'll be some bad mixed in with the good and you just gotta learn to take the one with the other." Winding Piper's Sunday hair ribbon around the brush's handle, Betty tucked them in the bag and closed it with finality. "You done went and chose your path and there ain't nothing your pa and I can do about it now."

At first Piper didn't understand what her ma was angling at, and then at once things snapped into focus in such a way that they did make sense. Betty had told her and told her not to fly. She'd warned her to keep her feet on the ground and Piper hadn't paid her any mind. Sure as anything, she'd gone and caught that baseball and everyone saw. The whole situation was out of her ma and pa's hands. Like a detective unraveling a case, Piper traced the steps she had taken to arrive at this moment. Leaving with Dr. Hellion was only the latest ramification of the choice she'd made to jump off the roof while lying on the tree branch that day. There wasn't anything she or her ma or pa could do about it now. It was Piper, and Piper alone, who had brought all this about.

"I didn't never think this was gonna happen." Piper breathed quietly, shaking her head in wonder.

Betty handed Piper the carpetbag. "Mind your manners now."

"I will, Ma."

"See to it you clean your plate." Betty sniffed, turning away quickly and roughly pushing the back of her hand against her cheek. "Best be getting a move on. Don't want to keep all them folks waiting on us." She left Piper's room abruptly and bustled down the stairs.

Piper took one last look around the only bedroom she'd ever known before picking up the old bag and reluctantly leaving. When she opened the porch door she noticed that the fancy cars were packed up and the men in dark suits were waiting next to them at the ready. Dr. Hellion smiled when she saw her. "All ready?"

Piper nodded sadly. Off to the side, Joe stood forlornly waiting.

"I'm going now, Pa."

Joe sighed, thrusting his hand into the pocket of his overalls and pulling out a beautifully carved wooden bird. He handed it to Piper and she took it gently, turning it over reverently.

"Was gonna be for your birthday," Joe spoke slowly. "I expect now's as good a time as any. Made it myself."

Tears sprang into Piper's eyes. "It's beautiful, Pa. Most beautiful I ever saw." Piper's fingers traced the delicate lines on the feathers of the bird that Joe had painstakingly spent hours creating. It was truly a labor of love.

"We'll be waiting right here for you when you're ready to come back to us." Joe patted Piper's shoulder awkwardly. He wasn't used to so much talking.

Piper nodded through her tears. She felt Dr. Hellion's gentle hand on her shoulder and allowed herself to be guided away. Agent Agent lifted her up into the helicopter and expertly fastened safety straps across her chest, which firmly held her against the soft leather seats. The next thing she knew, the door was closed and the engine was revving up. It was all happening so fast.

The helicopter lifted off and Piper watched the strong wind created by the blades blasting against her ma and pa. They stood stalwart against it and waved as the helicopter rose into the sky.

Piper kept her eyes fixed not on the sky but on the waving hands of her parents. Although she knew that they couldn't see, she waved back.

Long after all of the fancy cars had sped away and the dust had settled, Betty and Joe McCloud kept their eyes fixed firmly on the horizon where they'd last seen the helicopter. Neither of them moved for a long time.

CHAPTER SIX

THE HELICOPTER flew due north at such a speed that green forests quickly became white with snow. Then the trees disappeared altogether and there was an endless stretch of wintry tundra that reached in every direction as far as the eye could see. Not that Piper noticed any of it. Slumped over in the luxurious leather seat, Piper's thoughts stayed on the farm, her parents, and how much she missed them already. Dr. Hellion, who was seated next to Piper, reached out and gently squeezed Piper's small hand reassuringly.

"I've never been away from my ma and pa before. My ma always says she can't figure where I've come from. She says that there wasn't ever another McCloud like me. Sometimes I thought that was a good thing 'cause I don't want to be just like everyone else. But then I got to thinking and it got me worried. 'Cause *I am* a McCloud, and if I'm not a McCloud, then what am I? A person likes to feel like they belong some-where."

"For some people that path to belonging is more diffi-cult than others." Deep understanding resonated through each of Dr. Hellion's words. "I promise you I will help you find it, though."

"You reckon?"

Dr. Hellion smiled and nodded. Relieved, Piper smiled too. There was something about Dr. Hellion that was so calm and assured. Everything made sense to her in a way that it never had to Piper, and she longed for that same knowledge. Maybe she'd learn that at the school as well.

"Roger that. ETA is ten hundred," Piper heard the pi-lot say, and she began looking out the window to catch her first glimpse of her new home. Pressing her face against the glass, she scanned the white horizon. There was no end to the icy terrain and they'd already been flying over it for quite some time. After a great deal more flying, the helicopter finally began to slow and then descend by a lonely shack, no larger than a toolshed, sitting all by itself in the middle of the frozen desolate landscape.

"Is that it?" Piper was disappointed and confused by the shabby structure.

"Yes, we're here."

With mounting disenchantment, Piper eyed the feeble hovel that looked as though it might be ripped from its earthly troubles by the hungry wind at any given moment. An old rusted sign attached to the structure read GOVERNMENT FACILITY. TRESPASSERS WILL BE TERMINATED.

When the helicopter touched down, several men in white snow gear jogged out of the shack and quickly opened Piper's door.

"Piper McCloud?" The attendant had to yell over the roar of the engine to be heard. Piper nodded and her teeth began to wildly chatter as the subzero temperature jabbed her.

"I'm here to assist you into the facility." The attendant snapped free the many safety restraints and guided Piper from her seat.

When her feet sank into two feet of snow, Piper instinctively winced. "Dang!" The temperature was so far below zero that the thermometer had hit its bottom mark and stayed there months before. Inhaling actually hurt Piper's lungs and instantly froze her nostrils. She'd known hard winters, but this cold was like nothing she'd ever felt. It was the type of cold that prevented you from thinking straight.

"Right this way." The attendant hurried Piper toward the shack. At that moment any place that provided shelter from the cold became a splendid idea. Piper dashed toward it, thankful when another waiting attendant opened the door to speed her entry.

Heedlessly thrusting herself inside, Piper entered an entirely new and unexpected world. Underneath the shack's apparently flimsy exterior was a smartly outfitted lobby with thick, white marble tiles and clean steel walls. A chandelier of glass and steel hung from the ceiling, and at the far side, an elevator door took up an entire wall.

The clash between expectation and reality froze Piper to the spot. "Well, butter my butt and call me a biscuit!"

A moment later, Dr. Hellion swept inside and approached a panel next to the elevator. She touched it a certain way and it snapped open, exposing a very complex computer. There were flashing lights and buttons and all sorts of other things that Piper couldn't even begin to imagine the use of. Dr. Hellion, of course, knew exactly what to do with them and expertly maneuvered through a battery of security protocols that included a voice confirmation, fingerprint identification, and retinal scan.

"Your safety and well-being is of paramount importance to us, Piper," Dr. Hellion explained, seeing Piper's bewildered expression. "We don't take any chances and so we've created a security system that will ensure that you remain safe while you are in our care." A moment later the computer beeped loudly and the doors to the elevator snapped smartly open.

Dr. Hellion graciously stepped aside and allowed Piper first entry. Piper had never been on an elevator, especially not one as sleek as this. Gingerly stepping aboard, she saw that the entire back wall was comprised of thick glass and the whole ceiling glowed with light.

"Ready?"

Piper nodded, scared and excited at the same time. This really was an adventure.

"Elevator, commence." The elevator instantly responded to Dr. Hellion's command. The doors swooshed shut and they dropped downward as the elevator fell at an alarming rate.

Unexpectedly a voice filled the elevator. "Approaching level one. Single-celled organisms. Minimum-security clearance." The voice was female and without expression. Piper looked around for it.

"That's the computer voice," Dr. Hellion explained. "You can speak to her just like a normal person and she'll respond."

"Golly!" Piper looked up as though expecting to see the computer above her.

"Go ahead and try."

"Uh, computer, do cows have feelings?"

The computer did not respond. Several strange blipping sounds came from the overhead speakers.

"That's a great question, Piper, but the computer can only help you with questions that are more specific," Dr. Hellion coached, gently.

Piper thought about it for a moment before trying again. "Computer, does *my* black-and-white cow got feelings?" Yet again Piper had flummoxed the computer and the blipping sounds increased.

Dr. Hellion politely coughed. "Try asking the computer our current location, Piper."

"Where am I now?"

"This elevator is approaching level one in—Three. Two. One second." On cue the elevator emerged out of the darkness and descended into an incredible underground world. Turning around so that she faced the glass wall behind her, Piper's eyes snapped wide and then impossibly wider still, and yet somehow could not take in all the mind-boggling sights that lay before her.

"Elevator, pause," Dr. Hellion commanded, and they immediately came to a stop.

The elevator hung directly in the center of a cavernous man-made well. The facility was approximately the size of a mini Grand Canyon, but instead of rock it was all steel, and glass curved in a big sweeping circle around the elevator, which dangled in the middle. In an unprecedented feat of engineering, bridges extended from the curved sides to connect with the elevator, yet appeared to be supported by nothing and were nonetheless completely stable.

Everything was shiny and white and illuminated by

blue glowing light. Huge glass walls made it possible to see exactly what was going on inside each floor from the elevator, while at the same time allowing the inhabitants to look down over a central atrium which was at the very bottom of the well.

"Holy cow," Piper squealed and reached for something to steady herself. "As I live and breathe, I swear I couldn't imagine up a place like this even if I tried all my days and nights. Look how them walls is all curved! Like we're in the center of a glass circle. It's so shiny, it near hurts my eyes to look at it."

The lights of the facility were reflecting off of the glass of the elevator onto Dr. Hellion's face, and her excitement for the place was palpable. Indeed, Dr. Hellion suddenly seemed to be a girl herself and looked at the facility as though she were seeing it for the first time too.

"I remember when I made my first trip down here and I knew right away that I'd found not just a home but a whole world that were special. It's so clean and bright and everything makes sense here." Dr. Hellion pulled her eyes away and smiled at Piper. "Every time I leave I can't wait to return. Doesn't it take your breath away?"

"It sure does," Piper agreed.

"There are many extraordinary things here, Piper." Dr. Hellion smiled. "That's why you'll feel right at home. Starting on level one, we have single-celled organisms, and as we descend you'll notice that each level has more and more complex life-forms. On level two we have horticultural specimens and plant life. Level three, insects. Level five, marine life. Level seven is the aviary, and so on and so on. Everything you can imagine, we have it. Unparalleled facilities, cutting-edge technology, and the best minds in the world all under one roof."

Dr. Hellion placed her hand on Piper's shoulder. "I hope that you'll be as happy here as I am, Piper." Sighing, as though she wished they could stay looking down at the facility forever, Dr. Hellion finally tore her eyes from the glass. "Watch carefully. There's so much to see. Elevator, commence."

"Level one," the elevator reported a moment later as the elevator fell. Piper kept a keen eye on the glass elevator window, and through the large glass walls of the first level saw scientists hunched over telescopes and other pieces of equipment that Piper couldn't even begin to imagine the use of, let alone put a name to.

"Level two, entry granted. Horticultural specimens. Minimum-security protocols in effect," the computer reported.

A moment later Piper caught glimpses of laboratories filled with exotic plants, arboretums with vast rows of shrubs and trees, and facility staff carefully tending and monitoring it all. One particular scientist caught Piper's eye as he leaned forward to smell an exceptionally beautiful rose. Suddenly the rose's petals pulled back to reveal a mouth with sharp, thorn-like teeth. The rose fiercely lunged forward and bit into the scientist's nose. Although she wasn't able to hear, Piper could see the poor scientist yowl in pain.

"Look there!" She pointed for Dr. Hellion to see but the elevator dropped down another flight.

"We have special task forces that carefully monitor the globe to identify and locate any species that requires our assistance and protection. That way we can ensure its safety and, in the cases of some of these life-forms, the safety of the rest of the world," Dr. Hellion continued.

Piper watched as scientists gathered around a large insect. The insect suddenly gave itself a mighty shake and unraveled wide wings from beneath its many legs. Its wingspan was extraordinary, perhaps five feet, and adorned with incredible patterns. The patterns started to move and change hypnotically, and the scientists were beginning to fall asleep. Even Piper began to sway back and forth.

"Amazing!" Piper shook herself awake.

"The entire facility has been created as a 'smart building,' meaning that it has sensors that can detect and answer your needs. The computer voice can assist you with a lot of things, including giving you access to a wide variety of information."

Unexpectedly, the elevator came to a stop and a research assistant embarked, holding a glass specimen cage that housed a tiny black cricket. Piper moved closer and the cricket stood up on his back two legs and looked right at her. Intrigued, Piper leaned inward.

It was the cutest cricket she had ever seen and he was just as interested in her as she was in him. He moved to the side of his cage next to her and even took one of his tiny legs and put it up against the glass. Piper was entranced. This was like no other cricket she had ever set eyes on and she could have sworn he was sizing her up too. The spell was broken when the elevator stopped and the cricket and his handler disembarked. Unlike the other levels, the windows on the fourth floor were frosted over so it wasn't possible to see inside.

"Will I get to know about all these other things I'm seeing?" Piper wanted to see and touch everything.

"That might be difficult. Many of them are dangerous and most of them are being carefully studied. Unless we know all about them, it's not safe to risk your welfare or theirs." Piper was clearly disappointed by this answer and Dr. Hellion relented, adding, "Why don't we see how things go and, based upon your progress, perhaps certain exceptions can be made."

Piper grinned. Maybe she wouldn't need to travel around the world after all. It seemed like everything she was looking for was right there under one roof. There wasn't a place Piper could set her eyes where a startling and amazing thing wasn't happening. She caught glimpses of a fish that had fur like a leopard, a snake with wings, and something that looked suspiciously like a unicorn.

"Level thirteen. Humanoid life-forms. Maximum-security personnel only." The elevator had dropped to the very bottom of the well and could travel no farther when the doors swished open.

"Welcome to your new home, Piper."

Piper's feet found their way onto the highly polished stone floor and she looked about in wonder.

The thirteenth level had three tiers, each with a balcony that overlooked the atrium where Piper was standing. A magnificent fountain dominated the atrium and unusual plants and trees created a sense of division between small sitting areas and tables. It looked exactly the way Piper would have imagined a very grand hotel. It was all very clean and quiet, but also empty.

"Where is everyone?"

"The residents are currently busy. Why don't I show you around and then you can join them?"

Piper nodded excitedly and followed Dr. Hellion on a tour down brightly lit halls, past a huge library, through a gymnasium equipped with everything from a swimming pool to a trampoline, rooms that Dr. Hellion called "learning centers," spacious lounges, a science center, playrooms with brightly colored toy trunks, and finally, a gourmet kitchen where the aroma of fresh-baked cookies made Piper's mouth water.

In the housekeeping quarters, a seamstress was on hand to expertly sew together a uniform that would fit Piper's exact measurements. Dr. Hellion allowed Piper to select from a huge wall filled with fabric bolts of every color. It didn't take Piper long before her eye was caught by a beautiful sky blue material made of the softest cotton. Before she knew it, she was standing before a large mirror in her uniform, which consisted of a full-skirted sky blue dress with a white collar and white kneesocks. In addition to this, her wild tangle of brown hair was liberated from the two tightly woven braids and held back by a blue ribbon. The whole getup was very dainty and feminine, and for a girl accustomed to overalls with multiple patches and church dresses that had serviced generations of McClouds, Piper felt a mite conspicuous as well as a bit gawky.

"While it's necessary to have uniforms, we like to honor each student's individuality by allowing them to choose their own material and color," Dr. Hellion pointed out as she walked with Piper to introduce her to the class.

"This is a mite tight around the arms." Piper moved her arms about, noticing how the dress was snugly fitted about her shoulders. "Can I use my old clothes to fly in?"

"That's a great question." Dr. Hellion paused, turning seriously to Piper. "You know, Piper, I'd like to ask you a few questions about your flying."

"What about my flying?"

"Our agents interviewed many of the people in Lowland County who were at the baseball game and saw you fly," Dr. Hellion began carefully. "Do you know what they said about your flying?"

Piper shook her head.

"They said that it scared them. Some of them said that they didn't want someone flying around them, that it was dangerous and a threat to their safety. One girl, I think her name was Sally Sue Miller, said that she wouldn't ever want to be friends with someone who could fly because she can't fly and it would make her sad to be around someone who could."

"She said that?" Piper's face went hot with embarrassment.

Dr. Hellion nodded. "What do you think about that?"

Piper shrugged, too upset to respond. She tried to blink away the tears that were welling in her eyes.

"Piper, I care about your well-being. I want you to be happy and joyful but I wonder if flying is really bringing true happiness into your life."

"But I love to fly more than anything," Piper protested.

"Of course. I'm not suggesting that you don't. I'm asking you to think about your life as a whole: about your parents, about your community, and about other people. Do you think flying is a good thing for them?"

"I guess I never thought of it that way before." Piper suddenly realized that things were more difficult and complicated. Maybe she was hurting her parents and she certainly didn't want to do that. Maybe all of the folks in Lowland County had a point.

"Piper, I know that you are a very sensitive and caring girl. I also know that you'd never do anything to knowingly hurt anyone." Dr. Hellion paused, looking at Piper with deep kindness in her eyes. "Sometimes we have to make hard choices, though, and consider all perspectives and other people's feelings too. Sometimes our true happiness comes from creating a balance between what we like and what's in the best interest of others. And that's called being a grown-up."

What Dr. Hellion said made a lot of sense to Piper. She'd never liked deceiving her parents and flying on the sly. The urge to fly was just so overpoweringly strong, it got the better of her.

"I didn't mean to hurt anyone."

"Of course not. And I know that." Dr. Hellion put an arm around Piper's shoulder, comforting her. "Sometimes it's hard to figure things out on our own and we need help. That's only natural."

Dr. Hellion walked forward, gently guiding Piper next to her. "While you think about all that, and also for your safety as well as that of the rest of the class, I'd like you to consider staying on the ground. Would you be willing to do that?"

"You mean not fly?" Startled, Piper looked to Dr. Hellion.

"Just for now. Perhaps in a little bit we can talk about it more and see. Okay?"

The last thing Piper wanted to do was promise not to fly, but Dr. Hellion was so smart and had so many good points. Not to mention the fact that she'd been so kind to Piper. She didn't want to be ungrateful. "Well, I guess. If you think it's for the best."

"I do." Dr. Hellion smiled. "That's my girl."

CHAPTER SEVEN

WHILE DR. HELLION consulted with Professor Mumbleby, Piper stood helplessly at the front of the science laboratory. Like everything else Piper had seen that day, the room was equipped with only the finest and most innovative technology. Bunsen burners, glass beakers, gleaming silver metal instruments, and shining white plastic containers were readily available at each student's very own learning station, which had been constructed to meet their particular academic needs. Currently the learning stations were occupied by science projects, all of which were in varying degrees of completion.

Piper counted eleven children in all, ranging in age from about five to fourteen years old. They shared an acute curiosity about their newest class member and each pair of eyes was fixed intently upon Piper with a merciless stare.

"Not much to look at, is she?" Smitty whispered to Kimber. Kimber punched him in the arm. She was a very strong girl. "Umph," Smitty wheezed.

A whispering firestorm was sweeping through the rank and file as they unabashedly dissected Piper, who had been left before them like a sacrificial offering.

"What's her thing?" Lily Yakimoto wanted to know.

Job one with a new student, besides intimidating them or generally ignoring them, was to identify their particular talent. Once uncovered, that talent would determine their place in the class pecking order. Not every ability seemed to have a purpose, thus the more interesting, unusual, or powerful the gift, the higher the ranking. Figuring out where Piper stood was potentially going to affect each of their standings and so it was of immediate interest.

"She don't have the looks of a genius."

"Maybe she's a fire-starter."

"Betcha she's another thought-thrower."

"It's called being psychic, stupid."

"She's psychic? God, not another one. We just got rid of Beth."

"Ten bucks says she'll break. She looks like a crier," Smitty judged. It wasn't uncommon for kids to crack up when they first arrived—what with being away from home for the first time and missing parents and the like.

The class had turned this homesickness ritual into a game that hinged on the ability to accurately predict the break-down's exact timing. Betting often topped fifty dollars, competition was fierce, and dirty tactics the norm. Opponents would egg a new kid on by reminding them how much their parents missed them, or perhaps how a much-loved pet might die before their return home, all of which was said in a calculated effort to push them over the brink at the appropriate moment and thus win the bet. The bigger and more violent the breakdown, the better.

"Those tears'll be flowing 'fore lights-out." Smitty squished his face up in mock sobs. *"I want my mommy. I want to go home. Sniff. Sniff."*

"She's no crier," Violet shyly ventured.

"Shut it, Violet, unless you've got the dough to back it up." Like a chihuahua who fancied himself a pit bull, Smitty was a pimply geek who had somehow mistakenly developed the notion that he was actually a muscle-bound tough guy.

"I'll see your ten, Smitty." Kimber stepped up to the plate. With her fiery red hair and temper to match, she was the sort of girl who embraced challenges, conflicts, and anything that involved getting the best of Smitty.

"Like taking candy from a baby." Smitty smacked his lips. "Better kiss that money bye-bye, Sparky." Sparky was Smitty's pet name for Kimber because (a) he knew she hated it, and (b) Kimber's personality was best described as shocking.

"Uh-hum." Professor Mumbleby cleared his throat loudly, interrupting the roar of quiet chattering. "Zis is Piper McCloud. She vill be joining us from now on."

Professor Mumbleby was seventy years old if he was a day. His German accent was so thick it was often unintelligible, and while he should have retired years and years before, he proved to be the only teacher capable of keeping control of completely uncontrollable children, which made him utterly irreplaceable.

"You vill make Piper feel velcome," Professor Mumbleby stated flatly.

Despite Professor Mumbleby's decree, Piper could see absolutely nothing welcoming in the expressions of her new classmates. In fact, they appeared to be regarding her with a strong mixture of suspicion, dislike, and mischievousness.

"I'm right pleased to meet you all." Piper smiled, hoping to win them over.

"I'll leave you to settle in now, Piper." Dr. Hellion quietly brushed past her on her way to the door.

"No!" Piper whispered urgently. "Don't go."

"Not to worry. I've explained your situation to Professor Mumbleby. He understands that you lack classroom experience and he'll help you out." Dr. Hellion placed a hand on Piper's shoulder comfortingly. "Just relax and you'll have fun. I'm excited for you."

"But—" Piper wanted to grab hold of Dr. Hellion and never let go of her.

"My door is always open for you, Piper." Dr. Hellion smiled and then slipped away, leaving Piper alone with *them*.

"Ze class is presenting their initial work on science projects, Miss McCloud. I'll schedule a meeting zis week to decide on your project, yah?" Professor Mumbleby waited for Piper to respond and Piper stiffly nodded. "In ze meantime, you vill sit with Miss Bella Lovely and she vill help you follow along."

Professor Mumbleby nodded to a petite girl with long, golden hair who immediately pulled an empty chair up next to her. Piper tentatively settled into the offered seat next to Bella, thankful to be released from the center stage spotlight at the front of the room.

"Hi." Bella smiled and her smile betrayed the joyous, smiling nature of a very bright soul. Bella was endowed with an unrelentingly sunny and effervescent disposition, which was in no small part due to the fact that her mother was a painter, her father was a sculptor, and she'd grown up on an organic communal farm in the San Francisco Bay area, where she was daily pummeled with massive amounts of unconditional love. This had left Bella without a mean bone in her body and enough positivism to single-handedly reverse global warming.

"This is Princess Madrigal." Bella presented Piper to her plant that was blooming on the desk in front of them. "She's my science experiment and I created her myself. Wanna smell?"

Bella had cross-pollinated a rose with a daffodil, a lilac, and an orchid. The by-product of these unlikely parents was the most exquisite-looking and -smelling plant that anyone had ever seen, and which, under Bella's loving attention, was daily becoming even more remarkable.

"This yellow blossom is for hope and that red one is for faith and devotion. But look over here." Bella pointed excitedly to the other side of her plant. "This bud is just about to open and it's going to be a glorious pink. See?"

Piper had never much taken to flowers, but there was something really special about this one. Besides which, it was clear to Piper that she and Bella were sure to be fast friends. Any girl with such a keen appreciation for beauty was someone Piper could see eye to eye with. "Holy cow, she smells like . . . paradise"—Piper wasn't even close to exaggerating—"and looks like heaven. That pink bud will set off those purple bits."

"Exactly what I was thinking!" Bella sparkled, buoyed

by the praise and thrilled that someone appreciated her flower as much as she did. She smiled at Piper and Piper smiled back, each girl excited by the other.

"Class, ve vill now begin your science presentations." A groan emerged from several throats but was promptly silenced by one look from Professor Mumbleby. "Bring your project to ze front of ze room and tell ze class vhat progress you have made with it." As there were no volunteers, Professor Mumbleby quickly selected candidates and tolerated no excuses or resistance.

Piper leaned forward in her seat, excited to be part of her first real class.

"First ve vill hear from Mr. Mustafa and Mr. Mustafa." Professor Mumbleby had the habit of addressing all of his students in a formal way.

Ahmed and Nalen Mustafa, identical twins, presented a miniature but fully functional weather station. On the top of it was a rotating steel disk.

"This is called a—" Nalen (or possibly Ahmed) said, pointing to the disk.

"—sensor and it collects—"Ahmed (or maybe Nalen) continued spinning the disk.

"—atmospheric data and—" ditto,

"—reports it to these—" ditto again,

"—sensors that—"

Their presentation went on in this manner and Piper

was more riveted by the way the two boys completed each other's sentences than the content of their explanation. The fact of the matter was that in all of their twelve years, neither Nalen nor Ahmed had ever completed an entire sentence independent of the other. They were never apart, no one could tell them apart, and they never revealed who was who. After a while people started thinking of them as one person, which suited Nalen and Ahmed just fine.

As their presentation continued, Piper became aware of loud thunder. Not long after, a thick fog began to gather in the classroom and it got so that Piper could hardly see her own hand.

"Zat vill do, Mr. Mustafa and Mr. Mustafa." Professor Mumbleby cut their presentation short and asked them to sit down. Curiously enough, once the two boys were seated, the thunder ceased and the fog quickly dissipated.

Jasper, a small boy as thin as a whisper and the youngest in the entire class, was called up next. As soon as he came to the front of the room he began to whimper uncontrollably and cry so that he couldn't get a single word out. Professor Mumbleby finally had to ask him to sit down.

Then Myrtle Grabtrash, a tall, lanky girl with dirty brown hair, zipped to the front of the classroom so quickly and spoke so fast that she was back in her seat before anyone realized that she'd even started. As far as

Piper could tell, her project was about the velocity of light.

"Mr. Harrington, you vill be next."

The commanding presence of Conrad Harrington III swaggered to the front of the class. He had blond hair, perfectly even features, and was by all standards handsome, a fact that no one ever actually noticed because his face was always contorted into the sourest expression. His father was a very important senator and his mother was a British diplomat with a lineage that rivaled the royal family. They had passed onto their only son what Conrad's aunts called "good breeding," and promptly left him to his own devices. The general feeling between his parents was that good breeding alone was more than enough parenting and Conrad couldn't possibly expect or need anything else from them. As they later learned, that was not the case.

When Conrad arrived at the facility he was seven, and after four years, he had become the longest resident. (For those not good at math, that made Conrad eleven years old.) He also had the most acute and extraordinary ability ever recorded, which placed him, uncontestedly, as the alpha kid in the class. Without Conrad's permission, the other kids wouldn't dare breathe, let alone think.

"My project is on time travel," Conrad announced,

causing Piper to sit forward in her seat with anticipation. *This'll be mighty interesting,* Piper thought to herself.

Conrad approached the dry-erase board and began writing out a very long, very involved, and completely confusing formula. "To fully appreciate the complexity of time travel, the time/space continuum must be further broken down by . . ." Conrad spoke quickly and his hand moved even faster. By the time that he was finished, every single board in the entire room was covered with his numbers.

". . . therefore time, space, and matter intersect on the probability axis here, which creates the opportunity to slow time and possibly, under the right conditions, reverse it." He turned back to the class with a flourish.

Absolutely no one reacted or moved. Piper, along with the others, was completely confused, and by the looks of it, Professor Mumbleby was no more enlightened. An unmistakable look of disappointment moved across Conrad's face and his sour expression intensified.

"Hmmm, vhat is zis, Mr. Harrington?" Professor Mumbleby barked. "Ve agreed your project vas to be on effects of polarized magnets. No?"

Conrad threw down his marker on the floor so hard that it cracked open. Using his foot, he stamped on it. "And I told you that I wasn't going to do that."

"I say you vill." Professor Mumbleby was not one to be bullied.

"Like pearls to swine," Conrad mumbled so quietly that only Piper was able to hear it.

"Vat is this you say, Mr. Harrington?"

"This, this," Conrad fiercely said, pointing at his many numbers and formulas, "proves time travel. It proves it, and you want me to do a project on magnets?" Conrad looked like he was on the verge of throwing something.

Professor Mumbleby got to his feet and fixed Conrad with a stare that could turn water to stone. "Mr. Harrington, vould you care to speak of this to Dr. Hellion? Is that vhat you vant?"

It looked like Conrad was going to do something radical, but at the critical moment he took a deep breath and unclenched his fists.

"No."

"A vise decision, Mr. Harrington. And I expect your project on magnetism next week zhen?"

"Yes, Professor Mumbleby." Conrad sat down in such a way as to suggest calmness, but it was clear to Piper he was on the verge of exploding.

"Princess Madrigal has grown two inches since last week," Bella happily reported to the class after Professor Mumbleby called upon her.

Bella went on to explain her cross-pollination process while Conrad silently seethed, getting madder and meaner by the second. At that moment, he was meaner and madder than he'd ever been, but mainly at himself, which is the worst kind of mean and mad to be, because the only thing to do about it is to take it out on someone else. Which was when Conrad's attention settled on the perfect target—Bella.

Bella's science project had been a massive success. Conrad could not, quite frankly, have cared less about her stupid flower. Horticultural science to him was for lesser or feeble minds and certainly a waste of his time and energy. But that wasn't the point. The point was that he hated the plant so much and, in a way that he couldn't explain, he needed to see it dead. And for Bella to suffer the loss of it.

It would serve Bella and her sickeningly loving family right, Conrad reasoned. He could conjure a snapshot of Bella's daily home life in his mind.

"I love you, Bella. You are the perfect daughter and wonderful beyond measure." That is what Bella's sickening mother might say while covering her in kisses.

"But I love you more, Mother." This is how Bella would probably respond.

"And I love all of you unconditionally. Group hug! And then we'll eat some yummy tofu," Bella's stupid father would say and throw his arms open wide.

It was enough to make Conrad vomit. Which was why he was going to lop off the head of her stupid, ugly flower and watch it roll across the classroom floor.

Out of the corner of her eye, Piper caught sight of Conrad carefully folding a piece of paper, and then moments later lifting a paper airplane into the air. It was, of course, no common paper airplane. Having been designed by Conrad, it was more like a fighter jet. Piper watched as Conrad quietly but quickly took aim and launched it with great precision across the classroom.

And this is what happened—

The plane zipped past Smitty and surprised him. He jumped backward to avoid being hit by it and ended up knocking into Kimber.

Startled, Kimber grabbed hold of Smitty and delivered ten thousand volts of electricity into his arm.

"Yeaowwwww!" Smitty yowled with enough force to shatter a person's eardrum, smoke rising from the singed hairs on his arm.

Startled, Professor Mumbleby dropped the book he was holding right on Violet's head.

Thwack!

Piper stared in disbelief as Violet shrank to half of her normal size.

Because of her reduced state, so to speak, the fighter jet passed easily over Violet's head. Next it veered past

Daisy, course-corrected on Myrtle's earlobe, and set a target straight for Ahmed and Nalen Mustafa.

As the jet approached the weather station, both Nalen and Ahmed reached out to snatch the plane from the air. Because they both lunged forward at exactly the same time and in precisely the same way, they collided in midair and sent their science project flying.

Boom! The weather station hit the floor and the spinning disk on the tower snapped free, ricocheting through the air at a frightening speed. It made a menacing swooshing sound.

Meanwhile, the paper jet was running out of steam and was just about to hit the floor when the airstream from a vent propelled it on one last mission—straight at Piper.

Swoosh. Swoosh. Swoosh. All eyes were on the dangerously whirling metal disk, careening about the classroom. The children didn't have to wait long before its ultimate target was announced. . . . *Swoosh, swoosh*—right at Bella's Princess Madrigal.

Bella's eyes went wide. She reached for her darling creation.

Swoosh. Swoosh.

THWACK! In slow motion the metal bit into the green stem and the brilliant, bright, hopeful flower was guillotined from its stem and tumbled through the air.

Before Bella's eyes, Princess Madrigal fell to the floor, scattering petals where she lay.

A terrible silence followed.

Piper gasped, her hand coming to cover her mouth in horror as the paper airplane landed, almost unnoticed, on the desk before her.

Bella fell to her knees, cradling her precious blossoms. No one spoke.

Conrad drank in the sight of Bella prone over her now dying flower like a vampire lapping at an exposed artery. The grief, the sadness that Bella was experiencing filled him and stifled the terrible meanness and madness that had all but totally consumed him. He breathed a sigh of relief as the tension ebbed from his body, just as it seemed to descend on Bella.

"Miss Lovely? Are you alright?" Professor Mumbleby came to Bella's side. "Miss Lovely?"

Bella wasn't moving, just holding and looking at her flower.

Professor Mumbleby was not exactly the most sensitive of men, but even a stone would have felt sympathy for Bella under such circumstances. "Miss . . . Bella? Bella, are you alright?"

Finally Bella spoke, her voice trembling. "Professor Mumbleby?"

"Yes."

"I was just thinking that my flower is still so beautiful. Maybe if I put it in water it would still bloom, and perhaps it's a good thing that this happened because now I'll know how long it will stay fresh when I grow other plants." Like a phoenix rising from the ashes, Bella rose to her feet, holding up the flower. "After all, a bouquet of flowers is probably the happiest and nicest thing ever. Right? It might make someone smile." As always, Bella could find the silver lining in a dirty paper sack. She blinked away the tears that had been welling in her eyes and her face returned to its normal cheerful configuration. "Actually, I'd like to give this one to Dr. Hellion so that she can enjoy it." Like all of the girls, Bella idolized Letitia Hellion.

"I'm sure Dr. Hellion vill appreciate this, Miss Lovely."

Piper smiled broadly for her new friend and relief spread through the other watching faces . . . except for one.

Conrad couldn't believe his ears. Bella was happy? *HAPPY?* Was she crazy? What was wrong with her? The temporary relief he was beginning to feel was instantly replaced with double the meanness and madness that he had before. No more Mr. Nice Guy. Conrad meant business this time.

"Professor Mumbleby? I can help Bella to Dr. Hellion's office," Conrad offered innocently.

"How nice of you, Conrad. Very well. You may both go."

Conrad jumped to his feet and subtly jostled Bella and her stupid plant from the room. In the course of their travels he would see to it that Bella got the message once and for all. This time there would be no mistake.

As the children righted chairs and took their seats, Piper's attention fell on the paper airplane in front of her. Reaching for it, the paper instantly unraveled to reveal a message inscribed within. It read:

WATCH YOUR BACK, NEW GIRL. YOU'RE NEXT!!!!

Piper's eyes widened with alarm as the bell sounded for a meal break.

CHAPTER EIGHT

PIPER WAS pointedly ignored and left to tag behind the others like a lost dog as they did a walk/hustle to the dining lounge that was situated on the second-tier balcony overlooking the atrium. Piper was the last to arrive and found Nurse Tolle waiting for her. Nurse Tolle, as Piper was soon to discover, was in charge of the day-to-day operations and the general health and well-being of the residents of the thirteenth level.

"McCloud, Piper?" Nurse Tolle snapped, flicking open a clipboard and pen. He was a mack truck of a man who in a past life had been a pro football player with a reputation for a mean tackle that earned him the nickname Bone Grinder.

"That'd be me." Piper smiled.

"That's me, what?" he growled back.

"Uh, that's me, my name is Piper?"

"My name is Piper, sir!" he corrected.

"Sir," Piper echoed, rattled.

Nurse Tolle quickly checked off several lines on a form. "I'm Nurse Tolle and you're late, McCloud." Nurse Tolle glared at Piper as though she had purposely made herself late.

"Uh, I'm sure sorry," Piper mumbled. ". . . Sir."

"Don't let it happen again." Nurse Tolle shut his clipboard with a bang. "I'll let you off with a warning this time. We run a tight ship around here and have a zero-tolerance policy with rule breakers. Understand me?"

"Yes, Nurse Tolle. Sir."

Nurse Tolle towered over Piper and leaned down close. "I've got my eye on you, McCloud. Remember that. Now follow me." Nurse Tolle strode to the other side of the table, coming to a stop by an empty chair. The rest of the class was already seated and waiting impatiently to begin eating.

"Seating is assigned. This is your seat. Do not sit in anyone else's seat. Do not eat anyone else's food. Ever. Do you hear me?" Nurse Tolle spoke impossibly loud, making it unthinkable that anyone currently breathing in the entire thirteenth level would not hear him.

Piper nodded.

"I can't hear you, McCloud."

"Yes, sir. Nurse Tolle, sir."

"Good. Later this week I will schedule a time for you

to complete a full diet and food preference profile with our chef. Your meals will then be specifically tailored for you and you alone. Until then you will eat what is served to you. Do you understand me?"

"Yes, sir." Piper saw that each meal on the table was completely different. On her plate were two slabs of fresh sourdough bread with thick slices of American cheddar, lettuce, and tomato, drenched in a tangy sauce, which was artfully arranged next to herb-encrusted sweet potato chips and a juicy pickle. To top it off, a delicious slice of hot apple pie fresh from the oven was waiting for her for dessert.

"Sit."

Piper sat.

As soon as Nurse Tolle was seated at the head of the table and Professor Mumbleby at the foot, the kids hungrily dug into their scrumptious food. It became immediately clear to Piper why mealtimes were such a high point at the facility. She had never tasted food quite so good in all of her life. There must have been five different flavors she'd never experienced before in her first bite alone, and every part of her mouth sat up and sang.

Reaching for a drink, Piper was startled when her glass of water slid two inches to her right and away from her hand. Adjusting her reach, Piper grasped for it a second time, only to have the water glass slide into the center of the table.

For a moment Piper just looked at the glass in amazement. The drink was ordinary enough—plain water, not sparkling, no ice, no lemon.

A muffled giggle was quickly swallowed, tipping Piper off to the fact that a prank was being played on her. Somehow someone had rigged her water glass to have a mind of its own. Looking about, Piper soon saw that every single kid at that table knew precisely what was going on, while pretending to be utterly disinterested. She had to hand it to her classmates: They were shockingly good at playing possum.

This wasn't the first time the water glass prank had been played. It was a choice device to quickly gauge what a new kid was made of. For some newbies, a problematic water glass was enough to push them over the edge after a trying day. One kid started babbling incoherently, another started banging his fists on the table in an uncontrollable rage, while yet one other kid laughed hysterically and was unable to calm himself without medical assistance. The jury was still out on Piper, making her an excellent victim.

For her own part, Piper was darned if she was going to be bested by a wily water glass. Two could play this game, she decided.

Her first strategy was to pretend like nothing was at all wrong or unusual. She took a large bite out of her sandwich, chewing it thoughtfully, and then loudly sucked some lettuce out of her front teeth. Not once did she look at the water glass. In fact, as far as she was concerned, it didn't exist.

"Mmmmmmm." She smiled at the kids next to her.

Right on schedule, the water glass began sliding back toward her. At first it came only a few inches, but when Piper didn't take the bait it moved closer and closer.

Meanwhile, Piper carefully sized up possible suspects. She quickly eliminated the kids at the far end of the table because they were too far away to be so precise with the glass's movements. That left three possibilities: Smitty; Kimber; and the sweetest, most innocent-looking girl sitting directly across from her—Lily Yakimoto.

By her own design, Lily was more china doll than girl. She artfully employed a luxurious cream ribbon about her long, shiny black hair to perfectly frame her heart-shaped face and accentuate her red button mouth. When required, she opened her golden brown eyes wide and tilted her tiny chin just so, to become the picture of innocence and sweetness—a proven pose to break any adult's heart within a one-mile radius and thus achieve any desired means. Now six years old, Lily had all but perfected her doll facade—indeed, she would settle for nothing short of a delicate ivory silk (sent for at great expense from Paris) for her uniform dress, having loudly proclaimed, "You *can't* be serious! I'll walk around naked before a cotton blend will ever touch *my* skin."

It was only in quiet moments when Lily thought she was alone and unwatched that one might spy her practiced demeanor accidentally slide from her features and glimpse the spirit of a wild tiger wrestling to free itself. It would only last for a moment, of course, before Lily would banish it back to the dark shadows of her person. It was a testament to her amazing self-control that the wildness lurking beneath her placid surface was so skillfully contained and hidden.

While Lily's innocent veneer easily fooled Piper, Lily's baby finger did not. The more Piper ignored the glass, the more Lily's pinkie finger moved back and forth in the exact same timing as the glass.

Gotcha!

Despite all appearances to the contrary, Lily was at the helm of this naughty trick and once Piper figured that out, the rest was easy. Biding her time, Piper waited, waited until the precise moment. . . .

Suddenly Piper lunged forward, making a wild grab for the glass.

As Piper expected, Lily jerked the glass backward out of her grasp, and because of its position, the glass neatly collided with a plate, which in turn smashed into the glass of water in front of Lily. The glass was pushed into Lily's lap, drenching her precious ivory silk dress.

"Eeeee," Lily yelped as ice-cold water hit her skin.

"Yakimoto! What are you doing at my table?" Nurse Tolle barked.

Lily tilted her chin and opened her eyes wide. "I accidentally dropped my glass, Nurse Tolle."

"Well, clean it up!" Nurse Tolle hated any disturbance or anything out of the usual. If it wasn't on his schedule, it shouldn't be happening. "Then go have your dress seen to or the next thing I know, I'll be dealing with sniffles."

"Yes, Nurse Tolle." Lily got to her feet, and when her eyes met Piper's, she simply nodded her head in acknowledgment of a worthy opponent. The rest of the kids were impressed too. No one had ever done that before.

Piper silently enjoyed her small victory and treated herself to a generous mouthful of apple pie as Conrad swaggered into the room. Claiming his seat, he eyed Piper with a knowing smile. Piper wondered if Bella wasn't close behind him. After all, Conrad had escorted Bella, so it would seem logical that they would return at the same time.

Minutes passed and still there was no sign of Bella. No one else seemed to be taking any notice, but Piper continued to glance about for her new friend when IT

caught her eye. She was so startled, so surpr⸺
she rose to her feet and didn't move for a lo⸺

"Dang! Look at that RAINBOW!"⸺
shouted, accidentally spewing bits of apple⸺
overstuffed mouth. All quickly turned and saw . . .

. . . exactly what Piper claimed, *a rainbow*. And not
just any rainbow, but the brightest, most glowing stream
of colors stretched out across the atrium not more than
twenty feet away from them. It glimmered above the
fountain, each color of the spectrum proudly shining
forth as clear as a bell.

An instant later a stampede of feet charged for the
balcony railing, accompanied by loud exclamations of:

"She's right. Look!"

"It is a rainbow."

"The colors are so bright!"

"Is there a pot of gold?"

There wasn't a pot of gold at the end of the rainbow,
but there was Bella, twirling about in her bright yellow
dress. Her long, golden hair spun about her as she danced
across the atrium below her rainbow.

"It's Bella!"

Dancing to the fountain, she splashed her hands into
the water, and immediately streams of pink, blue, and
green water began flowing from the spigots.

"Awesome!!!" Daisy cheered.

Bella whirled to a large potted ficus. Placing her arms around its trunk, color shot upward, turning its leaves into a colorized fire display. From gold to red to orange to silver, the tree was caught in a color storm.

"Bella's a real, live color artist." Piper was gob smacked.

"Actually, to be precise, Bella is igniting a mutation at a molecular level in objects she comes into physical contact with. The by-product of the mutation is a temporary color transformation. But yes, you are somewhat correct. Bella is a 'real, live color artist.' Good of you to point out the obvious. It might have slipped our notice," Conrad wryly remarked. As always, he stood apart from the others.

"Go, Bella. Go, Bella," Kimber applauded.

Others soon began to chime in. "Go, Bella. Go, Bella."

Bella's twirling reached a frenetic pace, splashes of color erupting on everything she touched, when suddenly she stopped dead in her tracks, swaying dizzily. Looking up to her classmates on the balcony above, her bewildered eyes were unfocused, as if she'd complétely lost touch and was waking from a dream. It was only then that Piper noticed the tears streaming down her face. Others noticed too, and the cheering died.

"Bella's . . . *crying?*" Violet was aghast.

Smitty was equally perplexed. "Didn't think her DNA'd allow for anything but a smile."

Nurse Tolle rushed out below and quickly came to Bella's side. In a daze, Bella allowed him to lead her away without protest. Just before she disappeared into a corridor she stumbled, swayed dangerously, and then collapsed. Nurse Tolle caught her before she fell to the floor and scooped her up as though she weighed no more than a piece of paper. A moment later they were gone.

Piper wanted to run to Bella's side but Professor Mumbleby was already herding the children back to the table. "Zis is mealtime. Come, come, children. You vill eat now."

"You did this, Conrad," Kimber hissed.

Conrad shrugged.

"Back to ze table now." Professor Mumbleby's patience was at an end. Kimber stalked away and Smitty followed.

"But, Professor, Bella didn't look good." Piper held on to the railing, wondering how to get to her.

"Zhat is why Nurse Tolle is with her. Ve vill leave her be. No?"

"Can I help?" Piper pleaded.

"To ze table, Miss McCloud."

Finally Piper tore her eyes away and returned to her seat. Conrad remained at the railing the longest and when at last he did take his seat, he didn't touch his food.

CHAPTER NINE

ILY'S TELEKINETIC," Violet whispered softly. Piper was
seated next to Violet in the art room, where the class,
after all the excitement of the afternoon, was finally quietly occupied with basket weaving. Violet's voice was so
soft that Piper didn't realize that she was being spoken
to.

"Telekinesis means you can move stuff with your
mind. Lily does that thing with the water glass to kids all
the time." Violet never took her eyes from her task.

"You talking to me?" With the exception of Bella,
the only thing Piper had gotten from the kids up to this
point was a hard time.

"Shhhhh." Violet looked away nervously. It was rare
that anyone actually caught a glimpse of Violet's eyes,
which were filled with a saintly compassion so deep that
she was liable to shrink or grow in response to the emotional states of the people around her. Her ever-changing

size caused her no end of embarrassment, and in a futile attempt to mitigate her situation, she averted her gaze at all times, hid behind her dark complexion, and spoke with a voice softer than a gentle breeze.

"I'm Violet. Keep your eyes down and don't look at me." Piper did as Violet asked, and after a moment Violet started talking again in the same soft way. "That kid in front of you is Smitty. He's got X-ray eyes and he can see through anything, even steel. If he looks at your dress too long, he's checking out your underwear and you should belt him. And hard too. The big girl over there is Daisy. She's the strongest person alive. Shake her hand and she'd break all your fingers and all the bones in your arm too without meaning to. Don't worry, though, not all of us do big, scary things like them. See that kid over there? The small thing?" Violet nodded her head in the direction of Jasper.

"The little fella?"

"Voice down. Don't attract attention," Violet warned. Piper put her eyes back on her basket and listened more closely. "That's Jasper. He's the youngest. No one knows what he can do. Story goes that when he came here, Nurse Tolle yelled at him so bad, he forgot."

Piper looked at Jasper in amazement. She'd sure love to solve that mystery. "What about him?" Piper nodded at Conrad.

"Shhhhhhh." Violet's fingers accidentally snapped the twig she was twisting into place on her basket and Piper couldn't help but marvel at the fact that she also shrank several inches. "That's Conrad. Don't look at him and don't talk to him. He's trouble. Big trouble. Just stay as far away from him as you can. Conrad runs this place. Always has. He's a genius, but more than a genius. They say he's fifteen times smarter than Einstein. He's so smart they're all afraid of him, even Nurse Tolle. Conrad's mean and he does bad things. Terrible things."

"What sorta terrible things?" Piper's mouth hung open and she looked from Violet to Conrad.

"Things that will hurt you." Violet met Piper's eyes for the first time and Piper saw fear in her face.

"Was it him who did something to Bella?"

Violet shrugged and shrank several inches more.

"You reckon Bella'll be alright?" Piper persisted.

"You don't even know what you don't know yet and I can tell that you're the sort of girl who'll go and get herself into trouble. Get herself hurt. Like Bella." Violet shook her head sadly. "We have rules down here and if you don't know them or follow them, you'll pay the price. Rule number one: Don't mess with Conrad and if you value your health, you'll learn it fast."

"But Bella—"

"Listen to me, you've gotta get Bella out of your head. There's nothing we can do for her now."

Piper wanted to argue with Violet, but Violet turned to her basket again and didn't say another word.

"Professor Mumbleby." Conrad raised his hand politely. "The glue is all gone." He held up the glue container and turned it over to demonstrate its emptiness.

"Yeah, we're—"

"—out too," chimed in the Mustafa twins.

Professor Mumbleby sighed. The art room was on the third tier of the thirteenth level facing the atrium and the supply closet was on the first tier, about as far away as it could possibly be. He'd specifically arranged for double the necessary supplies to prevent just such a predicament.

"I see." Professor Mumbleby irritably got to his feet. "You vill all behave until my return." He fixed a few of the students with a pointed look.

Conrad shifted the twenty stolen glue bottles that he'd hoarded in his desk and waited long enough for Professor Mumbleby's footsteps to quiet in the hall.

Haughtily rising to his feet, Conrad assumed command of the classroom. "Jasper, what do you have there?" He sauntered through the rows, stopping at Jasper's desk, where the already tiny boy vainly attempted to make himself even smaller.

"This doesn't look like a basket to me." Conrad snatched up Jasper's half-finished basket and swung it back and forth at eye level in front of Jasper. "Are you trying to pass this piece of rubbish off as art? You think we're stupid? You think *I'm* stupid?"

Strangled whimpers started to emerge from Jasper's throat. By this point, Nalen and Ahmed were flanking Conrad. They enjoyed a good fight and loved it when Conrad stirred up a bit of trouble.

"Say what, Jasper? What did you say?" Conrad leaned in closer to Jasper as though he could hear Jasper saying something. "You think I'm wrong? You think your basket is good?"

Piper's agony at being forced to witness the spectacle of a small child being picked on by someone twice his size quickly morphed into a furious rage. Fidgeting in her seat on the verge of exploding, Piper's forearm was abruptly seized by the steadying hand of Violet. "Don't do anything, Piper. Sit down. Don't look at them."

"But he's bullying! That ain't right!"

"It's not your business. You can't do anything about it anyway."

Conrad started bashing Jasper's basket violently against his desk, and Jasper burst into sobs. A second later Piper could stomach it no longer and jerked her arm out of Violet's hold; she leapt to her feet.

"Hey, Conrad, you let him be," Piper yelled. "Din't anyone ever tell you it ain't right to bully? Why don't you pick on someone your own size!"

Violet sighed in the way you do when you know something bad is going to happen, but hope against hope that it won't, but it does anyway and you realize that you always knew it would and were stupid for having made yourself believe that you could stop it.

Piper came to the other side of Jasper's desk and confronted Conrad head-on, her eyes blazing. "Get back his basket to him."

Conrad smiled, like a cat that just swallowed a canary. "I'm sorry, what did you say? *Get back his basket?* Are you speaking English or is that some primitive grunting language? Unga bunga. Maybe if you could actually communicate like a human being and not a hayseed, I'd return the basket."

Piper shook with rage. "You know what I mean. It ain't yours. And you're bigger than him besides. Now give it back."

"You're confused, new girl. It's clear you need guidance on exactly how things work around here."

Nalen and Ahmed sneered and nodded their heads. The rest of the class waited with bated breath.

"Don't need no one telling me the difference between what's right and wrong. Especially the likes of you. And I know a bully when I see one. And that basket you're holding doesn't belong to you. Now get it back." Piper seethed. "NOW!" she yelled.

Conrad smirked. "Shucks, seeing as you puts it that way, I'm guessin' I'd best do as you says." Conrad held the basket out at arm's length in front of Jasper. "Well, what are you waiting for, Jasper? Here it is. Take it."

Jasper looked to Piper for guidance and she nodded for him to take it. Terrified out of his mind, Jasper reached out one thin, shaking arm. All watched the slow journey of his lone hand until it finally arrived at the basket and tentatively moved to grasp the handle. At that very second, right before his fingers could touch the wood, Conrad suddenly snapped the basket back, flung it around, and tossed it across the room.

Professor Mumbleby had opened one of the windows, but the basket avoided falling to the atrium floor by a mere three inches, and instead got caught on the rail above the window, which hung some thirteen feet above the classroom floor.

"You stinking piece of cow poo!"

"Be that as it may, there it is, Piper. If you'd like Jasper to have his basket back, I invite you to retrieve it at your earliest convenience." Conrad nodded to the basket on the rail, challengingly. "Allow me to rephrase that so you can understand—*go fetch, girl. G'on now. Fetch. Yeee-hawwww.*"

Piper was fit to be tied. "Don't think I won't!"

"Don't think? What I think is that you are a stupid hick who doesn't know a basket from a brick. And if there's any thinking to be done around here, I'll be the one doing it." Conrad moved around the desk and came face-to-face with Piper.

"Your fancy words don't fool no one. All that thinking that goes on in your head don't make you smart. Or didn't anyone tell you that yet?" Piper stepped around Conrad and marched across the classroom to the window.

Instantly the class abandoned their seats and crowded around Piper as she climbed atop a desk located directly beneath the basket. Reaching to her full height, she was still well below her goal of reaching Jasper's basket.

Ahmed and Nalen snickered knowingly.

Undaunted, Piper stacked a chair atop the desk and climbed both the desk and then the chair, carefully rising to her full height, only to discover that once again, the basket was still out of reach.

The kids murmured in anticipation as they watched Piper stack a second chair atop the desk and, with precarious movements, climb all three. Several times Piper lost her balance and Conrad, with gleeful anticipation, expected her to fall, while the other children gasped in horror.

Smitty leaned over to Kimber, speaking out of the

side of his mouth. "Four bucks says her tailbone gets an introduction to the floor."

"Make it ten."

"You're on, Sparky."

At her full height, above two chairs and one desk, Piper reached and her fingers fluttered a mere two inches beneath the basket. Her feet were stretched upward and she balanced on the very tips of her toes, but could go no farther. The chairs swayed dangerously.

"Careful, Piper," Violet urged. Lily watched through her fingers.

Piper knew that Conrad was already smugly anticipating her empty-handed descent. *Thinks he's so smart. But he doesn't know everything and I'll be darned if he gets the best of me.* She was going to do whatever it took to get Jasper's basket back to him and show Conrad a thing or two. Piper closed her eyes and silently said the words.

Because the rest of the class was closely gathered at the foot of the desk Piper was standing on, they weren't able to see what was happening above them. It was Conrad, haughtily leaning off to the side, who saw everything. Like everyone else who saw it for the first time, it took his breath away.

Piper flew. Not much. Just those two inches and then she grabbed the basket and got her feet right back onto the chair.

Conrad was shocked and surprised. Novel emotions for a genius for whom the unexpected was often anticipated with unerring accuracy. His facial muscles registered nothing of the electromagnetic firestorm of cognitive excitement that was instantly sparked inside his brain. In short order (meaning in less than two to three seconds, tops) Conrad processed Piper's capacity to fly, generated and then reviewed all options, selected a course of action, and then calculated its success to a two percent plus or minus degree. Thus accomplished, Conrad confidently set forth.

Piper turned triumphantly to the class, holding the basket like a trophy above her head.

"She did it!" Kimber shouted, excited to have won the bet with Smitty. Except for Nalen and Ahmed, the others gave out various cheers and excited gasps. Especially Violet.

Piper gently dropped the basket into Jasper's grateful little hands and he smiled nervously up at her and blushed in appreciation.

"Looks like you owe someone an apology." Piper grinned, noticing that Conrad's face kept a stony calm as the kids turned to him. He'd been the undisputed class leader for so long, it was both sacrilegious and exhilarating to have him challenged.

"You mean, apologize? To Jasper?" Conrad strutted

forward and the children parted to allow him a path to the desk. "Perhaps you're right. An apology is in order. But not to Jasper, to you."

"Me?"

"Yes, you." Conrad reached the desk. "For the record, I'm very sorry. Perhaps one day you'll know exactly how much." With that, Conrad reached forward and gently touched the edge of the bottom chair upon which Piper was delicately balanced. It was the exact amount of pressure placed at precisely the point required, as Conrad well knew, to send Piper toppling in only one direction.

"Whoa." Piper flailed, her arms swinging.

"Watch out," Violet squeaked.

Piper swayed first left, then right, then left again, and to the surprise of all gathered, except Conrad, at last fell backward, arms swinging like a windmill, out the open window directly behind her. A second later she was gone.

Silence.

Not a child moved, so shocked were they by the outcome of events. The classroom was three floors above the atrium floor—a fall that would have killed any one of them. Kimber's face went bright red. Violet's face went white and she forgot herself and all the rules completely and turned on Conrad furiously. "You killed her. You *killed* her!"

Conrad sauntered away unperturbed. "You think?"

Still none of the other kids moved and absolutely no one went to the window to look out, for fear of what terrible sight might be waiting for them on the hard stone of the atrium floor below.

Jasper, being the youngest and most fragile, began to cry.

"She's dead," Lily whimpered. And they all believed it to be true, except one.

Then suddenly, Piper shot upward, soaring through the air. "Ha. I told ya, you ain't none too smart, Conrad, or else you'd know well and good that you can't keep a good girl down."

Conrad snorted and rolled his eyes. Everyone else was rendered mute with astonishment.

"She can fly." Violet almost fainted with relief. "She's alright because she can fly."

"Man, would ya look at her fly." Smitty clapped his hands together.

The cheer that rose was deafening. Daisy pounded the floor and her strength was so great, the very room shook. Myrtle began clapping her hands together so fast, it sounded as though she was an entire stadium of fans. And the others just cheered.

"She can fly!"

"I wish I could do that!"

"I knew she wasn't psychic."

Piper smirked at Conrad and performed a few twirls

and loops for his benefit and to rub it in a little bit too. "How do you like them apples, Conrad?"

"I like them just fine. Please, carry on." Turning his back, he returned to his seat and casually sat down.

"Do another twirl, Piper," Lily called out, clapping.

"And go faster," Kimber prompted.

The kids hung out the windows raptly cheering Piper's every move, and Piper couldn't have been more thrilled. Not only did they accept her flying, they welcomed it. Truly, she had finally found a home! She completed a complicated twist loop combination in sheer pleasure.

So great was the excitement and distraction that no one heard Professor Mumbleby's approaching footsteps, nor see him stop dead at the threshold of the class and gasp. Except, of course, Conrad.

"VHAT IS GOING ON HERE?" he roared. Kids scattered like buckshot, clearly exposing Piper outside the window. Piper froze in midair, a deer in the crosshairs.

"PIPER McCLOUD!!! YOU ARE BREAKING ZHE **RULES**."

CHAPTER TEN

"NEIN. NEIN. *Sie nuss verwiefen werden!*" Infuriated, Professor Mumbleby had temporarily lost his English vocabulary entirely and was pacing back and forth in Dr. Hellion's office, spitting out German in such a way that his meaning was entirely all too clear.

Sitting behind her desk in her large, white office, Dr. Hellion was the picture of calm, composure, and rationality. Agent A. Agent stood silently behind her right shoulder like a statue, and behind him was a wall of glass through which you could see the rest of the facility. Piper, who'd been placed in the hot seat before the desk, sat on the edge of her chair, nervously waiting to plead her case, which was not an easy task with Professor Mumbleby and Nurse Tolle competing to be heard.

"She had Daisy pounding the floor," Nurse Tolle pitched in as soon as Professor Mumbleby momentarily paused for breath. "The entire building was shaking and now we've got structural damage on levels eight to thirteen. And I'm not even getting into Myrtle's clapping. Sounded like the Super Bowl and there's a snail with hearing damage on level three because of it. Not to mention the others . . ."

"Conrad went and pushed me out the window. I'da died if I didn't fly," Piper hotly protested in her own defense.

"We don't need another Bella."

"Zhis one is a bad influence!"

"She's a troublemaker."

"I keep tellin' you that Conrad was bullying a smaller kid," Piper repeated, all too aware that Conrad had, hands down, won the battle. She'd swallowed his bait, hook, line, and sinker, while he sat back enjoying the spectacle of having her unceremoniously yanked from the classroom. "It's not right. Surely you can see that. And I didn't jump out the window, I was pushed."

Dr. Hellion listened to Piper thoughtfully.

"I demand zhat you *send her home. Immediately.*"

All at once Piper realized that things were a lot more serious than she had first imagined. *They're gonna pack me off home with my tail between my legs? Then what?* Piper silently begged Dr. Hellion to give her another chance.

"Piper," Dr. Hellion interjected evenly before Nurse Tolle or Professor Mumbleby could interrupt. "Do you remember the discussion we had earlier today? You told me that you wouldn't fly. Isn't that right?"

"Yes, but . . ." Dr. Hellion raised an eyebrow and Piper stopped herself before she continued. "Yes, ma'am. I remember."

"I'm glad to hear that, Piper. Now, when you agreed not to fly, did you understand that you were making a commitment both to me and this institution?"

"Yes, ma'am."

"So, you understand that you broke that agreement?" Dr. Hellion quietly pointed out.

"But . . ." Piper gulped, feeling lower than a snake's belly. "I guess, well, yes. And I'm truly sorry. More than you'll ever know."

"Albeit you had your reasons, but Piper, you must understand that Professor Mumbleby is responsible for your safety as well as order in the classroom. If you have a problem, you must ask for help. Understand?"

Piper nodded contritely. "Yes."

"I'd like a moment alone with Piper if you wouldn't mind," Dr. Hellion said to Professor Mumbleby and Nurse Tolle. Reluctantly, they allowed Agent Agent to escort them from the office, closing the door after them.

"I'm awful sorry, Dr. Hellion," Piper stammered, tears welling. "I'm begging you not to send me home. I swear I won't fly like that again."

Dr. Hellion watched Piper closely. In the uncomfortable pause that followed, Piper shifted back and forth, waiting on tenterhooks for Dr. Hellion's verdict. After the way Dr. Hellion had been so nice to her, Piper felt just terrible for letting her down.

When Dr. Hellion finally did speak, she did so in the same even tones and rational manner that made everything make sense. "Piper, I am here to help you. We are all here to help you and the rules we have created are for precisely that purpose. They ensure your safety, protection, and growth. If you don't follow them it won't be possible for us to assist you, and if that's the case, there is no reason for you to be here or to participate in our program." Dr. Hellion paused, watching Piper to make sure she was really listening and understanding. "The reality of your situation is that there is nowhere else for you to go and no one else who can help you. We're it. This opportunity is the best you'll ever get."

Piper nodded, knowing Dr. Hellion was right.

Dr. Hellion stood up and walked to the large glass window in her office to look out over the amazing facility that stretched high above them.

"This is the bottom line, Piper. I have been doing this long enough to know that ultimately you can't force someone to do something that they don't want to do. Therefore I won't try to tell you what to do or what choices to make. Those decisions belong entirely to you and I will respect whatever path you take." Dr. Hellion spoke firmly, harshly even. "However, if you choose to stay with us, you *will* follow the rules. And that is non-negotiable. One more incident, regardless of who is at fault, and you will leave. From this moment on, if you choose to stay, you will be a model student and anything less is entirely unacceptable." Dr. Hellion turned, holding Piper's eyes in her own with a firm stare. "Is that understood?"

Piper's body flooded with relief. "Yes, Dr. Hellion."

"Good. I'm glad to hear it, Piper." Dr. Hellion smiled warmly. "Anyone can make a mistake. I understand that. I will be very disappointed, though, if I ever find out that you are willfully being disobedient. You see, Piper, I wouldn't be surprised if one day, not too long from now, you'll be standing right where I am and running this entire institute."

"Me?" Piper was shocked.

"Yes, you. I see so much of myself in you, Piper. I have faith in you and I know you have what it takes."

Piper was deeply moved. No one had ever said something like that to her before, let alone thought it. She wanted to be deserving of Dr. Hellion's high opinion and make her proud of her. "That'd be swell."

"Wonderful," Dr. Hellion corrected.

"That'd be wonderful," Piper repeated.

"You're like an innocent and naive lamb, Piper McCloud, just waiting to find your way back to the safety of the flock. I hope that you'll let me shepherd you back." Dr. Hellion sighed and returned to her desk, remembering herself. "Well, I think that is enough excitement for one day. I believe your classmates are all preparing for lights-out. If you hurry, you won't be late."

"Thank you, Dr. Hellion." Relieved and thrilled to have so narrowly escaped a near disaster, Piper rushed from the room before Dr. Hellion changed her mind. Passing through the adjoining waiting room, Nurse Tolle and Professor Mumbleby immediately shot her dirty looks.

"She can stay, for now," Dr. Hellion stated flatly when they came back into her office. It was clear that both Nurse Tolle and Professor Mumbleby adamantly disagreed, as testified to by the expression on their faces. Dr. Hellion either didn't notice, which was unlikely, or didn't care, which was closer to the truth. "But keep an eye on Conrad. He's up to something, that much is certain. He never does anything without a carefully calculated reason."

THE DORMITORY was on the third tier of the thirteenth level and each student had their own room. Piper's room

134

was toward the very end of the hallway and was a cozy retreat. A fluffy down duvet rested on a cushy bed. The small corner desk held a shiny, white computer above which rested shelves of books deemed by Professor Mumbleby as suitable for the development of young minds. Pictures of trees and forests and brightly colored flowers completed an overall cheerful and incredibly inviting effect.

Rushing to meet the bedtime deadline, Piper went to her closet, where a fresh uniform, pressed and ready for her to wear the following day, was waiting. Next to it hung a gym outfit, a nightdress, and a bathrobe, all arranged neatly in a row. They were all new and perfectly tailored to meet Piper's measurements. Despite the time pressure, she paused to run her fingers appreciatively down the soft robe before quickly shedding her uniform and slipping into her nightdress. A moment later she jumped into bed and turned off the lights.

"That's it, lights-out." Nurse Tolle's voice boomed up and down the dormitory hallway. "That means you, Smitty."

Nurse Tolle passed by and checked in on Piper, completing what would be the first of many night checks performed throughout the course of the evening.

"Good night and God bless, Nurse Tolle," Piper said as he passed.

Nurse Tolle stopped dead in his tracks and spun around to face Piper. "What'd you say, McCloud?"

Piper gulped, peeping over her covers at the hulking figure of Nurse Tolle lodged in her doorway. "Uh, good night and God bless. It's what my ma says every night before I go to sleep, sir."

"That right?"

Piper nodded.

"Huh." He turned to go and then changed his mind. "My mama said the same thing to me too." An unexpected softness blazed across his face, but he ruthlessly squashed it. "No talking after lights-out, McCloud. That's the rules."

"I'm sure sorry."

"I can still hear you talking, McCloud!!"

"But there's no one here to say it to me. It's the first time in all my days I'll go to bed not hearing it." Piper suddenly wanted her ma and pa so badly it hurt all over.

"That's tough, McCloud, 'cause you're not hearing it from me. So suck it up."

"But—"

"You got a problem, McCloud? You want me to call Dr. Hellion for you?"

Piper swallowed her tears as best she could. "No, sir. No problem."

"Glad to hear it. Now lights-out and no talking."

Nurse Tolle waited to make sure Piper really was good and quiet before he continued down the corridor.

"I can see that light on, Lily. One more bounce of that ball, Ahmed or Nalen or whoever the heck you are, and it'll belong to me."

Before long, all the noise died and the soft hum of the facility filled the air. It was the first quiet Piper had heard in what had to be the most exhausting and confusing day of her life. A wave of tiredness passed over her. She'd never slept anywhere but the farm, never on any bed but her own, and her day always ended with a "Good night and God bless" from her ma. But not tonight. Tonight she was all alone in a place far, far away, surrounded by strangers.

Snuggling down under her covers, she clung to the little wood bird her father had so lovingly carved and said a quick prayer for Bella, and her ma and pa, and Dr. Hellion, and all of the other kids too.

"Good night and God bless, Piper," she whispered quietly to herself.

"Good night and God bless, Ma. Good night and God bless, Pa."

CHAPTER ELEVEN

WITH SURPRISING ease, Piper settled into the routine at her new home. She discovered that she wanted for nothing, and everything from her soft bed to the delicious food was specifically tailored for her comfort. Like a five-star resort catering to the very rich and finicky, Professor Mumbleby and Nurse Tolle overlooked no detail no matter how small when considering the kids' needs—from arts and crafts to music to a varied athletic schedule.

"I can't turn this way or that without having to learn something new these days," Piper told Dr. Hellion one evening several weeks into her stay. Dr. Hellion often invited Piper to stroll in the atrium with her before lights-out, and Piper looked forward to their special time together more than anything else. Dr. Hellion never granted individual time to any of the other children, despite the fact that they were clamoring to get her attention, and Piper was grateful for her attentiveness and advice.

"Professor Mumbleby says that I'm pretty much the slowest student he's ever had. He says that for someone with so many grand ideas, I can't spell worth nothing and he thinks it's more likely we'll make first contact with aliens before I end up getting the hang of those multiplication tables. I can learn 'em fine—I just can't think up a good enough reason to pay them any mind. What's the point learnin' eleven times eleven anyways? Doesn't do anyone any good knowing such things. Besides, if someone's gotta know it, seems to me that Conrad's got that covered nine ways to Sunday. I asked Professor Mumbleby just the other day when I could fly again and he said it wasn't likely to be soon, and I thought I'd be real sad but I ain't. I mean, I'm not." Piper was trying to talk like the other children, and was making progress. "But I guess that's because we're doin' so much stuff I hardly have time to think straight. Didya know that Nurse Tolle said I'd get to be on the trampoline next exercise class and he's going to teach me somersaults? He sure comes off mean, but the other night when I said, 'Good night and God bless, Nurse Tolle,' he didn't once tell me I was breaking the rules like he normally does. Course he didn't say it back, but I bet he was thinking it, and it won't be long before he's saying it loud as you please. I reckon deep down he wants to. You think?"

Dr. Hellion considered the matter. "I don't see any harm in trying, regardless of whether he does or doesn't."

Piper liked the way Dr. Hellion always spoke to her like an equal and listened, not just pretended to listen. "Did I tell you that last week in gym class when Nurse Tolle told us to get partners, Violet asked me to be her partner? She did. Just like that she said real quietly, 'You wanna be partners?' and I said, 'You betcha!' right off. No one's ever asked me before. I've gotta admit I felt real special afterwards. Now whenever there's supposed to be partners Violet and I just know that we'll be partners. It's comforting to have that. And we walk to classes together too, and Violet waits for me to finish up in the morning and tells me not to be late 'cause of how sore Nurse Tolle gets about lateness. She doesn't even mind the fact that I like to talk so much. Ma says that I'd talk the hind leg off a donkey, but Violet says she likes it 'cause then she don't have to talk, which she doesn't like to do, as it makes her shrink. Wasn't that nice of her? I think that makes us friends. Don't you?"

"I think that does," Dr. Hellion agreed.

"She's my first friend ever. It's real nice having a friend. It makes you feel . . ." Piper thought for a moment, trying to put the right words to it, ". . . connected. Like someone is watching out for you and you're watching out for them."

"That's a nice way of putting it, Piper." Dr. Hellion received daily reports from Professor Mumbleby and Nurse Tolle, and although Piper may not have been aware of it, she was already very popular with most of the other children, which said a lot, because they were a prickly and difficult lot who routinely rejected and ostracized classmates, particularly new ones. Just the other day, Professor Mumbleby had recounted how Jasper wouldn't let Piper out of his sight and followed her around like a lost puppy. The others were starting to follow Piper's example and look to her for leadership too.

"D'ya think I'll get a letter from my ma and pa soon? I write to them almost every other day and I haven't heard a thing back yet. Course, it's getting close to harvesttime and things are awfully busy on the farm, so maybe they didn't get time. That's one thing about being down here, it's like time took a holiday and you can't tell one day from the next."

"I'll keep an eye out for any letter."

A bell sounded on the third tier, jolting Piper. "Jiminy, that's first bell. Lights out in less than three minutes."

"Good night, Piper."

"Good night, Dr. Hellion." Piper dashed off and thankfully slipped beneath her covers and switched her light off moments before Nurse Tolle's form filled her door frame.

"You're lucky, McCloud. You were almost late!"

"But I wasn't, Nurse Tolle, sir."

"I got my eye on you, McCloud."

"I know it, sir."

Nurse Tolle lingered a beat.

"Good night and God bless, Nurse Tolle."

"Huh." He gruffly turned on his heel and left. Piper could hear him moving from room to room as she settled more deeply beneath her covers. Something she hadn't told Dr. Hellion, probably because she didn't quite realize it herself, was that a calm had begun to settle over her like none she had ever known before, thanks to the structured and regulated environment. Her thoughts settled and slowed in such a way that they were more manageable and relaxing. She slept more deeply at night and the burning sensation that had relentlessly pushed her to ask, discover, and explore grew less persistent and bothersome. Piper found she liked it better this way.

As weeks quickly slipped by, Piper settled in further and this feeling deepened. It was exactly when Piper had reached the point of almost blissful relaxation and when everything seemed to finally all make sense that, as if on cue, things started to go very wrong very quickly. And Conrad was entirely to blame.

FROM THE very first day she arrived, Conrad Harrington had refocused all his energy on one single purpose—the demise of Piper McCloud. With unerring accuracy and a dark insight, Conrad systematically targeted Piper to the nth degree and caused her trouble at every turn. First Piper's homework assignment went inexplicably missing, then Nurse Tolle discovered her bed unmade (even though Piper swore up and down she had made it). In gym class the rope Piper was climbing broke and she fell to the floor, and then her pen exploded, leaving a large black ink stain on her dress. And that was only what Conrad did in the first week.

"I wouldn't be surprised if Conrad didn't even have a soul," Piper confided in Violet after Conrad locked her in a classroom, making her late for lunch. Piper couldn't begin to imagine what perverse satisfaction Conrad derived from orchestrating his malicious pranks. Whether he was motivated by boredom, or he enjoyed causing other people grief, or he just had a black heart, such cruelty was completely outside Piper's range of experience.

Piper fought against his onslaught with passive resistance, hoping he would soon tire and find other things to occupy his attention. To all outward appearances, she acted as though Conrad didn't exist and met all his mischief with calm equanimity. It must be noted that this was easier said than done, and much to Piper's credit, she had ingeniously devised a foolproof way of accomplishing this each and every time, regardless of Conrad's dirty tactics. With great care, Piper had used a ribbon to fasten Joe's wood bird around her neck so that it rested against her heart. Her precious wood bird provided her with a link to her parents and her home, giving her the strength, despite anything Conrad happened to be doing, to take the high road. Besides which, she learned her lesson after the art class incident and couldn't risk being expelled.

Unfortunately, nothing irked Conrad more and his fixation was violently inflamed by Piper's seeming indifference and Zen-like acceptance. Conrad first doubled, then tripled his efforts, until at last things reached the point of complete intolerability (and even Gandhi himself would have shaken his fist and shouted warlike cries) as he pushed Piper to the brink.

"Move it, fatso." Conrad gave Piper a sharp shove in the corridor on the way to morning class. He pushed her forcefully, throwing her off balance so that her books scattered every which way. Nalen and Ahmed snickered, enjoying the spectacle of Piper crawling on her hands and knees to collect her tangled books. The rest of the kids carefully kept out of the fray, except Violet, who stayed loyally by Piper's side.

"Don't pay any attention to him," Violet urged Piper.

"Aren't you supposed to eat like a bird, fly girl?" Conrad kicked a book out of Piper's reach. "You look like a turkey gobbling your breakfast. Or a pig. Gobble gobble. Oink. Oink."

"It's plain as day that you're green with envy." Piper calmly picked up her last book as her hand instinctively took hold of her wood bird. "And green isn't your color, Conrad."

"Envious of what? You?" Conrad laughed. Nalen and Ahmed joined him.

"I saw you spying on me last night when I was walking with Dr. Hellion. You were trying to listen to us too. It chaps your big toe knowing Dr. Hellion wants to walk with me and not you."

Piper's aim was true and Conrad flushed in response. Lashing out, he grabbed hold of her arm, holding it so tightly that she would notice bruise marks later on. "You're as dumb as a fence post, Piper McCloud." Conrad got into her face, staring her down. "Why don't you open your eyes?"

"I see plenty. Like how you're always stealing food from Jasper." From what Piper could discern, Conrad seemed to subsist on a diet of plain lettuce leaves and rice. A habit that, in Piper's mind, would turn anyone mean or crazy and went a long way in explaining his peculiar behavior. While he had no appetite for his own food, he routinely stole food from everyone else and his victim of choice was Jasper, who was too weak and helpless to defend himself. "In case you never learned it, when you take stuff that belongs to other people that's called stealing, and that makes you a thief."

Conrad's lip curled up and his eyes squinted in fury as the morning bell rang. In the mad dash to class, the meanness and madness deep inside Conrad bubbled to the surface and swallowed him whole. By the end of that very day, come what may, Conrad silently vowed that he would break Piper McCloud.

"Class, you vill be pleased to hear that Bella has completely recovered and vill be graduating," Professor Mumbleby announced as soon as Piper and Violet were seated. Immediately an eruption of surprised gasps and whispers rippled through the room. "Later zhis afternoon you vill all attend her graduation party and I expect zhat you vill be on your very, very best behavior."

Piper shared a gleeful smile of anticipation with Violet. Since Bella's collapse, Piper had lost count of the number of times she'd asked after her, only to receive the same response: "Bella's not feeling well and needs her rest." Piper was overjoyed at the prospect of seeing her again, and when afternoon finally came, she rushed with Violet to the atrium and found that it had been festively decorated with balloons and streamers and a large sign that read, GOOD LUCK, BELLA! in multicolored, bright lettering. While waiting for the guest of honor, games were

146

organized and played with much gusto. Graduations were few and far between and the excitement level was running high. As was often the case when something new and off of the ordinary schedule was allowed, which hardly ever happened, the students couldn't quite seem to control themselves. Try as they might, it just proved too difficult for most of them to remember the rules and restrain themselves when there was so much fun and excitement to be had. Needless to say, there were many slipups, both big and small.

During musical chairs, Myrtle's remarkable speed made her unbeatable, even when she wasn't particularly trying. At pin-the-tail-on-the-donkey, the blindfold was useless against Smitty's X-ray vision and he went on to win every single time. Lily reveled in a cat-and-mouse game that consisted of releasing her balloon into the air and teasing it with thoughts of freedom before telekinetically drawing it back down to her hand. Kimber managed to "toast" all of the marshmallows on the refreshment table until the smoke set off a fire sprinkler and put an end to her covert s'mores operation. Then Daisy's underhand toss during the dodgeball game shattered a massive window with such force that glass detonated outward like a bomb, and the kids were thereafter restricted to a game of Twister, which was thought to be far less dangerous and unlikely to result in the sudden death of a student, teacher, innocent bystander, or combination thereof.

As usual, Piper's joy was marred. During the Twister game, Conrad disqualified Piper by kneeing her in the stomach and pushing her off of the mat when no one else was looking.

"Hey, that's cheating!" Piper held her stomach, winded.

"So what if it is? What are you going to do about it?"

"I'm . . . I'll . . ." Piper stammered, splitting at the seams from the effort it took to restrain herself. No matter which way she turned, she couldn't get away from his nastiness and her patience was wearing thinner than thin. "I'll—" Piper touched her wood bird, which instantly made her remember to take a deep breath and count to ten.

"Just like I thought. You'll do nothing." Conrad looked ready to explode.

Violet grabbed Piper by the arm and pulled her away from Conrad. "Piper, c'mon. Dr. Hellion's just brought Bella. She's over here." Violet pointed to where Bella was surrounded by the others, and Piper was startled to see that Bella looked nothing like she remembered. For starters, her long, golden hair had been cut short and her bright yellow uniform had been exchanged for a pair of drab jeans and a gray jersey. She also looked very tired.

"We'll miss you, Bella," Lily said with genuine affection. It was impossible not to like Bella.

"Will you write?"

"What are you going to color up first?"

"Hi, Bella." Piper squeezed through the group to get closer. "Remember me? Piper."

Bella took a step away and smiled, unsure.

"C'mon, Bella. Just do one more rainbow," Lily begged.

"Yeah, and make it a big one with every color you got."

Bella looked between the faces in confusion. "I don't understand."

"You know, Bella, your colors!" Smitty persisted.

"Awww, just once more."

Piper could tell that Bella was genuinely flustered. Whatever damage Conrad had done to Bella, it was clear that she hadn't completely recovered from it. Yet one more reason that Piper could add to her already long list of why Conrad was trouble and needed to be avoided at all costs.

"Um, I don't know what you're talking about," Bella stammered, causing Dr. Hellion to come protectively to her side.

"I'm sorry, but it's time for Bella to leave now. Her parents are expecting her." Dr. Hellion eased Bella away from the throng and toward the elevator.

"Does Bella seem right to you?" Piper whispered to Violet. "You think she's just fooling about her colors 'cause Dr. Hellion's here?"

Violet shrugged.

"She didn't smile once. You see that? Not once. When I first saw her, she wasn't able to last more than a minute without bursting into a smile that'd light up the sky. It's like she's not the same person anymore."

As Dr. Hellion led Bella onto the elevator, Piper pushed forward once again with a last-ditch effort at reaching her. Since Bella's absence, Jasper had taken care of Princess Madrigal, and almost overnight new blossoms had appeared, and even the stalk that had been severed had regrown. Amazed at the plant's miraculous recovery, the kids had anticipated Bella's joy at seeing how it was thriving.

"Hey, Bella, if you want I can go fetch Princess Madrigal for you," Piper offered, hopefully. "She's got a new shoot pushing up and you can show her off to your folks."

"Princess Madrigal?" Something passed behind Bella's eyes and then she flushed. "No. No, thank you. You can take care of her for me."

Piper gasped. Bella didn't want to see her flower??? "But—"

"Elevator, commence," Dr. Hellion commanded.

"Bye, Bella!"

"Don't forget about us!"

"Come back and see us soon."

Bella raised her hand to wave but the doors of the elevator closed before she was able to complete the gesture. Rushing around to the other side of the elevator, the kids were able to see Bella through the glass as she went up, up, up, and finally disappeared to the surface above them. It was the last any of them would ever see of Miss Bella Lovely.

"Sure wish I got to see my parents."

"Must be nice to go home."

"Alright then, we've got more cake here that needs eating. Back to the party." Nurse Tolle guided Lily and Jasper back to the refreshment tables.

After a respectful moment the rest of the kids returned to their games; Kimber found another marshmallow to covertly toast, and Nalen and Ahmed reverted to beating each other over the head with balloons. Only Piper remained with her eyes looking upward, her thoughts consuming her. *Bella didn't want Princess Madrigal? She loved that plant.* It didn't make sense that she would leave it behind.

Piper's deep confusion was so acute that she let her guard down and became oblivious to the people and events around her. Conrad, who had been carefully observing Piper, realized that this moment was exactly the opportunity he'd been waiting for. Piper's distracted confusion made her into a sitting duck, which was just what he needed to complete his plan!

With silent stealth, Conrad crept forward, then quickly darted around to Piper's side. Oblivious, Piper's gaze remained upward. Positioning himself just so, Conrad prepared himself mentally and physically and then struck like a cobra. He lashed out and grabbed at Piper's chest.

"Ahhhh," Piper yelped, harshly jolted back to reality. Instinctively, she jumped away, but Conrad moved faster. With a violent tug, Conrad broke the ribbon around Piper's neck and wrenched her wood bird free.

It felt to Piper as though Conrad had ripped out her very heart. Her precious wood bird, no larger than a golf ball, with a monetary value no greater than a dollar fifty to Conrad and all the world, had a meaning and resonance held deep in the very fiber of her DNA. That little piece of wood had been nourished by the soil of her home, where her kith and kin patiently awaited her return. It was a physical piece of her pa's love, a tiny sliver of the safety, love, and belonging without which she was suddenly cut adrift with no link to her past or key to her future. She needed it like she needed oxygen.

"This is a piece of garbage!" Conrad sneered, twirling

the bird out of Piper's reach. "Your father can't carve worth crap!"

"You give that back RIGHT NOW, Conrad, or I swear by the stars that I'll—" Piper's face was red with fury and her breath was coming in gasps.

"You keep saying that, fly girl, but you don't do anything. Do you know why? Because you can't. You're useless!" Swinging it around above his head, Conrad pumped his arm, causing the bird to move faster and faster until it became a blur in all of the whirling.

"Conrad! Stop that!!" Piper tried to command Conrad, but her voice sounded more like she was begging him, which, of course, was the truth.

Impervious to Piper's pleas, Conrad bided his time until all eyes were on the bird, and then he flung it at the waste disposal chute. His aim could not have been more accurate—the tiny bird neatly flew through the air. Before Piper's horror-filled eyes, it was swallowed whole, disappearing forever into the mouth of the filthy pit.

And that was Piper's breaking point.

CHAPTER TWELVE

"AHHHHHH!!" A furious scream rang out, raising the small hairs on the back of the neck of anyone who had the ears to hear it.

Piper catapulted herself at Conrad. Unprepared for the ferocity of Piper's attack, Conrad crumpled and the two fell in a tangled, wrestling, furious heap on the floor.

"Fight!" Nalen gleefully announced (or maybe it was Ahmed).

"Fight!" repeated Ahmed (or maybe Nalen).

Arms, legs, teeth, and hair went flying.

It took Nurse Tolle *and* Professor Mumbleby *and* the attending agent on duty, not to mention all of their considerable strength and tactical effort, to separate the two, and even when she was firmly restrained by the agent's grasp, Piper was still swinging.

"I want my bird! Get it back!"

"McCloud! Harrington!" Nurse Tolle panted between furious and terrified gasps. "Dr. Hellion's office. NOW!"

During the elevator ride to the fourth floor, Piper's eyes threw daggers at Conrad, and all appearances suggested that not only couldn't Conrad have cared less, but that he was smugly congratulating himself on a job well done. Nurse Tolle deposited Conrad on one side of Dr. Hellion's waiting room and Piper on the other and sat with them until he was sure that Piper was calm enough to restrain herself. When the meal bell rang, Nurse Tolle left them with strict instructions not to move a muscle, or speak or fight or do anything else that would get on his last remaining nerve until Dr. Hellion's return.

"What does it feel like to have something so precious taken from you?" Conrad taunted as soon as Nurse Tolle left the room. A smile was playing on his lips and Piper's hand had an almost irrepressible desire to wipe it clean off of his face.

"Do you think your bird will burn fast or slow? I think slowly," Conrad baited. They both knew that the disposal system employed suction to draw all waste through tubing to the incinerator room on the fourth level, where it was burned once a day.

"The incinerator's starting in twenty minutes."

Suddenly Piper sat bolt upright in her chair as a fragile hope welled in her. If Conrad was right (when was a genius not right?) and the garbage hadn't yet been incinerated, it meant her bird was still safe and maybe, just maybe, she had time to get to it. *Ma always says, "Where there's a will, there's a way." I'm sure willing, so there must be a way.* Passionately swearing to herself that she was going to have her bird back, Piper leapt to her feet.

"But the real question is, if a wood bird burns in a garbage heap and no one hears it or sees it, does it really burn?" Conrad mused.

"Aww, stuff a dirty sock in it, Conrad." Piper made for the door.

"You'll never make it in time. The incinerator is on the other side of the testing lab and the lab doors have four security safeguards," Conrad scoffed. "It's more likely you'll get struck by lightning than get past those doors."

"Then I'll be real careful of that lightning once I'm on the other side of them." Piper didn't waste another moment of her precious time on Conrad and slipped out of the waiting room and into the corridor with a plan. All she had to do was find the laboratory doors, and to do that, she followed the garbage ducts. Several breathless minutes later, and after many wrong turns, Piper arrived at two doors painted bright red and labeled MAXIMUM SECURITY— EXPERIMENTAL TESTING LABORATORY. Sure enough, they had four different security measures, just like Conrad said they would.

Keep your wits about you, Piper coached herself. She tried fiddling with the security keypad and the screen, but it had no effect. In desperation, she banged the side of it, hoping to shock the system into releasing the doors. It did no good.

"Hey, Moo, grab the dolly. They'll be heavy," a gruff voice shouted from behind the doors. Piper ducked out of sight, and a moment later the red doors swung open and a fat man wearing a utility uniform waited impatiently in the threshold. He tapped his foot until Moo appeared, wheeling a dolly.

"Quit with the rushing. Every week's the same, Jessie. The new specimens will be ready by five-thirty like always. You get yourself all hyper over nothing." Moo, who was even fatter than Jessie, had a small stick dangling from his lips that he pressed this way and that out of some sort of nervous habit. Chronically bored and seriously ill-tempered, the two men lumbered through their well-worn routine in a state most closely compared to sleepwalking. It took very little effort on Piper's part to grab for the red door and slip inside once they ambled down the hall.

As the red doors closed behind her, Piper was amazed to discover that the testing laboratory covered over half of the entire fourth level. Rows upon rows of scientific experiments stretched a considerable distance.

"Geez Louise." Piper shook her head at the sheer vastness of it all. There were more scientific doohickeys and whatchamacallits than a person could lay a name to. With no time to dawdle, she quickly located the waste tubes coming from a nearby garbage chute and followed their path through the laboratory. Several rows in, Piper's eyes were suddenly caught by a red rose fastened between the tongs of a specimen stand. She stopped dead in her tracks.

"I remember you!" She'd seen that rose when she first arrived and it had bitten a scientist's nose!

To test her theory, Piper very carefully extended her hand toward a petal, and sure enough, the petals pulled back to reveal a small mouth with teeth hidden inside.

"Grrrrrr," the rose growled.

Piper quickly pulled her hand away as the rose snapped at her, biting the air. "You have yourself a real temper."

"Grrrrrr." The growling rose was perfectly prepared to bite at anyone who might poke or sniff it. It was gloriously in full bloom and its red petals were positioned in front of a spray gun–like machine. Suddenly the machine whirled to life and a black mist shot out, squarely hitting the flower and also landing on Piper's forearm.

The rose coughed, spitting out the foul chemical, and

Piper found herself coughing too, as the skin on her arm started to painfully burn.

"That smarts!" Piper plucked up a nearby cloth to wipe the chemical off of her skin.

"O! A! A! O!" It was a small noise, the sort of sound you would make at the back of your throat if you were in pain, and it was unmistakably coming from the rose. When only the very smallest touch of the black stuff had burned her own skin, Piper could only imagine its effects on a delicate rose. Despite its tough pretense, this rose was suffering a slow and painful death.

"Here, little fellow. Let me help you." Piper reached out with the cloth to get at the black coating on the red petals.

"Grrrrr."

"If you'd hold still a minute, I'll help you some. I can't do anything if you're biting me."

The rose was unconvinced, perhaps because it was yet to experience a human hand that wasn't interfering with it in some way. At the same time, it was so weakened by the chemical that it didn't have much fight in it, and after a short struggle it finally relented to Piper's ministrations. She carefully cleaned off the wilting petals and then showered the rose off with water. The rose shook itself, gratefully.

"Why are they spraying this stuff on you?" Piper moved the rose a safe distance from the chemical.

"Grrrrr."

Piper was sure that Dr. Hellion would want to know about this. Obviously Moo and Jessie were up to no good, and the first chance she got she was going to expose them and put things right. In the meantime, time was running out and Piper had to get to the incinerator.

Breaking into a run to make up for lost time, Piper said good-bye to the rose and then sped past several more rows until her sight was arrested by a turtle with a lead block stuck on its back. The block was so heavy that it was slowly crushing the life out of the turtle and its legs were flailing about helplessly.

"What in the name of Jehoshaphat happened to you?"

Piper stopped dead in her tracks, confronted by a critical decision—if she helped the turtle, there was no way she could get to the incinerator in time. If she left the turtle until later, Moo and Jessie would likely return and she wouldn't be able to do anything about it without being caught.

"Gosh, darn it all!" Piper's heart couldn't leave the turtle to suffer. She was simply going to have to find a way to live without her little wood bird. Once again, Conrad had seen to it that he got his way.

"Hey, little fella, looks like you got the whole world on your back. I reckon you'd appreciate a little bit of help." Piper unlatched the cage and angled her arm so that her fingers could get at the metal hook that held the lead block in place. Pushing this way and that, she finally managed to snap it free and the heavy block tumbled away.

"That's better. Isn't it?"

The turtle happily stretched his legs out and was able to get to his feet. Piper stepped back to admire it, when suddenly the turtle began to leap. It was the fastest, springiest turtle, and the very next thing Piper knew, the turtle leapt right out of the cage.

"Hey, get back here!" Piper jumped after the turtle, but it was leaping ten to fifteen feet into the air, and before she could count to two, it was across the room and had leapt out a window that opened to the central atrium.

"Dr. Hellion's not gonna like that." Piper turned away in dismay, only to discover that her actions were being carefully observed by a little black cricket. He was peering at her from behind a glass container, and looked to be the exact same cricket that Piper had been introduced to in the elevator. With the same soulful eyes, his antennae moved forward just as before when she crouched down to look at him.

"So that's where you've been hiding!" Piper was excited to see him again. This time the little black cricket didn't come to the side of the cage to greet her and Piper soon saw why. A gooey glue-like substance had been splattered all across his legs, binding them together and fixing them to the cage. The cricket was courageously waging a battle against the goo by thrashing his legs with all his might. Unfortunately, the more he fought, the more the sticky glue was spreading across his body.

"Hey, little guy. Remember me? Hold on there. You keep moving like that and you'll be covered in the stuff. Here, I'll help you out. Hold still now." Piper opened the cage and plucked the cricket out and onto her hand. "There, see, it's not so bad." Piper held him at eye level and girl and cricket regarded each other. "You need a little bit of help maybe?"

The cricket gazed at Piper, unblinkingly. Piper found some nearby Q-tips and used them to absorb most of the chemical. "Who'd go and do something like that? It's not right. It's just not right."

Grateful for the assistance, the black cricket trustingly remained still and allowed Piper to daub away much of his grief. Piper shook her head at the thought of someone hurting such innocent and beautiful creatures.

Delicately cupping her hand around the cricket, Piper was determined to bring him back to show Dr. Hellion what was going on. This laboratory was nothing short of a torture chamber. From her position alone, Piper was forced to witness one atrocity after another—a purple swan swam in a pool of bleach, an eight-armed monkey had all but two of his arms in a straitjacket, and a walking daffodil was leashed to a stake to keep it planted. The more Piper saw, the less she wanted to see, and the more it was painfully obvious that many terrible things were going on in the testing laboratory. Such torture and in-humane treatment of any living creature was hard for Piper to stomach or comprehend.

Bang! Bang!

A loud thumping sound startled Piper and she ducked down out of sight, convinced that Moo and Jessie were about to catch her red-handed. The little black cricket fidgeted about nervously.

Bang! Bang!

The source of the noise was a small room at the end of the row, where Piper was crouched. The more she lis-tened, the more it was apparent that the noise was some-what unusual. The sort of noise that wasn't of human origin.

Bang. Crash.

The door to the room was cracked open and Piper crept forward and peeked inside. Unfortunately, the room was pitch-black, making it impossible for her to see any-thing.

Bang! Bang!

With a trembling hand, Piper quietly pushed the heavy

door open slowly, inch by inch. Light from the laboratory spilled in and cut a swath down the room in direct proportion to the opening of the door.

Bang. Bang. Piper held her breath. Against the back wall of the examining room was a large beast cloaked in the blackness of shadow.

A trembling moved up and down Piper's legs and her breathing came in terrified gasps. She could hear the creature breathe too, and through the darkness see its eyes watching her.

"Howdy."

Tentatively moving one foot in front of the other, she took one step into the room, and then another. Silence.

"Whatcha doing in here?" One step more. Silence.

"You wanna come out of that corner? It's mighty dark. Me, I don't like the dark all that much. I'd turn a light on for you if I could find it." By this point Piper was in the middle of the room, halfway between the beast and the door. She dared not go any farther. She could feel it watching her and sizing her up.

Bang! Bang!

Piper flinched, expecting the beast to lash out. In actuality, it was shifting its position and uncoiling its long neck. Then, slowly, the beast stretched that neck out toward the small, trembling girl in the center of the room. As soon as its head hit the shaft of light, Piper saw that the beast was actually a beautiful silver giraffe! He was covered in dirt and looked terribly thin and tired, but there was no mistaking his regal beauty. He stretched his neck out and came face-to-face with Piper.

"You've got yourself in an awful fix. Don'tcha?"

Piper's eyes adjusted to the darkness and she could see that thick and ghastly chains were binding the giraffe's body to the floor and cutting into his flesh. His long legs were cramped and arranged at odd angles—the banging noises came from his attempts to get comfortable.

The once proud and beautiful creature was broken and beaten and Piper inwardly raged with a ferocity at the terrible injustice. She wished she could break the chains with her bare hands and free him that very instant.

Instead she used her hand to gently stroke the giraffe's head. "Hey, there."

He leaned into her touch, hungry for the gentleness of a kind word and gesture. Piper brushed the silver patches on his head, and they were so smooth that it felt like stroking velvet.

"You're so soft. Beautiful." She caressed the giraffe's delicate face and he held still, lest he miss even a moment of her sweet and gentle attention. While there was no way for Piper to know it, her kindness was the first he had felt in a long time, and it took his mind off of the agony of cramped and crumpled legs and the heavy chains that held him to the ground. His sad heart was lifted and the room mysteriously filled with a flickering light that grew brighter and steadier.

Initially Piper thought the overhead light in the room had been turned on, until she realized that the giraffe's silver spots were literally glowing like spotlights.

"Holy moly, you're like a giant lightbulb!" The beacon inside the giraffe, activated by Piper's kindheartedness, was blinding.

"Don't you worry yourself. I'll get some help for you and you'll be outta here in a jiffy. Soon as Dr. Hellion hears about this, she won't stand for it. You just wait and see."

A gruff male voice came from the lab just outside of the giraffe's room. "Set up the new experiments between the insects and plants."

Jessie and Moo had returned! Piper quickly rushed to the door and eased it closed so that she could peep out without being seen. Moo was pushing a dolly full of specimen containers holding harried-looking spiders the size of golf balls. As they crawled about, they rapidly changed color from fluorescent green to orange to yellow, and then back again.

Piper was on the verge of being discovered, and there was no telling what Moo and Jessie might do if they found her. Rushing back to the giraffe, she gave him one last pat. "I'll be back. You hear? I'm not gonna leave you like this. Just you hold on." Then as quiet as a mouse, Piper slid out of the giraffe's room, crouching low and out of sight. With the little black cricket in one hand, Piper scuttled from one workstation to the next, making a beeline for the red doors. Only two rows shy of success, the red doors came bursting open and a team of scientists entered. Thinking fast, Piper ducked out of sight and remained hidden under a table as the bevy of scientists stopped inches away from her position and conferred.

"Specimen four–two–alpha is still not responding to treatment protocols. Clinical trials show no improvement or any change whatsoever," a bald scientist smartly reported in an overly educated, nasal voice.

"This is a compiled list of the specimen's pertinent data," a second scientist continued. "Note here the use of electric shock treatment, chemical cocktails, hydrotherapy, and of course, physical restraint. None provided any statistically significant results."

"Mmmm."

Piper froze.

The last voice was low but familiar, and it sent a chill down Piper's spine. Her line of sight was obstructed by several white lab coats and she craned for a better view.

"Exterminate it then. It's unfortunate, but we can't dedicate resources to life–forms who resist rehabilitation."

Once again, it was that same familiar voice that spoke. It was not only familiar, but unmistakable. Piper knew it all too well but even so refused to believe what her senses were telling her.

"Two separate teams have been dispatched to capture additional species today," the soft and gentle voice continued. "Uncooperative specimens must be destroyed to make room. By whatever means necessary."

The lab coats parted and Piper saw . . .

NO!!!!!!! It was a silent scream. The sort that your soul yells when a piece of it is crushed and dies. *NO!!!!!!!*

As always, Letitia Hellion's face was breathtakingly beautiful, and she was the very picture of composure. Even as she ordered the extermination of exquisite and delicate life-forms helpless under her care, she did so with the same ease you might ask for more sugar in your tea.

"I have compiled a list of specimens"—Dr. Hellion handed out pages to the scientists who nodded their heads and took notes—"that must be collected and terminated. Let's begin with specimen four-two-alpha." Dr. Hellion led the way and the group followed.

Piper wondered what had happened to all of the oxygen in the room, because none of it was getting into her lungs. How was this possible? Dr. Hellion was nothing short of an angel, or at least she looked like an angel. But would an angel use words like *destroy* and *terminate*? Did angels bind giraffes, slowly kill roses, and torture crickets? Dr. Hellion's outwardly beautiful surface had deceived Piper. She'd believed in her, loved her, and had placed her very life in her hands, and now, God help her, she was at her mercy. If Dr. Hellion was capable of such things, then what was in store for Piper? What terrible things would Dr. Hellion do to her and the other kids?

And yet . . . despite everything, a part of Piper wouldn't believe what her senses told her. The tender, dreaming part of her held out hope that she was wrong and mistaken and that Dr. Hellion was the savior she presented herself to be.

Dr. Hellion came to a stop at the lab station where specimen four-two-alpha should have been waiting. But specimen four-two-alpha was not waiting. Instead, the group found an open case with white chemicals in the bottom of it. Dr. Hellion immediately looked to the team leader for an explanation.

"But . . ." The scientist blathered, looking around the experiment station. "It was right here an hour ago."

"What's the physical description, Dr. Fields?" Another scientist took the chart from Dr. Fields and flipped through it.

"It's the *voculus romalea microptera,*" Dr. Fields quickly explained, scrambling about the station. "Easily mistaken for the common field cricket."

Shaken from her stunned trance, Piper looked at the black cricket sitting in the palm of her hand and swallowed hard. *This is not good,* Piper quickly realized.

"Dr. Fields, the specimen has been released." Dr. Hellion stated the obvious.

"But . . . but . . ." Dr. Fields spluttered. "We've never, it's never happened before."

"Be that as it may, I'm alerting security." Dr. Hellion flipped open her phone. "Agent Agent, we have a situation in—" Dr. Hellion paused in midsentence as her eye rested upon a single stray Q-tip. Very carefully, she lifted it between two slender fingers and turned it around. A hushed silence fell over all the gathered scientists as the full implication of the Q-tip became clear to them. "—ah yes, Agent Agent, correction, we've got a red alert and a possible intruder on level four. I want all surveillance tapes and . . ."

Piper didn't exactly know what a red alert was, but she knew that it wasn't good and that the place was soon going to be crawling with agents. She had to act fast or be trapped. A steady stream of lab personnel had been moving in and out of the red doors since Dr. Hellion's arrival, preventing an escape without being seen. Piper slid the little black cricket into her pocket and ever so quietly whispered to herself, "I'm as light as a cloud, as free as a bird. I'm part of the sky and I can fly." When the tingling started, she reached on top of the table above her head and grasped the first heavy object she came upon. Without so much as a glance at it, she tossed it to the opposite side of the room.

BANG! A glass beaker exploded, scaring the science team out of their wits. Taking advantage of the distraction, Piper leapt across the aisle and then dashed across the room until she came to the panel of frosted windows that overlooked the atrium, a dizzying number of stories far, far below. With wild abandon, Piper threw herself out an open window.

Dr. Hellion turned on a dime. She saw something out of the corner of her eye. That much was certain. She ran to the window and looked down and then up and then side to side. She saw . . . nothing.

"Agent Agent, I want the exact current location of Piper McCloud." Dr. Hellion hadn't gotten to be head of the facility for no good reason—she knew that someone had been in the lab. "In my office? Thank you."

It required every ounce of Piper's energy to fly into Dr. Hellion's office through the open window. Her body felt like it weighed a hundred million pounds. She hadn't flown in months and it was almost as though she couldn't remember how. "Like the birds, I will fly." She said it over and over again. "I'm part of the sky and I can fly."

Panting and puffing and pushing, her feet touched

down and her first thought was to call for help. The telephone was sitting in plain view on Dr. Hellion's desk and Piper immediately reached for it and dialed home.

It must have been hours before the phone began to ring.

"C'mon, Ma, pick up." They rarely received any phone calls from one month to the next at the farm and it would probably catch her mother off guard to hear the unfamiliar ringing. That is, if she was close enough to the phone to hear it at all.

One ring. Two rings. Three rings. Four rings.

"Please hear it. Please be there." Piper expected Dr. Hellion to burst through the door at any moment.

Ten rings. Eleven rings. Twelve rings.

"Hello?" Betty McCloud said on the other end of the phone and Piper almost wept with joy.

"Ma—"

Click. The phone went dead.

Piper gasped and looked down to find a finger resolutely pressing the disconnect button on the phone. That finger belonged to Conrad Harrington III.

"What are you doing? Don't you know what's going on here?"

Conrad didn't react, but instead took the handset away from Piper and, with quick movements, took it apart. A moment later he plucked a small, round disc the

172

size of a button from the earpiece. He held it out so that Piper could see it.

"Bugged."

Piper looked at Conrad as though seeing him for the first time and, in truth, this was the first time he was actually letting her see him. Everything about him was different. He looked taller and more confident and nothing like the whiny, mean child who had been making her life miserable for the last few weeks.

"But . . . what—"

"Shhhh. Don't speak. Just listen."

Conrad reached into his pocket and pulled out Piper's little wooden bird, silently handing it to her.

Piper clutched the precious wooden bird to her heart and tears obscured her vision. Was nothing she knew or saw real? With her own two eyes she'd watched Conrad throw her bird down the garbage chute. "But how—?"

"I created a replica," Conrad quickly explained, putting the reassembled phone in place. "I took your bird with one hand and threw the replica in the rubbish with the other."

Piper's mouth opened, but there were no words.

"There isn't time. Dr. Hellion is on her way. She'll suspect you but she'll have no proof. I was watching your progress on the surveillance cameras and know everything. I've done what I can but you must follow my lead and make sure the cricket stays in your pocket. If she catches you or it, all will be lost. Just do what I tell you to."

That was when Piper knew that Conrad knew everything, had always known. That he was actually trying to protect her and that they needed each other.

And that was when Piper McCloud's greatest enemy became her only ally.

As fate would have it, Piper was given less than four seconds to retroactively relive all of the events of her last months in a staggering journey that reordered by 180 degrees everything she'd accepted as real and true to be fake and lies, so that her head was spinning and her knees were shaking and she no longer knew which way was up or down. It was that precise moment when the door to the office burst open, and Dr. Letitia Hellion stood on the threshold and fixed her piercing eyes upon Piper's white, trembling face.

CHAPTER THIRTEEN

LETITIA HELLION was gently panting from her sprint out of the testing lab, Piper was on the verge of hyperventilating, and Conrad subtly slumped his shoulders and allowed his facial features to return to their normal look of sullen complaint. For an agonizing three seconds, there was silence.

At the precise moment that Piper was sure her chest might break open, or that she'd burst into tears or faint, or some combination of all three, Conrad threw himself upon the awkward quiet. "It's Piper! She's hiding something," he blurted, roughly shoving Piper forward at Dr. Hellion.

Piper's mouth flew open. What happened to the Conrad she had just been speaking to? He had become an entirely different person.

"Is that true, Piper?" Dr. Hellion was amazingly calm, her eyes gentle and kind. "Are you hiding something?"

"Tell her." Conrad sulked.

Piper looked at Conrad in mute dismay. What was she supposed to say?

"What is it, Piper? You can tell me."

"Bella stole something and Piper saw it," Conrad tattled.

"What?" No kidding, now Piper was utterly lost.

"I saw everything and if you don't tell I will." Conrad turned to Dr. Hellion. "Bella had this little, black bug in her hand when she was leaving. It looked like a cricket and she showed it to Piper when no one else was looking." Conrad smugly turned to Piper as though he'd just put one up on her.

Piper looked at Conrad and marveled at his complete genius.

"Is that true, Piper?" This revelation made Dr. Hellion relax and sit down at her desk.

"Well." Piper didn't have as much practice as Conrad, but she tried her best to play along. "Bella was walking and . . . well, I saw it in her hand and, um—"

"And then Bella let Piper touch it before she hid it in her pocket," Conrad finished quickly.

Dr. Hellion nodded carefully, looking between the two children. Her eyes gave nothing away, and as usual her face was as calm as a lake of still water. "I see."

"I warned her she had to tell."

"Piper, for your information, students aren't permitted to interact with specimens unless supervised. Conrad is correct that it is your duty to report this."

"I'm sorry, Dr. Hellion. I don't want to break any rules."

"Yes, I know that, Piper." Dr. Hellion paused, looking between the two of them. "And what is this I hear about a fight?"

Conrad looked genuinely surprised, and even consulted Piper with a confused expression as if to see if she knew what Dr. Hellion was talking about. "No. There was no fight."

Piper couldn't get over how convincing Conrad was. It was eerie.

"Nurse Tolle reported that Piper's bird was thrown in the garbage," Dr. Hellion persisted. Once again Conrad's amazement could not have been more genuine.

"As you can see for yourself, Piper's holding her wooden bird right now." Conrad nudged Piper and Piper held up the bird.

"I see." As usual, Conrad had all of his bases covered. Something told Dr. Hellion that if she asked the other children, they would tell a similar story, and it was even possible that by tomorrow Nurse Tolle would claim that he'd misreported the incident. There was nothing to be gained from questioning them further, even though

Piper's eyes were as wide as two moons and her knees were shaking. "Well, that certainly explains everything. Thank you for coming forward. You may return to the dormitory now."

"Good night, Dr. Hellion." Conrad turned to leave and Piper followed him. Before they could reach the door, Dr. Hellion's phone rang.

"Yes, Agent Agent. What about the surveillance tapes? What sort of computer error? I find it hard to believe that nothing can be retrieved. I see."

Conrad didn't look or speak to Piper all the way back to the dormitory, and by the time they returned, it was already bedtime.

"Lights-out." Nurse Tolle patrolled the dormitory hallway.

In a state of shock and anguish, Piper waited for thirty agonizing minutes in her room after lights-out. During the wait, she tried to calm her nerves by tending to the little black cricket, whom she decided to name Sebastian. She'd never known anyone named Sebastian, but it struck Piper as a very grand name, and the more she watched the cricket, it became clear to her that he was a very, very fine and elegant creature indeed. She created a little house for Sebastian on her desk using a small box, and he seemed thankful for her efforts and settled into his box for the evening.

The instant Nurse Tolle completed his second night check, Piper flew out her window and landed in Conrad's room, where she found him completely dressed and calmly packing a case on his bed.

"What is going on here?"

"I would have thought that was obvious even to you by now." Conrad wasn't in the least surprised to have Piper suddenly come flying through his window, and continued to calmly place books and files into his case.

"But, but, they're hurting all those beautiful creatures," Piper blathered, on the verge of hysterics. "I saw that giraffe and the turtle and the rose and so many others. It's not right. We've gotta get out of here."

"For once, you are absolutely correct on all accounts. I couldn't have put it better myself. Unfortunately, getting out of here wasn't possible to do until you arrived. I needed a flier to make an escape work. But now that you're here and you've got your head on straight, we can go." Conrad closed his case and Piper realized that he had actually packed up all of his belongings and was ready to leave that very instant.

"You mean we're gonna leave right now? Just like that?" Piper took a step back, unprepared. Too much had happened in too short a space of time and she was reeling.

"Like you said, what are we waiting for?"

"But . . . well, I mean, shouldn't we tell someone? Do something?"

Conrad sighed, put his case down. He seemed older than his eleven years, and he crossed his arms over his chest and looked at Piper like a parent would a confused child. "Oh, so you want to go through all that song and dance. Alright, let's get it over with so that we can get out of here.

"I'll start at the beginning. Here, you'd better sit down, this might take a while." Conrad pointed to the bed and Piper sat on the edge of it, her eyes wide. He spoke with strained patience, as though he'd gone through this a million times, which he had, if only in his own head. "First of all, did Dr. Hellion ever tell you what this place, this institute, is called?"

Piper thought back and realized that Dr. Hellion hadn't, nor had Piper ever asked. "Uh, no, she sure didn't."

"And what about the logo? Have you seen this around?" Conrad pointed to a piece of stationery with the letters I.N.S.A.N.E. printed neatly across the top. Piper nodded. She'd seen it everywhere, they all had. She'd never given it any thought, though. "These letters stand for the Institute of Normalcy, Stability, And NonExceptionality, or I.N.S.A.N.E. to make things a little less wordy. I.N.S.A.N.E. is a perfectly constructed, faultlessly operated facility with only one purpose—to make everything and anything that passes through its doors normal. It is one hundred percent effective in this task. Since its inception, it has crafted a seamless and systematic process that ensures absolute results."

Conrad reached for the lamp on his desk and switched it on. Because he'd taken out the normal lightbulb and replaced it with a black bulb, the light suddenly exposed to Piper white writing on every square inch of Conrad's room. Late at night when everyone else was sleeping, Conrad had been hard at work. Trust a genius to devise a foolproof way to hide his secrets in plain view. Formulas were scrawled across walls, there were diagrams on his door, charts covered the desk, and even the ceiling wasn't spared his handiwork. All of which was undetectable without the black light.

"Holy moly!" Piper had to crane her neck to take it all in.

Conrad pointed to a diagram on the door, trying to focus Piper. "Over here you can see how it all starts with tracking devices that have been positioned across the globe. They quickly identify and isolate a specimen that shows itself to be exceptional, whether it be a bird or a fish or a human." Conrad next pointed to a larger diagram with an array of arrows and formulas. "As soon as a positive identification on a creature is established, it is then flagged by satellite. Retrieval units are immediately dispatched to apprehend it. From the moment the specimen is flagged, an electronic surveillance net is thrown over it, making it a sitting duck. By the time it is brought down here into the facility its fate is sealed. Make no mistake, there is only one way out of here, and that is Dr. Hellion's way."

Conrad smartly tapped the corner of what appeared to be an ostensibly ordinary Snoopy calendar that hung on the wall. Immediately it unraveled to the floor like an accordion, revealing still more diagrams, charts, and numbers. "First the specimen is placed under observation and carefully studied; scientists document and record all physical and behavioral characteristics, creating an exhaustive dossier of information, which is then used to isolate a chemical that will stop it from doing whatever it is that they do not consider normal. After years of trial and error, they have found that the appropriate drug administered to the specimen will promptly alter its brain patterns and physiological chemistry. Once that is accomplished, the bulk of their work is done, and all that they need is time before the specimen will revert to normalcy. They know that if the specimen does not use its ability for a certain period of time, the ability will be lost forever. In other words, you have to use it or lose it."

Conrad paused to let that information sink in before moving to the formulas on the opposite wall and continuing more quietly. "While the vast majority respond to the right drug, there are exceptions to the rule, and in those rare cases Dr. Hellion will resort to more radical and invasive means. She'll have the specimen surgically torn apart and put back together again. She'll use gene therapy, alter its DNA, maim the offending exceptional characteristic, and finally, if all else fails, destroy the specimen altogether. That is what they are doing on level four."

Piper's face was deathly white, and she was trembling slightly. As she didn't seem like she was on the verge of completely losing it, Conrad took a breath and continued.

"But the human specimens, like you and me—well, we are their greatest challenge. Other creatures only require physical and biological alterations, but with us, with the human animal, an additional layer of difficulty is added because of this." Conrad pointed to his head. "The psychological, intellectual, and emotional aspects of the human being make us much more difficult to manage and control. It's taken the researchers a while, but they now understand that to successfully rehabilitate us and create lasting normalcy, they must make us want it, embrace it, and see its value. Otherwise it doesn't work. And how do they do this? By befriending us, giving us what we want, making us comfortable, and if at all possible, gaining our unwitting complicity in our own demise. Something they accomplish all too easily in most cases." Conrad gave Piper a pointed look and Piper filled with shame, looking away miserably. Why had she wanted to believe Dr. Hellion? Why had she said that she wouldn't fly when flying was all that she'd ever loved?

"It's all very subtle, of course, and their reasoning is flawless and logical. If it didn't make sense, our brains wouldn't accept it and we wouldn't go along with it. They know if we don't use the ability we will soon lose it, and they're astute enough to realize that the most effective way of accomplishing this is by distracting our attention and refocusing it onto the normal and mundane. Old Hell has a masterful grasp on the delicate balance between encouragement and gentle persuasion toward normalcy, while at the same time negatively reinforcing any unapproved behavior until all traces of the talent are extinguished altogether. Too firm a hand and we'll resist and rebel. It's much easier and more effective to distract us and keep us happy and calm. They don't truly teach us anything to keep our brains quiet and inactive. Their rigid schedule is designed to lull us into a stupor, while they silently and secretly go about the real work of killing our talent once and for all."

Conrad's words, not to mention all the numbers and diagrams, began pressing in on Piper and her head started to feel like it was spinning. She held on to the bed to steady herself while Conrad leapt atop his chair and started pointing to his work on the ceiling.

"You see, they employ a two-pronged approach. Breaking a subject down mentally is half the battle; the other half requires drugs. And how do they do this, you ask? In the food. The delicious, entirely amazing food that is perfectly tailored to your taste buds is made precisely so that it will mask all of the chemicals they're shoving into it. And they're pumping a lot of chemicals into you each and every day, make no mistake. All the while they carefully observe your reaction to them until they isolate just the right drug that is going to make you a little slower, stop you from thinking quite like you did, maybe even make you mildly happy, but extremely docile.

"As soon as that happens—and they are getting better and faster at it each and every day—you no longer want to use your ability, and at the same time the physiological balance inside your body alters, never to be the same again. Their methods are simple, effective, and foolproof. One day a kid wakes up and seems to remember that there was once something that they could do—something special, something different—but for the life of them they can't remember what it is. But they won't mind so much because they've got an incredibly comfortable bed and their thoughts stretch only as far as their next meal and how good the food will be, and for the most part they are given anything and everything they ask for. So they figure, why fight it? Without actually realizing it, they've sold themselves out for a cushy bed and a raging food addiction.

"We're like rats in a maze down here and the only way we'll get out is by being normal."

Piper hadn't realized that she'd stopped breathing somewhere in the middle of Conrad's speech, and suddenly she gasped like a fish pulled out of water.

"No." She shook her head. "No."

"Are you going to lose it? Because we're on a schedule here and we really don't have time for you to get into a flap."

"Sorry to ruin your night and all, Conrad, but it's not every day you figure out that folks have got it in for you."

"Yeah, well, get over it. You're not in Kansas anymore, Dorothy."

"What? My name's Piper and I'm from Lowland County."

"Right, forget it. Can we go now?" Conrad picked up his case for a second time.

"So that's why you won't eat anything and you're stealing Jasper's food." Everything was suddenly falling into place in Piper's mind. "You didn't want to eat the drugs and Jasper's drugs don't affect you 'cause they're meant for him."

"Right, right." Conrad nodded impatiently. "Jasper's scheduled to graduate next and I was trying to prolong it as much as I could to give him a chance to remember his ability. Clearly, it's not working."

Piper was glad she was sitting down. "Not Jasper!"

"Afraid so. They've got you good and hopped up too. Obviously they've hit on just the right chemical combination because you're walking slowly and you've got this dazed look in your eyes. If you stay it will only be a matter of time."

"It will?" Now that she thought about it, Piper had been feeling very sedated and slow. She had chalked it up to being relaxed, but now it was all clear to her. "You're right. So you were picking on me 'cause . . ."

"Because I needed to wake you up and the drug was slowing you down. I needed you to figure out the truth fast and I had to push you a little bit. Dr. Hellion's taken a particular interest in you and it's dangerous to your health. From the moment you arrived and I discovered that you were a flier, I knew there existed the possibility of escape. That changed everything."

"But what about the others? Do they know?" Piper had a million questions.

"No. I tried telling them but it doesn't work. They won't believe you, or if they're too firmly hooked into Hellion's reality, the shock of the truth will drive them crazy. Like Bella."

"Bella? That's what happened to Bella?"

"I tried my best with her but she couldn't take it." Conrad hated defeat of any kind.

"But can't we do something for her now? I mean, if she was to listen and understand, couldn't she get her ability back?"

Conrad shook his head. "She passed the point of no return. That point is different for everyone, but once they make you give it up, I mean really, truly give it up, you won't ever get your ability back. Bella gave it up. You could see it in her eyes."

The sheer tragedy of losing Bella and her extraordinary gift was almost more than Piper could bear. Bella's light had shone so brightly. Undoubtedly she'd been destined to bring so much joy and beauty to the world. Instead she was now gray and lifeless, a fate the silver giraffe was being threatened with at that very moment. And what of all the other nameless, faceless children who suffered a similar fate? What was to become of them and what could be done about it?

Conrad didn't want to give Piper any more time to dwell on the news or to get lost in her thoughts.

"Alright, so now that that's sorted out, I need to know if you've ever carried anything or anyone when you've flown. Can you estimate a comfortable weight range? And I'll need an approximate flying distance before you'll require rest."

"But why? Why do they want to do this to us?"

Conrad swallowed hard and reminded himself to be patient. "Because they consider us dangerous and they can't control us. The Mustafa twins could start a tsunami in their spare time. Daisy can lift a tank without breaking a sweat and Myrtle can run so fast they don't even have instruments capable of clocking her. Unless we're normal, there's no place for us in their world and that's why they've got us locked up down here."

"So we escape and get help. Is that the plan?"

"What help? No one will help us. If we ever tried to come back, they'd capture us and that would be the end of it. No, we've got to get out of here and hide where they'll never find us."

"But the others? What'll happen to 'em?" Piper thought of Violet and her gentle kindness and Lily's mischievous pranks, not to mention the giraffe tied up in a darkened room on the fourth level.

Conrad shrugged, then sighed. "There is nothing we can do. They'll have to stay here. It's better that two get out than none. We can't do anything for them."

"You mean just leave 'em here? Do nothing?"

"Listen, I've done all the calculations and there are little to no statistically significant probabilities that we can get them out. More people generate more variables, which creates more risk. It's too dangerous." Conrad didn't even want to try and explain all the mathematical work he'd done on organizing this escape. If Piper was having difficulty comprehending what, to him, was an obvious and plain situation, there was no way she was going to be able to absorb higher mathematical reasoning. "This is the only way."

"I don't believe you. Even if you're right, I don't care. I won't leave 'em behind." Piper was adamant. "There's gotta be another way."

"There isn't." Conrad's patience was at its end. He picked up his case for the last time. "Now let's get out of here!"

Before Conrad could reach Piper, she shot off of the floor and flew out of the window, hovering just out of his range. Conrad rushed forward.

"What are you doing? Get out of sight before someone sees you!"

"I can't do it, Conrad. I just can't leave without 'em. Violet's my friend and all those animals and things I saw on the fourth level—they nearly broke my heart. Where am I going to hide that I won't remember them?"

Conrad didn't have an answer. Piper knew that she might not be as smart as Conrad, and she even knew that she was probably in shock and wasn't thinking straight. But even so, she knew that she couldn't live out the rest of her days knowing that she'd left the others behind.

"Either we all leave together or we don't leave at all. And that's the end of it. If you're such a genius, you'll just have to figure out a plan that works."

"I'm telling you I can't. Nothing will work. Piper, we're not some comic book characters with happy endings all mapped out for us. Half these kids have got abilities that are all but useless for the purposes of mounting an escape—or for anything else, for that matter."

"All the same, I reckon you'll find a way to make it all work out." Piper floated back and forth.

"I knew you were going to be a problem."

"I'm not aiming to cause you problems, Conrad. The way I see it, we've got no one but each other right now and so we'd best figure a way to get along." Piper started to fly back to her room. Over her shoulder she said, "You'll think up a real good plan. And don't you worry yourself, I'm gonna help out too."

Piper help *him* think up a plan? If Conrad wasn't worried before, he was now.

CHAPTER FOURTEEN

CONRAD WAS desperate.

His desperation meant he needed Piper McCloud, and Conrad Harrington III had never needed anyone. It's certainly safe to say that no one had ever needed him, let alone cared about him. Both his father and mother saw to it that he had absolutely anything and everything except their time, attention, and affection. A child was a necessary accessory in a politically motivated power couple, and they were overjoyed when Conrad III arrived. He was exactly what he should have been, only more. Unfortunately, much more. His acute intelligence was something neither of them wanted, and initially the only use they could find for it was as a dinner party diversion.

"Thank you, Nanny. Do put Connie on my lap." Abigail Churchill-Harrington accepted the boy outfitted in a spotless silk sailor suit and held him as one slightly afraid, like he was a wild chinchilla or an exotic snake.

Dinner guests instantly cooed on cue, their dessert forks pausing en route to their lips, dripping with zabaglione and balsamic-roasted strawberries.

"What a lovely child."

"He looks just like his father."

"You must be so proud!"

"Yes, yes, thank you." Abigail smiled, turning to the guest seated at her right. "You know, Mr. Vice President, our little Connie has already memorized all the presidents and states too. Such a wonder for a two-year-old, don't you think? Of course, both Galileo and Newton are in my family tree, but that is neither here nor there. All the same, you simply can't get away from good breeding. Nanny, why are Connie's eyes closed? NANNY? Oh, they're open again. Connie, dear, recite the states and their capitals for our nice guests." Abigail proudly held her child until he had finished his recitation and the guests applauded, whereupon Nanny whisked the child out of sight, not to be seen or thought about again until he was required at the next dinner party, or tea party, or photo opportunity.

At the age of six, darling little Connie's performance schedule was cut short when he questioned his father on a matter of foreign policy in front of the Chinese ambassador at the annual Thanksgiving cocktail party.

What had begun as a lovely diversion was proving to

be an embarrassment and liability to the family. Conrad's intelligence was so extraordinary that no teacher could surpass it, let alone match it, and no other school would accept him, particularly the best ones. Not long afterward, Conrad started to—in the words of the best child psychologist in Washington D.C., at a rate of five hundred dollars an hour—"act out." At seven years old, little Connie's acting out culminated in a foray into the national Defense Department mainframe, where he remotely reprogrammed an orbiting satellite armed with nuclear missiles. When the CIA notified the Oval Office, the president found he was not well disposed toward a seven-year-old having his finger on the red button. Rather than deal with the embarrassment, Abigail and Conrad Harrington willingly handed little Connie over to Dr. Hellion when she came knocking on their door, no questions asked, thus neatly avoiding any political fallout from the debacle.

Incidentally, the satellite that caused the kerfuffle in the first place had a new trajectory, thanks to Conrad, which prevented a collision with an aging Russian space station that had slipped from its orbit. No one, least of all the president, bothered to attach any significance or thanks to this factoid.

Conrad's ability was at once a blessing and a curse. With relative ease, he immediately saw through Dr. Hellion's lies and understood the true nature of I.N.S.A.N.E. Unfortunately, that same intelligence informed him that there was nothing he could do about it. Conrad and Dr. Hellion were equally matched opponents; Conrad's intelligence versus Dr. Hellion's security systems, agents, research, and drugs. While Conrad couldn't escape, he took effective countermeasures that made him immune to Dr. Hellion's tactics. Had Conrad's parents not been such political powerhouses, Dr. Hellion would have eagerly employed the more drastic rehabilitation means at her disposal, but in Conrad's case the Harrington name bound her hands.

Conrad couldn't escape. Dr. Hellion couldn't make him normal. Thus they remained in a deadlock year after year with no end in sight. Escape was all Conrad thought about. It was the only thing that mattered. And escape was absolutely impossible.

For four long years, Conrad remained buried alive on the thirteenth level in a state of unspeakable agony. His brain activity was relentlessly in motion, analyzing, creating, problem-solving, calculating, its capacity exponentially growing in staggering leaps and bounds. Day and night it worked nonstop, yet Conrad had no vent for any of it (Dr. Hellion made sure of that), no way to turn it off, and it gushed inside him—a raging river of intellectual power battering against the feeble dam of his body, demanding an outlet. Year after year, he existed like a half-starved dog chained in a dirt yard under a burning sun without shade or water, and the pain and pressure turned Conrad mean and mad.

If he didn't get out soon, Conrad Harrington knew that he was going to go insane. And escape was absolutely impossible.

Until there was Piper McCloud.

The probability of a flier is so rare, so completely out of the ordinary, and it was the very thing Conrad needed to make an escape plan work. The minute he saw that Piper could fly, he knew hope. He carefully plotted and prepared for every eventuality except one—Piper's refusal to leave without the others.

How can she be so colossally stupid??!! Didn't she understand?

To make matters worse, Piper had somehow developed the mistaken impression that they were now friends. Each night when Nurse Tolle finished night check and Conrad sat down to plan the escape, Piper made a habit of flying through his window and chattering nonstop about anything and everything that was going on inside her head. (Some information, even a genius like Conrad dreaded to know.)

"I saw Violet eating that chocolate brownie at dinner, and I nearly split, I wanted to warn her so badly. You reckon we'll be able to tell 'em soon?" Piper sat on Conrad's bed, holding Sebastian and gently stroking him. The little black cricket was fully recovered and liked to hop between Piper's fingers.

"Mmmmm," Conrad mumbled, not really listening.

"I know I've been down here a good long stretch already but I've got to admit, it's like I wasn't here at all. Like my eyes were taken right out of their sockets and I was walking 'round as blind as a bat. It's as plain as day to me now that this whole place is crazy. Like how all we do is weave baskets and memorize the same names and dates over and over again. Sure we're busy but we're not learning or doing anything useful. It just doesn't sit right with me. I gotta tell you that when I saw what I saw and you told me what you did, I felt awful in here." Piper pointed to her heart. "A person wants to believe in folks and trust in things, and when you can't, life doesn't seem worth living anymore. That's exactly how I felt. Like it was hopeless. But the more I got to pondering it, the more I just figured that even if some folks are bad, there's others who aren't. So I reckon I just won't ever give up my flying for anyone ever again. I don't care what they tell me. There's just some things you gotta keep for yourself, no matter who asks you or how nice they're being. Then it doesn't make any difference if folks are good or bad 'cause they can't do anything to me if I won't let 'em. Know what I mean?"

"Mmmm."

"You sure are working hard, Conrad. I'm fixing to help you too, if you tell me what to do." Conrad didn't respond. "I'm real useful if you give me half a chance. Even my ma says I can husk a corn faster then anyone and she's stingy in the praise department."

Conrad not only doubted that Piper could help but, except for her flying, it was clear to him she was a terrible liability. So when the very next night Piper landed in his room in a state of great excitement and grandly announced that she'd figured out exactly how to help, he braced for the worst.

"I got to thinking how you explained about Dr. Hellion and her way of getting us not to use our gifts. How she explained things in such a way that we'd think we didn't want to do it anymore. And we wouldn't. Well, it makes sense then that if we wanted to use our gifts again then we would, right? So then I got to wondering how I'd get the others to want to and it came to me right off. Just like that. They need to *dream*! You know, think up what they would do with their talents, and get them real excited about it, and then they might get a hankering to follow that dream."

"Ahh," Conrad said out loud.

That is absolutely ridiculous and won't work, Conrad said inwardly.

All the same, Conrad knew that if Piper's time and attention were occupied, she was less likely to get in his way, or otherwise screw up an already difficult situation, and so he let the matter go.

"So I got right to it and I started with Violet and you know what she told me? She said that if she was to get out she'd be an archey—an archeyolo-something. It's when folks go to far-off lands and dig up stuff from way, way long ago. Like tombs and crypts and the like. Violet explained the whole thing to me. She says when they get to digging, they find things all sealed up and so she figures she could shrink down really small and go inside before the others. She reckons she'd be the first one in places that no one's been near in hundreds, maybe thousands of years, and see stuff painted on the walls and look at old King Tut. Soon as she gets herself an eyeful, she'll come right out and tell the others what was what and how to get in without hurting anything. Isn't that something? I told Violet that she had herself a real good plan." Piper looked to Conrad but he didn't turn around or acknowledge her presence in any way.

"That Conrad sure don't say much," she whispered to Sebastian later on as she settled into sleep. Piper chalked his silence up to all of the hard work he'd been putting into planning the escape, and the next morning approached her day with a renewed vim and vigor, excitedly reporting her findings to Conrad that night.

"You ask folks a question and they'll tell you the most amazing things. Things you've never heard of or would've thought up, even if you lived to be a hundred. Like Smitty's got everything all worked out. He's gonna be a detective and solve all the real hard crimes because he can see stuff other people can't. Isn't that something? I told him he'd be really good at it and I'd hire him, and his chest swelled up like he'd got a balloon in it.

"And then Lily, she's all small and dainty, but I can tell you right now that her insides are as strong as steel. Lily's gonna join NASA and be an astronaut. You know why?" Conrad didn't answer and Piper didn't notice. "'Cause she says that when they go up in space, it's real trouble-some moving stuff outside the spaceship and Lily figures she can do that easy as pie. Don't that just take the cake? I can see it too. Lily, all fine in her space, outfit, looking out the window of some ship, picking up space rocks or fixing a broken engine. She'd be a real credit to us all and it'd be a shame if she didn't get to go up to the moon and I told her so straight out. She told me that when you're on the moon and you look down on Earth, it's real pretty and promised that she'll take a picture to show me. Think of that!"

Once Piper got started, she learned everything about

her classmates. She learned that Myrtle Grabtrash, a tall, thin, gawky girl, whose dark hair somehow managed to completely conceal her face, was her mama's twelfth child. Myrtle was born in a one-room shack on a piece of real estate shared by the railroad tracks of the Georgia Amtrak, and at the moment of her birth, a train crashed right through their tiny shack. The train, which had been mistakenly rerouted onto the abandoned tracks, didn't bother to stop, and so it took a whole week before Myrtle was finally apprehended at the Peachtree, Georgia, station. Her mama liked to say that it was the first time Myrtle ran away. It wasn't to be the last.

Myrtle's best friend was Daisy, and Piper discovered that Dr. Hellion apprehended Daisy after she picked up a whole bulldozer and threw it upside down to prevent the construction of a hazardous waste dump. Only after persistent questioning and great patience was Piper able to extract from Daisy the information that the dump was going to destroy a family of pygmy rabbits burrowing in the soil of the proposed land.

"Small," Daisy told Piper in her slow way, and then held out her large hand and cupped it in the approximate size to show Piper exactly how tiny the fluffy gray-and-brown rabbits were. "Extinct. Too small, not strong enough." Daisy didn't exactly have a way with words.

After Daisy tossed about a few more large pieces of

heavy equipment, including a crane and an asphalt machine, the developer got a little antsy, and Daisy earned herself a one-way helicopter trip to I.N.S.A.N.E., leaving behind a family of pygmy bunnies to wage their own battle against a multinational construction company. Every day, Daisy worried about her miniature bunny family, wondering if they had managed to escape and find themselves a new home.

"I told Daisy that them tiny rabbits got out, no problem. They might be small but I bet they can run, I told her. So you know what Daisy and Myrtle would do if they got out? They figure they'll work together and make homes for things that don't have homes anymore. They don't have it all worked out yet exactly but Myrtle's gonna do the legwork and Daisy'll handle the heavy lifting and they've got a mind to get a piece of land and just collect up plants and animals and people that's looking for a place where folks will let them be."

Conrad snorted. Without a doubt, that was the most ridiculous idea he'd ever heard, until, of course, the following evening when Piper related how Nalen and Ahmed's grand plans were so detailed that they had already selected a name for their company, *Mustafa Weather Solutions*, and had a business plan that included a bread-and-butter base of helping farmers get rain, as well as dabbling in government contracts to reverse global warming.

All of that work would support their main passion—hurricane wrangling, tsunami interception, and possibly even some covert operations in counter-weather terrorism (that last part was, of course, very hush-hush). Hearing this, Conrad just about threw up his hands in disgust at the craziness of it all.

Two nights later, Piper excitedly reported that Kimber's dream was to use static electricity to create an act for the Cirque du Soleil in which she would be called "Mistress of Electricity." Kimber's act was going to be so electric, so amazing, that her audience would give her standing ovations each and every night. (No comment from Conrad.)

There was one stumbling point that Piper endlessly discussed with Conrad but had no success overcoming. No matter what Piper did, Jasper could not remember his ability and had no dream other than getting home and seeing his grandmother, who promised him a puppy whom he planned to call Rex.

"It's like they went right into his head and took a piece out," Piper complained to Conrad. "Jasper just plain doesn't know. I reckon I've asked him every which way to Sunday and still he doesn't know. It's a right shame too."

As soon as Piper sensed that the uprising of enthusiasm and excitement for their dreams was firmly established among the class (with the exception of Jasper), she began posing subtle questions designed to cause suspicion and fan the flames of discontent.

"I sure miss my ma and pa. Don't you miss yours? Dr. Hellion keeps telling me she'll pass on any letters they send but she doesn't. Are you getting letters from your folks? No? Huh, why d'ya think we don't get to talk to them?"

The more Piper prodded and poked, the more she got the others to think hard about things that hadn't yet occurred to them.

"But Dr. Hellion says that if I go around using my telekinesis all the time, I'll get really bad headaches and she doesn't want to see me in pain," Lily said with wide eyes.

"But did you ever get a headache before?"

Lily thought hard for a moment before saying slowly, "Well, no, I guess I didn't. I can't ever remember having a headache."

Piper nodded meaningfully. "Well, then it's a mighty strange thing for Dr. Hellion to tell you, don'tcha think?"

"I said it to her just like that," Piper reported passionately to Conrad. "I said, 'That is a mighty strange thing for Dr. Hellion to tell you,' and I could see Lily got to thinking the same thing. And when I pointed out to Kimber that we kept learning the same lessons over and over again and asked her why she thought they weren't teaching us anything new, it was like you could have knocked her over with a feather. She just plum didn't realize they were teaching the same things day in and day out. Did you notice how she was all fidgety and angry all afternoon and asking all those questions? It's 'cause she knows something's not right."

Piper paused, considering her next words carefully. "Conrad, there's something else. I've been getting this strange feeling. . . ." Piper reached for phrases that could communicate the peculiar feeling of being watched and followed that had been steadily building inside of her over the last few weeks. It was as though just out of her line of sight there was a shadow lurking, ready at any moment to pounce upon her. Try as she might, Piper had never actually seen or heard anything. If she hadn't known better, she would have sworn that it was exactly like that fateful morning in her bedroom at the farm, when she'd heard that man's voice, the one Dr. Hellion had warned her about.

"What I'm getting at, Conrad," Piper began again, "is that I'm being followed—"

"Finished!" Conrad, who, as per usual, hadn't been paying any attention to what Piper had been saying, put down his pen and stepped away from his desk.

"You're finished! You got the plan!" Piper shot upward several feet into the air.

"It's a plan. I can't guarantee it'll work," Conrad warned.

"It'll work. We'll *make* it work!"

Conrad didn't share Piper's wild enthusiasm, nor belief in many of his classmates' random and ineffective talents. Nonetheless, twenty-four hours later he contrived to disable the security surveillance in the girls' bathroom and arrange a midnight meeting that would be attended by all the residents of level thirteen. Conrad insisted that Piper be the one to break the truth to the others, since the whole plan was her idea in the first place. He warned her not to be disappointed if the kids were already too brainwashed to accept the reality of their situation. He also prepared her for the fact that even if they did believe her, they'd probably be too scared to even consider the idea of an escape, or worst-case scenario, lose their marbles completely.

In the early hours, Piper finished explaining everything to a wide-eyed audience who sat slack-jawed and immobile. ". . . so we've got to get out of here. All of us. Conrad's thought up a right good plan and all we gotta do is follow it."

"And do what once we get out?" Kimber wanted to know.

"Where are we supposed to go?"

"My parents don't want me anymore. What am I gonna do?"

"But we can't stay here. They're putting poisons in us. Who wants that?" Piper reasoned. She tried her best to sound confident despite Conrad's pessimism. "With all of us working together we'll be out in no time. If you stay, the only way out is being normal."

"But is it such a bad thing to be normal and like everyone else?" Myrtle had spent her life running away from conflict and was ready to accept any option that would exempt her from having to face a fight.

"You wanna be *normal*, Myrtle? And never again run like the wind? Is that what you want?" Piper challenged, unable to understand how Myrtle would even consider staying at I.N.S.A.N.E.

"But are you sure about all of this, Piper? Maybe you're mistaken about Dr. Hellion or got confused," Lily hoped.

"It's even worse than the way Piper presented it. Much worse," Conrad weighed in, and the children knew better than to question his intelligence.

"I dunno if this is such a good idea." Kimber shook her head. "What if we're caught?"

"Can't be much worse than what they're doing to us now. Right, Conrad?" Piper argued. Although the others didn't notice, Conrad was strangely quiet on this point. Piper continued regardless. "C'mon, y'all. It's not a crime to be scared but we can't stay here if it's bad for us. We got something to fight for. I heard what y'all told me. How you have things you gotta do in this world. Don't tell me you don't 'cause I know you do. Sure, they gave us nice beds and fed us fancy food, but that's nothing. Not really. Not compared to going in tombs or floating in space or wrestling a tsunami or seeing our families. It's not right what they're doing to us. It just isn't right and that's the truth. I say we don't stand for it anymore."

Silence. Each child thought about this. It was a big decision.

While Conrad couldn't believe how well things were going (after all, the kids were stunned, but not out of control, and none of them had gone ballistic), Piper was exceedingly disappointed. Now that they knew the truth, wasn't it simply a matter of common sense that they would take action? Piper couldn't fathom how— knowing that they were being slowly poisoned, not to mention brainwashed, and that the institute was not a school but a prison—that they wouldn't immediately want to escape. And yet, they didn't. Piper hadn't realized what a difficult task it was trying to set a person free.

She dug deep and tried again. "My ma told me that there isn't anything in this life worth having that comes easy. She told me that every road I walk down's gonna have a price. But what she didn't tell me and what I learned since I've been here is that if you don't choose the road you're gonna walk, sooner or later someone else'll do that choosing for you. Now maybe Myrtle's right and there's nothing wrong with being normal like everyone else. But the truth is that we aren't like everyone else. We're like the way the good Lord made us and wouldn't that be a terrible thing to turn our backs on? I can't promise you that every-thing on this road is gonna be okay 'cause sure enough every road I've ever been on has got a bend or two and a few hills and valleys besides. I do know this, though—I know that I was meant to fly and I'm not gonna walk out of here, I'm gonna fly out. And I know what road I belong on 'cause I feel it here." Piper pointed to her heart. "So you gotta choose your road right now. And you'll know which one it is 'cause you'll feel it here too."

Piper held her breath while fears were considered and weighed against dreams. For some, it was dead even. For others, the fear spoke more loudly.

A small voice finally spoke up. "I think Piper's right. I say we escape." Violet shrank a good five inches from the effort.

Slowly, reticent heads began to nod.

"If we're caught, I'll electrocute you till you're black and crispy." Kimber wagged her finger at Piper.

Before anyone could change their minds, Conrad spread a schematic of the facility on the floor in front of them. "Alright, listen up. Here's the plan."

It was a brilliant plan, which surprised no one. It was complicated, though, depending heavily on precise timing and each kid using their talent. As most of the children had been unknowingly consuming the drugs for such a long time, some of them didn't even know if they still had their ability.

Conrad set a rigorous seven-day schedule for preparation. He allowed a forty-eight-hour period to flush the drugs out of their bodies and budgeted seventy-two hours of practice and additional mental preparation. The escape was far from easy and he needed them at their best.

From that moment on, mealtimes brought a new challenge. Kids had to look as though they were eating so as not to arouse suspicion, while consuming only the list of foods that Conrad knew were incompatible with drugs. The list was extremely small: carrots, most fruits, potatoes, rice, and salad without dressing. As a result of their restricted diet, the kids dragged themselves about, starving and quietly complaining to one another.

"I'm so hungry I could just die," Lily whined to Smitty.

"I'm so hungry I ate some of the leaves off Bella's

plant," Smitty confessed. "With a bit of salt, they don't taste half bad, either."

"You think you could score some for me?"

In addition to this, Conrad had worked out a practice schedule so it would be possible for all of the kids to use and strengthen their talents, an absolute necessity if his plan was going to have any chance of working. Violet shrank at night in her room for a whole hour between nine and ten o'clock, and then again in the morning for another half hour. Daisy snuck into the gym and alternated between lifting the entire climbing apparatus and the trampoline. Smitty and Lily performed random acts of X-ray sightseeing or telekinesis throughout the day. Though many wished Lily wouldn't, she was unable to resist playing pranks. It was harder for Piper to fly since most of the ceilings were too low, and Conrad insisted that the atrium was too risky. Piper did what she could and saw to it her feet were off of the ground and in the air as much as possible. As for the Mustafa twins, a random hurricane above the facility or rain clouds in the shower was simply going to attract too much attention, and they were given strict instructions to restrict their preparation to mental planning.

The escape was set for Friday at midnight, and as the days passed, tension built and the kids got increasingly jumpy and snappy. By the Friday morning of the escape, the residents of the thirteenth level were roused from a restless and sleepless night and started what they hoped was their last day in the facility with frayed nerves and a wild look in their eyes.

"It's the waiting that gets to you." Smitty paced nervously in the library that afternoon.

"Sit down." Smitty was getting on Kimber's last nerve. "You're attracting attention. Conrad said we've got to act like normal."

"You're one to talk. Like they didn't notice that you shorted the gymnasium electrical grid and blew out a hundred and twenty lightbulbs this morning. Yeah, that was subtle, Sparky."

Smitty and Kimber weren't the only ones the pressure was affecting. At breakfast Daisy had somehow managed to break the dining table in half, even though it was made of steel and unbreakable Kwarx glass. A strange mist kept swirling around Nalen and Ahmed, and Violet had spent the entire day at half her size and her hands were shaking so badly that she couldn't turn the page on the book she was pretending to read.

"Tomorrow morning we'll all get to watch the sun rise," Piper soothed them. "You'll see. It's gonna be as easy as pie." Listening to her words and the conviction in her voice calmed them. Smitty nodded and sat down, Myrtle's rhythmic rocking slowed, and Violet grew two inches.

"Piper's right," Conrad weighed in, convincingly. "Relax."

"There isn't a thing we have to worry about. Everything's planned and it'll go just as it's supposed to. Nothing will go wrong now."

"Harrington. Front and center." Nurse Tolle's booming voice startled the group from their discussion. He appeared out of nowhere, glowered at the door of the library. "Move it. Dr. Hellion wants to see you. Now."

As nonchalantly as possible, Conrad strolled from the room, leaving behind nine kids, who accelerated from tentative relaxation to full panic in less than sixty seconds flat. It took Piper the better part of an hour to calm them so that Kimber stopped giving off spontaneous electrical sparks and Violet could return to something close to her normal size. Conrad returned just as the evening meal bell rang, much to everyone's relief. He was relaxed and smiling and instantly put everyone at ease.

"We're in the clear. Dr. Hellion knows nothing and suspects even less. It's a go."

CHAPTER FIFTEEN

PLANNED COMPLETION OF ESCAPE	12:05 A.M.
PLANNED COMMENCEMENT OF ESCAPE	12:00 A.M.
CURRENT TIME	11:55 P.M.

ABOVE THE facility, a thunderstorm raged. Violent cracks of lightning stepped on the heels of booming thunder, courtesy of the Mustafa twins. Silently standing opposite each other in their room over one mile beneath the surface of the earth, they swayed to the rhythm of a music that only they could hear, while throwing an energy force, which only they could see, back and forth between their hands.

According to the plan, at 12:05 a.m. the residents of the thirteenth level would revel in their first breath of freedom. As it was only 11:55 p.m., eleven children lay stone-cold awake with nothing but sheer panic and terror coursing through their veins as they anticipated the five agonizing minutes they still had to wait, as well as the five demanding minutes that would follow.

There was only one person who waited with anticipation and not dread, and for that person failure wasn't possible.

Lying on her bed, Piper imagined the stars that she would be gazing at in the night sky at exactly 12:05. And not just the stars but the bright futures that were awaiting each of them—Smitty solving his first case, Lily on the moon, Violet uncovering treasures from the past. She tingled from head to foot and, as her excitement and expectation ballooned, she had to hold herself down by gripping the sides of her mattress, or she would have floated right out of her room.

CURRENT TIME   12:00:01 A.M.

BOOM! CRACK! BOOM!

It was up to the Mustafa twins to knock out the exterior power conductors by hitting them with lightning. Hardly an easy task, particularly as it required a direct hit, and they were without the benefit of practice. This feat was supposed to be accomplished no later than twelve midnight, which made them officially behind schedule.

Nalen and Ahmed's movements became frenzied. Outside of the facility, the thunderstorm was so intense that lightning pummeled the ground like grenades, and even thirteen levels below the surface, the chaos in the skies above was loud, violent, and ever present.

CRACK!!!!!!! A direct hit. The hallway lights in the dormitory flickered and died.

CURRENT TIME   12:00:20 A.M.

Nalen and Ahmed silently performed a victory dance. Auxiliary power kicked in. In sixty seconds the facility's computers and security systems would reboot.

A flurry of motion erupted in each dormitory room. Kids shot out of their beds fully clothed, their feet hit the ground running. Myrtle flashed from room to room checking to make sure that each child was awake (as though they could still be asleep!). Deployment of the teams commenced immediately.

Omega Team, tasked with surveillance and security, depended upon the combined efforts of Smitty's eyes to see and Myrtle's speed to relay any pertinent information to the others. Smitty got into his lookout position on the third-tier balcony and began scanning for any possible threats. Myrtle took her first lap through every corridor of the thirteenth level. She had less than fifty seconds to complete each circuit, at which time she would report to Smitty with her reconnaissance and receive any messages.

Alpha Team consisted of Violet, Piper, and Jasper. As Conrad quietly and urgently pointed out to Piper, everything rested upon her. Piper had to fly up to the very top of the elevator shaft and manually reroute the elevator back down to the atrium. It was Violet's task to shrink as small as possible and ride in Piper's pocket, to assist with any unforeseen difficulties that might come up at the top of the elevator shaft. Jasper was tasked with waiting at the bottom of the atrium so that when Piper sent the elevator down, he could hold the doors until all of the others were safely aboard.

Lily, Kimber, and Daisy were on Team Mayhem. Each had to create a disturbance in a specific location at a specific time to distract attention away from the main thrust of the escape. Daisy headed for the security center, Kimber ran for the control room, and Lily's job was to create blocks at critical entry points.

Conrad, as always, worked alone and was in charge of hacking into the computer and destroying data.

CURRENT TIME   12:01:19 A.M.

Myrtle completed her first lap and checked in with Smitty.

"All clear," Smitty reported.

"Roger that." Myrtle flashed off again.

Alpha Team was in position, Jasper waiting at the foot of the elevator, Violet shrunk down to the size of a Barbie doll. With Violet in her right pocket and Sebastian in her left, Piper took a running leap off of the balcony and shot up the elevator shaft.

Like clockwork, Daisy breached the security control room and locked the lone agent in a closet. Conrad arrived on Daisy's heels and swiftly cracked into the computer mainframe, destroying the databases and deleting all information.

CURRENT TIME   12:02:45 A.M.

Nalen and Ahmed arrived in the atrium and began creating a thick fog cover so that the floors above would be unable to see their activities.

Conrad released security access on the control room just in time for Kimber to gain entry and locate the fuel cells. Taking several deep breaths, she generated what she hoped was one hundred thousand volts of electricity and pumped it into the cells.

Smitty caught sight of a maintenance crew on tier two and dispatched Myrtle to warn the others to keep clear of that area.

Piper reached the top of the elevator shaft and found the access space so tight that her hand became streaked with blood from straining to reach the red wire that would release the elevator.

"It's no good. I can't get at it." She wiped the blood away on her skirt.

"Let me. I'll do it." Violet wiggled in Piper's pocket.

Piper pulled Violet free and placed her on the ledge. Violet shimmied along the narrow strip of metal and then grabbed the red wire as hard as she could. "Uhhh, uhhh."

BOOM! Kimber miscalculated her voltage, and so instead of just shorting out the fuel cells, she ignited them.

CURRENT TIME   12:03:30 A.M.

Jasper kept his eyes fixed on the elevator shaft but it was empty—the elevator nowhere to be seen. It required thirty seconds to make the journey from top to bottom, and according to the schedule it should have been arriving in the next fifteen seconds. Nalen and Ahmed had successfully created a thick fog cover.

"Pull, Violet. You're nearly there," Piper coached, floating back and forth.

"It's, uh, so, uh, so hard," Violet grunted. Sweat was pouring down her face from the effort, and she had planted her feet on the side of the wall and was bracing them to create additional leverage. "Ahhhhh." With a burst of energy, Violet gave it her all.

Snap. The wire broke free, sending Violet flying. Or more to the point, free-falling off of the ledge. "Ahhhhhh!"

"Hold on, Vi." Piper flew after Violet as the elevator sprang to life. Because the elevator traveled at lightning speed downward, Piper was suddenly in a race against time. Violet was free-falling directly below the elevator's path, and if Piper didn't get to her first, the impact would undoubtedly be fatal.

CURRENT TIME   12:04:10 A.M.

Daisy and Lily ran across the atrium to join the others. "Where's the elevator? It's supposed to be here!" Lily demanded. The fog had become so thick that it wasn't possible to see more than a few feet in any direction.

"We dunno—" Nalen (or Ahmed) panted.

"—what's happening. That's Piper's—" (ditto)

"—job. Go ask her."

"Ahhhhhh!" a wee voice screamed.

Violet tumbled through the fog and a moment later Piper snatched her to safety.

Singed and coughing from her accidental fuel cell explosion, Kimber stumbled into the atrium with an unmistakable look of pride on her face. Just then Piper's feet hit the floor and the elevator arrived. Seeing the elevator, Kimber let out a whoop. "We're getting out of here!"

CURRENT TIME · 12:04:20 A.M.

Myrtle and Smitty stormed the open elevator, joining the others inside.

"We're gonna make it," Smitty smiled broadly.

The first stirrings of excitement could be felt.

CURRENT TIME   12:04:23 A.M.

"What are we waiting for?" Myrtle fidgeted. "Let's go, go, go."

"Wait, Conrad's not here," Piper insisted.

Smitty stuck his head forward and quickly found him. "Conrad's leaving the security room now."

"What the heck?" Kimber practically yelled. "He's gonna blow it for all of us, and after he lectured us about being on time and sticking to the plan. What was he doing anyways?"

"Maybe it just took him longer than he thought."

"Yeah, right." Kimber sarcastically snorted. "Like Conrad didn't calculate everything down to the last second. And he's never wrong."

She had a point.

CURRENT TIME   12:04:28 A.M.

"Go, go, go," Conrad roared as he ran for the elevator, diving inside.

Pulling wires from the control panel, Kimber wove a blue wire to a red one. "Elevator, commence," Kimber commanded. The doors slid shut. "What took you so long?"

"Nothing. Nothing. We're alright."

CURRENT TIME   12:04:39 A.M.

Each kid silently counted down as the elevator passed upward.

"Level eight." The computer voice spoke evenly.

With every floor successfully achieved, hearts grew lighter and anticipation peaked.

"Level five."

Jasper couldn't contain himself and he started to jump up and down excitedly. Lily's smile broke her face wide open and Violet grew four inches and squeezed Piper's hand.

"Level three."

"We're free!" Kimber squealed.

"I'm gonna see the world again!"

"Level two."

Myrtle, in a fit of euphoria, threw her arms around Daisy, and Piper turned to Conrad. "What'd I tell you, Conrad? I knew we'd do it. I just knew it."

Conrad couldn't look at Piper's dancing eyes and smiling face and he turned away. Piper looked at him in confusion as—

"Level one."

Bing! The elevator chimed and slowed. Then it stopped.

"What's going on?" Shocked eyes searched out fearful faces.

"Why are we stopping?"

"What's happening, Conrad?"

Hearts fell like stones. No one breathed. All suffered silent suspense as time slowed and they watched helplessly as the doors to the elevator opened. . . .

"Oh no!" Piper whispered.

Click! was the sound the elevator doors made when they were fully retracted, exposing a brigade of agents, several lines deep, positioned in rows and armed with weapons aiming into the elevator.

There was a moment that lasted no more than a heartbeat. In it, the children's dreams of freedom continued to flicker before their eyes so brightly that they were unable to reconcile the reality of being surrounded with their fervent need to escape. The two contradictory ideas effectively short-circuited their brains, causing them to go completely blank.

Alas, the stillness would not stand.

Agent A. Agent lunged forward and seized Piper. Pandemonium ensued.

Everything happened so fast—there was no time to prepare and certainly no time to organize any sort of resistance. There was a loud scream. It sounded like Lily. Myrtle tried to run but they had a net. Someone cried out. Probably Jasper. Daisy was the only one who proved difficult. Several agents had broken arms and legs before a tranquilizer dart lodged itself in her arm and she fell to the floor with a thud.

The agents had prepared for everything. Each team was assigned to a child and prepped for their particular ability. Had the children been primed, or even had an inkling that they'd been discovered, they would have had a fighting chance. In the end, it was the element of surprise and the agents' strength that effectively made them sitting ducks.

The escape had officially failed.

The time was 12:05:59 a.m.

The kids were promptly escorted down to the thirteenth level. Each child was guarded by three agents, who were not only armed to the teeth, but looked more than ready to use the weapons at their disposal. Agent A. Agent lined the children up in a row on the atrium floor.

From the moment she'd been seized and restrained, Piper was so shocked that she was almost completely unaware of her surroundings. "I don't understand," she whispered quietly to herself, over and over again. "It doesn't make sense. It just doesn't make sense."

Conrad stood next to Piper in the atrium lineup. On the verge of losing control, her feverish utterances hit his ears in unremitting waves. "Piper, stop it. It's over. You've got to snap out of it."

Nothing prepared Conrad for the look of haunted horror that had come over Piper as she turned to him. It was worse even than when he'd told Bella the truth about I.N.S.A.N.E. and she'd torn the precious petals off her flower in savage movements. It was even worse than Ang Chung, who started to hit himself and wouldn't stop.

"But we had a plan. We were all working together. I knew here"—Piper pointed to her heart—"that it would work. I felt it. I knew it. How . . . ?"

"Thank you, Agent A. Agent." Dr. Hellion swept into the atrium, perfectly outfitted and absolutely calm. "Quite an evening you have all had." Moving down the line, she looked each child in the eyes and, without exception, they all looked away.

"I've been so worried about you all." She shook her

head sadly. "So concerned for your safety and well-being. What could possibly be going on that you felt the need to—?" Unable to actually use the word *escape,* Dr. Hellion waved her hand, indicating the events of the evening. "I've been wracking my brain as to the cause of all of this. And then it came to me. Someone *lied* to you.

"It's a terrible thing to be lied to. That person probably told you things that aren't true. They made them up. Lied. I can imagine how easy it would be, once you have mistakenly accepted the lies for truth, to jump to a conclusion where your only option is, well, to do what you did this evening." She paused and smiled, and there was nothing but warmth and understanding about her person. Her whole being said, *I understand and you can trust me.* "I see your actions tonight as nothing more than a call for help.

"Rest assured, I'm here to answer your call." Dr. Hellion sighed and spoke as though she was sharing a terrible secret. "I can be sympathetic to those who were misled. But at the same time, the person who told you the lies really needs my help the most and I wouldn't be doing my job if I didn't help that person. So"—Dr. Hellion smiled in the most kind and caring way—"which one of you will tell me whose idea this was?"

No one moved. Even though Piper knew better, Dr. Hellion's sincerity was so persuasive that despite herself, she began to doubt. What if she had been mistaken? If she had been so wrong about the escape, then maybe she'd been wrong about everything. What was real? Who could she believe? Certainly not herself anymore. She'd proved that, that very evening.

"Of course, if you feel that you can't tell me, then I'm compelled to help you all equally. Certainly not my choice. But I will respect your wishes. Nurse Tolle?"

Nurse Tolle came forward with a cart. On it were eleven hypodermic needles. It didn't take a genius to figure out that they were filled with drugs.

"It came to Nurse Tolle's attention this week that you have not had appropriate nutrition. Undoubtedly this has contributed to your confusion. Nurse Tolle and I would like to rectify that immediately. Nurse Tolle, please bring Jasper forward."

Nurse Tolle and three agents dragged a squirming Jasper front and center. The other children were forced to witness his feeble attempts to resist. "N-n-no," he stuttered. "P-p-please, Dr. H-h-hellion. P-please don't."

Piper's eyes couldn't believe what they were seeing. Poor Jasper, the weakest and most helpless, was twisting and turning like a bird with a broken wing before a pack of hungry dogs. Dr. Hellion watched him without mercy and, with the slightest nod of her head, Nurse Tolle plunged the needle into Jasper's thin arm. Jasper yelped and the kids averted their gaze, unable to watch.

A moment later, Jasper's eyes clouded over and his body became limp and relaxed.

Dr. Hellion waited, but still no one came forward. "Very well, Nurse Tolle, please assist Lily."

"Nooooo." Lily's high-pitched voice hovered in the cadences of true panic. Her cry struck Piper to the quick.

"Wait!" Piper stepped forward. "Wait."

Dr. Hellion nodded to Nurse Tolle, who pulled the needle away from Lily's arm. "Yes, Piper?"

"It was all my idea, Dr. Hellion. They didn't do anything. Please let Lily be."

Dr. Hellion carefully looked at the others. "I see. And no one helped you?"

"No, it was all me. And I'm sure sorry."

"I understand, Piper. I really do. There's no need to be sorry. Why don't you come stand here by me?" Dr. Hellion waited for Piper to shuffle forward and come to her side. "There is something I can help you understand, Piper, and it will change your life. It's very important." Dr. Hellion bent so that she was eye level with Piper. Lowering her voice, she spoke with a quiet intensity. "When you fly, people get hurt. Your flying causes pain and it hurts everyone you love."

Piper got lost in Dr. Hellion's eyes and doubt took advantage of her confusion, taking firm root and quickly spreading its poison.

"Piper, I am here to support you, but it's important for you to see the consequences of your flying. You may proceed, Nurse Tolle."

"But, Dr. Hellion, please. They didn't do anything. You don't have to do that to Lily."

"You still don't understand, Piper. *I'm* not doing anything. It is *you* who are doing this to them."

"I am? But—" Piper fought with the notion, but as the needle plunged into Lily's arm, her gut-wrenching scream took away all of Piper's ability to form rational thought and left in its stead guilt, remorse, and pain.

And that wasn't even the worst of it. As Piper was forced to stand and watch, Nurse Tolle went down the line and one after another picked out a terror-filled, writhing victim and injected them with the drugs. Daisy cried. Smitty covered his eyes. Myrtle tried to run. But nothing could save them from the needle. Before the injection they struggled and resisted; afterward their bodies were limp and their eyes vacant.

Each one broke Piper's heart. How could she have been so wrong? If she couldn't trust other people and she couldn't trust her own heart, then there was nothing left for her to believe in and trust.

And right then and there Piper's heart broke in two.

CHAPTER SIXTEEN

PIPER DIDN'T resist when Agent A. Agent and Dr. Hellion escorted her to the fourth level. Led past row upon row of experiments, she saw the rose covered with black soot and a closed door behind which the banging of the silver giraffe was no longer heard. Finally, at the far end of the laboratory, Piper was led into a room protected by more security protocols than any other in all of I.N.S.A.N.E. At the center of that room stood a strange metal contraption. It looked to Piper like a giant metal frame shaped into the outline of the human body, almost like a life-size version of what her mother used at Christmastime to cut out gingerbread men from cookie dough.

Dr. Hellion approached the contraption reverently and ran her hand down the cold, shining metal with admiration. "This device, Piper, is specifically designed to help clear your mind. It's called a Molecular Orienting

Limitation Device or M.O.L.D. for short." Dr. Hellion's face appeared very helpful and kind. "At a core level, it will adjust you so that you can enjoy a more normal way of life."

At Dr. Hellion's command, Nurse Tolle and Agent A. Agent lifted Piper up and placed her into the center of the metal shape.

"As we input your information on this computer over here"—Dr. Hellion indicated where a scientist was working by a monitor against the wall—"it communicates with the M.O.L.D. and instructs it to create the exact normal specifications for someone of your age and sex. While you relax, the M.O.L.D. will help you discover what it feels like to be normal just like everyone else. Wouldn't you like that?"

"I—I can't rightly say." Piper didn't know what she wanted anymore. She no longer had any frame of reference.

With a few more keystrokes, the scientist completed his data entry and the metal frame began to contract around Piper from all sides. It quickly went from feeling snug to pressing against her with a force that made her scream out in agony.

"Ahhhhh!"

"You'll learn to love that feeling, Piper." Dr. Hellion caught the scientist's eye. "I think it would best serve Piper if you increased the intensity, Dr. Fields."

Dr. Fields's brow furrowed and he looked as though he wanted to object, but then thought the better of it. Silently, he complied, and after a few more pecks at the computer, the metal instantly responded to the commands and squeezed Piper even more tightly.

"Owwwww." Piper's eyes widened and she couldn't catch her breath. The M.O.L.D. was literally crushing the life out of her. It took all of her strength just to stop herself from begging for mercy.

"I'm told that the more you resist, the more painful it is. When you learn to relax and accept it, you'll feel nothing but comfort and safety." Dr. Hellion smiled reassuringly. "Dr. Fields, I believe that Piper still requires greater assistance. Please increase the intensity."

This time Dr. Fields was not able to restrain himself. "But, Dr. Hellion, it's already at the maximum level."

Letitia Hellion turned with icy calmness and fixed Dr. Fields with dead eyes. "Is there a problem?"

Dr. Fields inched forward and lowered his voice fearfully. "Dr. Hellion, if I increase it any more, it could cause permanent damage, maybe even cripple her. It's not . . . I can't . . . it isn't recommended."

"Thank you, Dr. Fields, for that information. Shall I ask someone else to come in and take over your responsibilities?"

The beads of sweat on Dr. Fields's brow became tiny

rivers. His hands hesitated and then trembled as they returned to the computer. Even as he did it, Dr. Fields knew that on the day he died, this was the moment he would remember with the most regret. He couldn't bring himself to look at Piper as the metal responded one more time and somehow, although he couldn't imagine at this point how it might be possible, pushed Piper in farther.

"AHHHHHHH." Piper would have begged if she had been able to speak. It took all of her resources just to draw breath.

"Perfect. That's much better," Dr. Hellion approved. "Now, Piper, when I see you again, you will not only never remember the fact that you flew, but you will never have the desire to do so again. Flying is a nasty habit. It hurts people. It hurts you."

"B–b–but"—Piper had to struggle through the pain to remember how to speak—"I love flying."

"No, Piper, you don't. You just *think* you do. Soon you'll *know* that you were mistaken. Just like you were mistaken about the escape." Dr. Hellion snatched Piper's wooden bird from around her neck, smiled brightly, and left the room. Nurse Tolle and Agent A. Agent promptly followed on her heels, leaving Dr. Fields behind.

"I'm so sorry," Dr. Fields mumbled and fled. He sealed the door and left Piper alone with her agony.

"Oh, it hurts. It hurts. Make it stop. Make it stop," Piper begged no one in particular. The pain was unmanageable. The word *pain* couldn't even contain the feeling. It was like being hit by a train, specifically the moment after you're hit but before you die (and are given the comfort of oblivion).

"Oh, Ma, Pa, help me. Someone help me."

A tiny wiggling motion moved against Piper's leg. Then it wiggled some more and traveled up toward her waist, until the white linen handkerchief her ma had given her was pushed out of her pocket and fell to the floor below. A moment later Sebastian squirmed free of the pocket, hopped over the metal, and found a perch on the wall at eye level with Piper. He settled himself across from her.

The sight of her dear black cricket brought tears to Piper's eyes. "You're a sight for sore eyes." She was so grateful that she wasn't alone.

"I guess you're not far from where I first found you, huh? I'm sure sorry about that. Probably I should've got you out sooner. But see, over there." Piper moved her eyes, the only part of her capable of movement, toward the direction of a vent. "You could use that if you had a mind to. Bet that leads somewhere."

Sebastian saw the vent but turned his black face back to Piper and didn't move. He obviously had no intention of going anywhere.

"If you change your mind, I won't hold it against you." The pain caught up with Piper again and she fought it with everything she had.

"Piper?"

Startled, Piper's eyes darted about the room, but she could see nothing.

"Piper McCloud?" The voice spoke again.

It was the same voice Piper had heard in her room back in Lowland County—the one Dr. Hellion had warned her about. Just as Piper had suspected and feared, it had been stalking her.

Suddenly a shadow passed before the door. Moments later, the overhead security camera violently snapped free from its casing and fell to the floor. Terrified, Piper couldn't move away or defend herself, and was forced to watch in horror as the shadow moved toward her closer and closer. The nearer it came, the more substance it gathered, until the shadow morphed into a man.

He was dressed in black, a backpack about his shoulders. He had a wiry frame that was perpetually in motion and rippled with muscles. He had the harried look of someone who was constantly on the run and under the gun. The dark circles under his eyes spoke of hard decisions and a life lived with deep regrets.

"Piper McCloud?" he asked with a quiet authority that reverberated throughout the room.

"I—I am. How'd you do that?"

"Do what?" He had already slipped the backpack off his shoulders and thrown it to the ground in quick motions. Unzipping it, he pulled out specific instruments with practiced motions.

"You weren't there and now you are. How'd you appear like that?"

"Oh, you mean how was I invisible? I don't know. How do you fly?"

No one had ever asked Piper that before. "I dunno."

"Then I don't know either." The man placed gray plasticine against the computer control panel. "Listen to me, we don't have much time. I'm J. and I've been following you and watching you for a long time. I am here to get you out."

"Dr. Hellion told me you were up to no good."

He quickly looked up from his work. "And you believed her?"

Piper didn't answer.

"If I wanted to hurt you, you'd be dead already. I'm here to help you—to get you out."

After all Piper had been through, she wasn't sure what to believe anymore. Seeing her hesitation, J. put down his tools. "Look at me. Unless you trust me, they're going to make you forget you ever flew. Is that what you want?"

"No." As Betty always said—beggars can't be

choosers—and Piper was hardly in a position to be choosy.

J. nodded and went back to work. He was an expert at what he did. Retrievals were never easy and sometimes things went terribly wrong. He had to be careful and make sure Piper was up to taking direction. "You'll have to do what I say when I say or they'll snap you back in here so fast it'll make your head spin." He was attaching wires between a small clock and the plasticine.

Relief washed over Piper. In precious moments this man could take away the terrible pain and freedom would be hers. Her prayers had been answered and tears of relief clouded her vision. "Did you get the others already? Or do you need me to show you where they are?"

"I'm only here for you." J. was definitive on this point.

"And you'll come back for them later?"

"That won't be possible. It's taken me weeks to reach you undetected. With the security in this place, I'll be lucky to get you out in one piece."

"But—" In a matter of mere moments Piper's top-of-the-mountain elation fell to twenty-leagues-beneath-the-sea despair. "But we can't leave them behind."

"It can't be helped. There's only so much that I can do." J. was a realist and he didn't candy-coat anything. Life was hard, and as far as he was concerned, people were better off dealing with cold hard facts.

"You have to try. . . ."

"Try?" He shook his head in disbelief. "Don't talk to me about trying. It's all I've done my whole life. You don't know what's been happening. There used to be thousands of us. But now you down here are the only young ones left. Letitia Hellion has seen to that. You're it."

"But—"

"I'm here for you." J. set the clock on the timer and it started to count down from sixty seconds. "You're exceptional, Piper McCloud. Do you know how incredibly rare it is to do what you do? To fly? It's unheard of."

"But—"

"Close your eyes, there's going to be a small detonation." He took cover at the side of the room.

"I *won't* go without them."

J. looked up, shocked.

" 'Cause of my flying, they're all in trouble. Dr. Hellion says that if I break the rules again she's gonna take it out on them. If I leave and they find out I'm missing, there's no telling what'll happen to my friends."

"You can't make yourself responsible for what she does. It's not your fault."

"I still can't go with you."

"I won't take no for an answer."

"I CAN'T!!!!" Piper screamed. She didn't have the

strength to fight the pain and J. at the same time. "If you try to take me, I'll scream and I'll let 'em know what you're up to. You won't get more than two feet out that door before they'll be all over us."

J.'s clock was counting back from thirty and he began to pace back and forth and pull at his hair. Piper had the distinct feeling he was itching for a cigarette by the way his fingers were twitching and going to his mouth, like he was expecting to find one dangling there.

"She's already brainwashed you. If you let me take you out of here, I can fix that."

"No." No matter what, Piper wasn't going to hurt anyone else ever again.

J. visibly deflated and sighed with defeat. Rushing to the clock, he quickly unwired it. A simmering rage seemed to bubble up inside of him. "We don't have the resources she has. Every day she stamps out another species, snatches another kid, and we have to sit and watch her do it." Suddenly he violently punched the wall. "What will become of us?"

"I'm sorry." Piper wept miserably.

J. ran a hand through his hair, sorting through the rubble of the debacle. "It's not your fault. I was too late. I should have found a way to get to you sooner." He gathered up his bits and pieces, shoving them aimlessly into his backpack.

Piper didn't know what to say. She couldn't be sorrier or feel worse. After J. put the last of his instruments away, he picked up Betty's white linen handkerchief off of the floor and held it in his hand. He ran his fingers slowly over a tiny embroidered bluebird.

"I'll be back for you, Piper." J. had steely resolve in his eyes and he gently placed the handkerchief in his pocket closest to his heart. Slowly he began to fade, and then he disappeared altogether. The room appeared empty, but J.'s voice was close by. "I'll find a way."

After J. departed for good, Piper was left with only Sebastian and the terrible pain to keep her company. Through the darkest hours of the night, she bravely waged her silent battle. It wasn't until dawn approached that her last reserves of energy dwindled. Her breaths came in short rasps, and Sebastian drew close.

"The—pain—" Piper whispered to Sebastian, "it—I . . . can't." She wanted to apologize to Sebastian for not being able to save him, but was too weak to talk. Sebastian watched as her body went limp. Beside himself, he jumped up and down, but Piper remained silent and still. In desperation, Sebastian stood upright on his hind legs and inhaled deeply. Opening his mouth wide, he began to sing—not with the voice of a cricket, but with the deep, rich sounds of an operatic tenor.

"I have seen the coming of the dawn."

Sebastian's voice was so extraordinary that Piper's eyes flickered and then opened, and she managed to focus on the little black cricket singing his heart out.

"Unconcernedly watching the passing of the day,
Whiled away my hours in joyful play—
I live to simply sing the song of love
And play the music of my heart—"

The music filled up every space in the room and then spilled outward through the vent, and quickly traveled through the entire facility of I.N.S.A.N.E.

In the laboratory the silver giraffe raised his head, listening to the music. Stretching his long neck so that he could press his ear right up to the vent on the ceiling, he drank in every note. The red rose, no longer feisty, paused in its coughing to listen to the music.

In the facility's main security room, sensors promptly notified Agent A. Agent of the sound disturbance. He instantly activated the silent alarm and reached for the phone. "Dr. Hellion? Yes. We have another situation."

After the events of the evening, no one had been able to sleep on level thirteen. As the music wafted down the dormitory hallway, kids sat up in their beds and listened in wonder.

> *"Dancing and playing in the light,*
> *I am filled with passion and delight."*

In her nightdress, Lily came out into the hallway as though in a trance. She was soon joined by the others.

"Where is that coming from?"

"It's so beautiful."

"It's the cricket," Conrad stated plainly.

"That tiny cricket's making all that sound?"

"They find them in the floorboards of opera houses." Conrad shrugged and returned to his bed. He didn't want to be with the others. He couldn't look them in the face.

> *"My voice is free.*
> *It rises and floats away from me—*
> *I am unable to escape these walls.*
> *My body will not float like my song's plaintive calls."*

Piper's chest swelled and the power of the music banished any pain. Her body tingled and, emboldened with Herculean strength, she effortlessly pushed against the M.O.L.D., causing it to groan under the pressure.

"It's coming from the testing laboratory."

"How is that possible?" Dr. Hellion was applying her lipstick faster than she would have liked. Agent A. Agent had met her in the elevator and they were on their way to the fourth level.

"We have agents standing by."

"This is the second disturbance in one night." Dr. Hellion's voice was almost irritated. "Before Piper McCloud showed up we went seven years without an incident. Seven long years and now we have two in one night." She snapped her lipstick shut. "This stops now!"

"Only in my mind I float free as my song
And I fly to a home where I belong.
There, those who know my heart well
Sing, sing, sing with my song's spell——"

The sun was just about to rise in Lowland County, but Joe McCloud had not been able to sleep. Sitting on the windowsill of his bedroom, he gazed at the fast-fading stars in the morning sky. It was going to be a good, clear day.

"Mr. McCloud, you'll catch your death from that morning air." Betty turned over, discovering Joe in his underwear on the open windowsill. The weather had turned cold, but Joe didn't seem to notice.

"Hmmm." As usual, Joe didn't have much to say, but Betty knew what he was thinking all the same.

"She'll be home soon enough."

"She'd sure have liked this sky," Joe sighed.

"They snatched my voice,
Held me against my choice.
I forget all that was mine
Yet I reach to dream it one last time."

The cricket's voice sang not for the ears but for the heart. His words resonated with a strength and truth that transfixed all nine children in the dormitory hallway, as the music permeated their very cells. In no time at all, the song hit at their core and a sharp pain stabbed them squarely in the chest. The drugs Letitia Hellion had pumped into them were neutralized—and all fears, both big and small, were forced out, leaving their mouths buzzing with the taste of freedom.

"Piper was right," Kimber chirped. "We've gotta get outta here."

"You got that right!" For once Smitty agreed with Kimber.

"We'll escape," Nalen said forcefully, and Ahmed was silent.

The singing affected Conrad too, but his heart was so

crowded by meanness and madness that the beauty of the song was too painful to bear. He writhed in pain, his bed-sheets tangling around his legs. As much as he resisted, the song gnawed at the meanness and madness inside of him.

"I struggle to the last
But my light is fading fast,
A lone warrior waging a brutal fight
Against an endless night."

Dr. Hellion, Agent A. Agent, and a security team burst into the room where Piper was being held. As the door opened, the music crashed against them, battering their defenses.

"Over there, Dr. Hellion." Agent A. Agent pointed to where Sebastian sang.

"I fight for escape even if the notes of this song
Are the only part of me to leave."

Examining the cricket, Letitia Hellion came as close as she had come in a long time to feeling an emotion. As it started to bubble up inside of her, she firmly clamped down on it, and instead turned to Agent A. Agent. "Give me your shoe!"

Agent A. Agent immediately complied.

"I rise up out of here,
Reaching for the things I hold dear."

The *voculus romalea microptera,* which was the name scientists had given to Sebastian, wait their whole lives to sing one song. When they start to sing that song, it often lasts days, and sometimes weeks, and they sing about everything they have heard and seen and learned in their lives. As Sebastian had only spent a few short months in the Vienna State Opera House before being captured and imprisoned inside I.N.S.A.N.E., the only thing he had experienced that was worth singing about was inspired by the time he had spent with Piper McCloud. But that was enough.

"I will not stay silent,
I shall not remain still."

In the laboratory, the glow created by the silver giraffe blinded the spiders that made cobwebs in the ceiling of his cell. In one great shake, the red rose shook off all of the black soot on its leaves and bloomed with rebel daring.

In the dormitory hallway, the children cheered and cried, while Conrad screamed in pain as the meanness and madness was driven from him.

Dr. Hellion snatched the offered shoe from Agent A. Agent and raised it high in the air.

"Nooooo!" Piper shrieked.

"I sing. I sing to the end."

In one swift motion, Dr. Hellion hit hard and did not miss her mark. Sebastian's voice was forever silenced.

From that moment on, Piper would remember nothing.

CHAPTER SEVENTEEN

CONRAD HAD betrayed Piper, had betrayed them all. He'd cut a deal with Dr. Hellion and told her everything. It was the only logical choice available to him at that time.

On the afternoon of the escape, when Dr. Hellion summoned Conrad to her office, he knew that she knew something. She knew he knew she knew.

"Conrad, please sit down."

Conrad remained standing. Letitia Hellion's fresh coat of lipstick glistened and she leaned back in her chair with an expression that was welcoming and conveyed warmth.

"I know you are up to something. I know the others are involved too." In the end, it had been Piper herself who had tipped Dr. Hellion off. The week before when Letitia had arrived at the dormitory to invite Piper for an evening stroll, she had found the girl mumbling about being tired, and she was unable to meet her eye. Piper's sudden hatred for her was as transparent as a picture window, and so intense that the child wasn't even able to pretend otherwise. This unexpected turn of events prompted Letitia to quickly return to her office and order a special security team to investigate the matter.

It went without saying that Letitia Hellion's greatest fear was that J. had, despite all her precautions, gotten to Piper. For weeks she'd sensed his presence and, knowing J. as she did, Letitia could expect him to be reckless, unpredictable, and willing to go to any extreme. There was a lot of history between the two, and that history had taught Letitia, in no uncertain terms, never to underestimate J. Indeed, he was the one person who posed a real threat to her plan, while at the same time being the very same person that the facility's security could neither repel nor contain.

To her very great relief, the security report had come back detailing secret midnight meetings on level thirteen, among many other things. Naturally, Letitia Hellion not only knew exactly what was going on, but how to deal with it.

"It's an escape, I presume." Dr. Hellion watched Conrad closely, but he gave nothing away, and his features leveled into an inscrutable neutral expression.

"You alone are smart enough to understand that it

won't work, which is why I'm talking to you. I assume the others don't know the consequences they'll face when caught? No, I wouldn't have told them either. How can a child face torture, or having the very life squeezed out of their body and enduring a living death? With stakes so high, they probably wouldn't be able to go through with it. I worry for the little ones the most, don't you? Can Jasper survive it? Or Lily? They're so young, and fragile, and under the circumstances it'll be necessary to use extraordinary means."

Conrad wasn't about to be enticed into joining the discussion until Dr. Hellion's hand was laid bare and all her cards were on the table.

"I'm not trying to scare you, Conrad, and I know that you understand that these are not empty threats. I realize that you don't have all the information at your disposal to make the best decision for you personally, though."

Dr. Hellion retrieved three sheets of paper—her *pièce de résistance*. She tossed them in front of Conrad. "I spoke with your father this morning."

Conrad looked up, startled.

"Such a nice man. I've been urging him for some time now to allow us to perform a new procedure that would greatly assist you. This morning he finally signed this release form." Dr. Hellion flipped the page over and pointed to his father's signature. "See? It is now at my sole discretion to determine whether to perform this wonderful new operation or not. It's called a—"

"Lobotomy?" Conrad's mouth hung open as his eyes jumped ahead, speed-reading the form.

"Well, that's a dramatic way of putting it. It's much more localized and specific. We believe that you are suffering from frontal lobe disease. Meaning the part of your brain that is responsible for your higher reasoning, planning, and problem solving is malfunctioning and causing you great distress. Therefore, it naturally follows that it must be removed." Dr. Hellion paused. "It would really help you, Conrad, to think more clearly. To slow down and not be so . . . agitated. I think you'd be very happy with the results."

Conrad had no words. Her plan was brilliant, even he had to admit that, and the stakes compelling. If he tried to escape and was caught, his frontal lobe would be removed. Conrad knew Dr. Hellion well enough to know that she wasn't bluffing. Undoubtedly, she already had the entire facility on high alert and lockdown, which meant escape was already impossible.

And Conrad was desperate.

Desperate times call for desperate measures. This left him with only one option and one question—

"What's in it for me?"

After Conrad left that day, Letitia Hellion sat at her

desk and carefully reapplied her lipstick. She performed this action each hour on the hour without fail. The name of her lipstick was Red Giggles, but Dr. Hellion had never giggled once while wearing it. This was probably because Letitia Hellion hadn't felt anything, either physically or emotionally, for years, least of all like giggling. She gave masterful impressions of emotions, which she created by carefully contrived movements of her eyes or lips—simulating caring or happiness or understanding.

Except for Conrad, no one had ever seen through Letitia's pretense—but then people were so ridiculously easy to fool. Most of the time they saw what they wanted to see, which was precisely why she invested so much time and energy in constructing a perfect outward appearance. Exquisitely groomed hair, lipstick always in place, beautiful couture clothing, and an elegant posture all worked to cleverly distract people from actually seeing *her*—the real *her* underneath it all. The Letitia Hellion who once upon a time had felt waves of panic, nausea, and revulsion whenever she encountered anything abnormal or unusual, and who unequivocally decided long ago that the world was a much, much better place without such things.

This pivotal decision became a simple equation to live by: normal = good and abnormal = bad; ergo, all abnormality must become normal or be destroyed.

To this end, Dr. Letitia Hellion devoted her life's work.

The upside of her decision was undeniable; her frayed nerves became instantly soothed as the world divided into black and white, manageable and containable. At the same time, her banishment of the murky grayness of it all effectively buried any feeling she ever had. And it was precisely the lack of feeling that allowed her to calmly witness unspeakable torture in plants who had no voice, in animals who had no one to understand their cries, and in children who were too weak to fight back. Without feelings, she had subjugated her humanity to a monstrous and play-acted version of a real person.

With her lipstick artfully painted across her delicate lips, Letitia pressed them together one last time, satisfied with the effect, and began preparations to deal with the escape.

The morning after the attempted escape, Conrad had demanded to see Dr. Hellion, but she made him wait a full week before she finally granted him an audience, by which time he was trembling with rage.

"We had a deal. You said that if I told you about the others that you'd release me. I told you everything. I handed them all to you on a silver platter and now you need to honor our agreement!!"

"You are correct. That was the deal." Dr. Hellion was working on her computer and could only give Conrad half of her attention. She had a lot of work to do and Conrad was no longer a top priority. She tossed him his release papers. "There is just one last detail to complete and you may go."

"What detail?" Conrad picked up the papers and quickly scanned through them.

"On page three, I need an adult guardian's signature, accepting legal responsibility for you from this point on."

"What?" This had not been discussed and Conrad was in no mood.

"When you came here I became your legal guardian, and in order to be released from that position someone else must claim it. An eleven-year-old boy cannot be released on his own recognizance, it's against the law. So I need a name." Dr. Hellion waited. "Any name."

"I'll have my father sign it when I return home."

"Unfortunately, you can't be released without a signature. Under the circumstances, I'm prepared to accept a verbal commitment. To expedite the process, I have your father on line one and he will speak with you right now."

"My father?" Conrad was shocked. He hadn't spoken with his father in over four years. At first when he'd arrived at the facility, he'd cleverly orchestrated ways to get to phones and call his father's office in a desperate bid to get help. Each time some snot-nosed assistant would inform him that Senator Harrington was unable to take his call. Then one day a new assistant accused Conrad of maliciously playing some sort of prank, because everyone knew the senator had no son, but that he and his wife had just become the proud parents of a baby girl. And that was how Conrad learned that he had a sister, and he marked that the last day he ever tried to contact his father.

"Conrad? As I said, your father is on line one." Dr. Hellion wanted to get this over with. She didn't like to waste her time or energy on a hopeless case.

Conrad hated himself for getting excited, but he was. He yearned to hear his father's voice. He picked up the phone with a quivering hand. "Hello? Father?"

It was noon in Washington D.C. and Conrad Harrington II was about to be late for a very important lunch. He juggled files and the phone as he left his office.

"Hey, sport, good to hear from you."

"Father, I—"

"Dr. Hellion tells me that you're doing one heck of a good job and your mother and I are proud of you." Senator Harrington dashed for an elevator. "Keep up the good work."

Conrad recognized the tone in his father's voice; it was the one he used to glad-hand his bigger campaign contributors. "Father, listen to me, I can come home now and I—"

"Oh yes, Dr. Hellion mentioned something about that, sport. The thing is that your mother and I feel it's a little bit too soon, especially as things are going so well for you there. Like I always say, if it's not broke, don't fix it."

"No, Father, I *need* to come home now, I—"

"Aw, Connie, it's real great hearing your voice, sport. You sound fantastic. Let's talk soon."

"No, no, don't hang up. Wait, you need to understand that—"

Conrad stopped talking when the dial tone buzzed in his ear. Still he couldn't let go of the phone. After all that had happened, after everything he'd done, it had all come down to this phone call, and he'd hardly said more than a few words. He'd failed. He'd sold out Piper and the others too, and now he had been sold out.

"Well, Conrad, I'm sorry that didn't work out for you the way we'd hoped."

"You never had any intention of letting me go. You lied to me."

"No, Conrad, we were both lied to. Your father also retracted his approval for that cranial operation, which means that neither of us gets what we want. I don't want you here any more than you want to stay. Frankly, I think you're a bad influence and make everything more difficult for everyone. And as much as I'd like to help you, I can't. My hands are tied."

It was a stalemate once again and they were back to where they'd started.

Conrad should have known better than to negotiate with Dr. Hellion. What was he thinking? Maybe, just maybe, Piper had been right. Maybe he wasn't as smart as he thought. . . .

"Conrad?" There was nothing left to say and Dr. Hellion needed Conrad to get out of her office. He was a living, walking reminder of her failure, and no one wants that hanging around. "Is there anything else? Conrad?"

"Huh? Oh." Conrad was drawn back from his thoughts to find that he still had the phone in his hand. It took all his concentration and willpower to open his fingers and place it back in the cradle.

Conrad left Dr. Hellion's office in a daze, and he remained that way for over three weeks. In class Conrad gazed off blankly and did not answer questions, did not participate, did not argue that the theory of relativity was outdated and limited. At mealtimes he ate mechanically and without thought, and he went to bed at lights-out and didn't work on his secret projects. His transformation was so startling that Professor Mumbleby even reported to Dr. Hellion that there might be opportunities to rehabilitate Conrad Harrington yet.

During those weeks, only one thought dominated Conrad's existence. He wrestled with it endlessly to try to understand it.

How was it that I failed? I thought of everything. I weighed every option, considered every aspect, I made all the right choices and still I didn't come to the right answer. How is that possible?

Finally it came to him. His mind—all-powerful, brilliantly calculating, analyzing, processing—didn't have the answers. His mind, Conrad realized all at once in a luminous flash of understanding, had *information*, not *answers*. The answers, Conrad suddenly knew, came from somewhere else entirely.

The revelation was so stunning that it immobilized Conrad completely.

"Harrington, you got something wrong with your ears?" Nurse Tolle barked when Conrad failed to get out of bed. "That was the breakfast bell, boy, and if you don't hustle, you'll be on my list."

Conrad still didn't move, didn't respond. Later that day when a doctor was called for, Conrad remained unresponsive.

"He's in no danger," the doctor whispered to Nurse Tolle. "He's had a nervous breakdown. Just let him rest. He'll snap out of it sooner or later."

Conrad wasn't having a nervous breakdown and he didn't care if they thought that he was. The problem was that Conrad couldn't figure out where his answers were going to come from, and until he could he wasn't sure how to go on living. His mind was the only thing he'd ever relied upon and no one had told him or even hinted that there could be another way. So how was he to find the answers if they weren't in his mind? Where were they hiding? How could he get to them?

Piper had known. Something in her had just known what to do and she wasn't even that smart. Conrad wasn't being mean, only factual. Piper simply didn't have the same capacity for intellectual thought that he had and yet she knew things that he didn't. How was that possible? Where were her answers coming from?

Days turned into weeks and Conrad remained silent and still. Kids began talking in hushed whispers in the dormitory hallway by his room, and Dr. Hellion contacted Senator Harrington to apprise him of his son's situation.

"Fine, fine, Dr. Hellion. Thanks for the call. I've got to jump into a meeting right now and you don't need to contact me again unless his situation gets worse. Is that clear?"

Dr. Hellion understood perfectly. Conrad was her problem and the senator didn't want to hear about it. He wanted him out of sight and out of mind and her calls were an irritation at best and a threat to his peace of mind at worst.

Several weeks more passed and Conrad sank deeper and deeper into blackness, until a single flickering ray of light, like a tiny candle on a gusty day, broke through.

Piper had the answer and had always had it, Conrad realized as he lay curled up under his covers. (*Why, oh why, hadn't he paid closer attention and listened to her before?*) And if Piper knew, then as soon as she was released, he could ask her, and then he would know too. It was a slender and feeble hope at best, but Conrad clung to it and it provided him with enough incentive to get out of bed and function such that he could attend class again. Each day he found himself sitting on the edge of his seat in a state of expectant anticipation. Was today going to be the day that Piper would return? Would he discover where to look for the answers that day?

It was a hard winter that year, and the snow got so deep that for a time the facility was blocked off from the outside world altogether. Spring came late and struggled to slough off the snow, but at long last the white cold melted away and a tentative green covered the earth.

As was often the case, Smitty was the first to see. "It's Piper. She's out! She's out!!" Smitty came screaming into the library. Conrad leapt to his feet and violently grabbed Smitty's shoulders, shaking him.

"Where? Where is she?" Conrad hadn't spoken in weeks and his voice was hoarse.

"The dining—"

Conrad ran before Smitty could even complete the sentence. The others were hot on his heels. Myrtle was,

260

of course, the first to arrive and discovered Piper sitting quiet and still at the dining table. A sandwich sat neatly on a plate in front of her and she was slowly chewing.

Although Conrad was not aware of it, all of the kids had waited for Piper's release with impatient fervor. More than anything, they wanted Piper back. Nothing was the same without her.

After the mad dash, the kids all stopped dead, feasting their eyes on Piper.

"Piper?" Violet trembled, afraid of what might happen next. Piper looked up from her meal and smiled. Relief spread through the waiting faces and they rushed to gather around her, excitedly reaching out to touch her.

"Piper, we missed you!"

"We knew you'd be back."

"Guess you showed old Hell a thing or two? Huh?" Smitty was overjoyed.

Piper smiled. Conrad watched her closely. He saw that she was paler and thinner. There was also a fragile quality about her, like she could be blown away by a hard wind. All of that was understandable, though, considering what she must have gone through over the last few months.

"So what happened?" Kimber pressed.

"Yeah, where've you been hiding?" Ahmed asked.

Piper shrugged.

Lily moved in closer and whispered, "Can you still fly?"

"Fly?" Piper smiled.

"Maybe you can fly tonight after lights-out!"

Piper shook her head. "I don't understand."

"You know, Piper," Smitty persisted, "flying. You fly."

Piper became more flustered. "Fly where?"

"No, you fly." Kimber helped.

"You're a flier, Piper."

Looking between the hopeful and expectant faces surrounding her, Piper's confusion mounted. "What do you mean?"

Conrad's heart sank, his worst fear realized. "She doesn't know what you're talking about. Leave her alone." Conrad turned away.

"No, she knows." Violet couldn't believe otherwise. "You remember, right, Piper?"

Piper's eyes were blank and her smile vacant. She nodded, but there was no understanding behind it. All of the people around her looked as though they were familiar, but Piper couldn't quite place them. They were talking so fast and nothing they said made sense. She wished that they would slow down. She was trying her utmost to follow along, but her mind couldn't quite seem to grasp words.

"I'm Piper." Piper smiled at the girl closest to her. "What's your name?"

"*My name?* Piper, it's *me*, Violet." Violet took Piper's hand and squeezed it with alarm and fear. "Just think, Piper. Think hard. You can remember if you want to. I'm your friend. Violet."

"I'm Smitty. Remember, Piper?"

"Remember the escape?"

"And Sebastian and how he sang?"

"Yeah, we all heard it, Piper. It was so beautiful."

"And we've been waiting for you so that we can escape again. Except this time it'll work out."

Piper's confusion mounted. "Escape what?"

"Stop it. Just stop it. She's gone." Conrad banged his fist on the table. "She's not Piper anymore."

Silence fell over the group. Piper returned to placidly chewing on her sandwich. Just like countless others Conrad had seen over the years, Piper had been reduced to an empty shell—a blank slate for Dr. Hellion to write on.

A bell rang in the distance, calling them to afternoon classes.

"Better not be late." Piper smiled. With her hands, she pushed herself away from the table and reached for two silver canes that were propped up against a chair. In all of the fuss they'd escaped everyone's notice.

With painful difficulty, Piper struggled her way up to a standing position, heavily reliant on metal support braces that had been wrapped around her mangled legs.

Even with the canes and the braces, Piper's movement was pure agony. Not only could Piper no longer fly, she could no longer walk. Dr. Hellion had crippled her.

Lily gasped and tears came to Violet's eyes. *"What have they done to her?!!?!"*

Ten children mutely watched through clouded vision as Piper hobbled pitifully away, bent and broken.

CHAPTER EIGHTEEN

EVERYONE WAS late for afternoon class. Normally this would have been instant cause for Professor Mumbleby to become irate and mete out detentions. Fortunately, it had been a busy morning at I.N.S.A.N.E.

"Class, a new student is joining us. Hiz name is Boris Yeltsinov. I expect you to all make him welcome," Professor Mumbleby declared.

Boris slouched at the front of the class. He was a stocky boy who looked to be about nine years old, and was shyly hanging his closely cropped head. His intense social embarrassment was serving no useful purpose— absolutely no one in the class was paying the least bit of attention to him. Lily didn't care what his gift was. Smitty wasn't placing any bets and, like everyone else, Kimber couldn't take her eyes off Piper.

"Maybe if we push her off something she'll remember how to fly," Nalen whispered to Conrad.

"You're not pushing Piper off anything." Violet turned in her seat and confronted Nalen with blazing eyes.

"Mr. Yeltsinov, you may sit with Mr. Mustafa and Mr. Mustafa over zhere and zhey will assist you." Boris approached Nalen and Ahmed, who were less than hospitable hosts. Just that morning Boris had been transforming street rats into stone and then lobbing them at local gang members in a Moscow slum. His battle was suddenly halted by a flurry of frenzied activity that culminated in an introduction to Dr. Hellion and a helicopter ride.

"Now we vill be reviewing zhe spring science projects." Professor Mumbleby paused to allow for the customary groaning, followed by the rolling of eyes. Neither reaction materialized and the funereal atmosphere in the classroom threw him off. "Uh, vell then, let us begin. Mr. Harrington. You vill be first. Come to ze front of the room and present your science project."

Conrad shuffled to the front of the class like a zombie. "Mmm hmm," Conrad cleared his throat, "my project is on . . ." Suddenly Conrad couldn't remember anything about his science project. It had gone completely out of his head. "Uh, my project is on, ah—it's on—"

Time bent around Conrad. It slowed and changed. A noise roared in his ears, like a big wave approaching. *Piper is gone. Another one lost.* Conrad saw Piper. He saw the faces of the others looking at him. He saw Boris but he was Ang Chung and then Bella Lovely and so many, many others all at the same time.

"Mr. Harrington?" Professor Mumbleby prompted.

"Uh, yes. My—project, my science project is about . . ."

The roar of a wave that only Conrad could hear hit him full force. He was and wasn't himself all at once. He was in the classroom and watching the classroom from afar all at the same time.

"My, *my* project is—"

And then it happened.

SNAP. Like the cosmos had become a chiropractor, Conrad's vertebrae popped into place with one swift jolt. **POP.** The wayward pieces of him got whipped together and then rearranged into a new order.

His eyes refocused and he stood in an endless ocean of stillness and silence.

"My science project is on time travel." Conrad's voice filled with quiet confidence and conviction.

Professor Mumbleby couldn't believe his ears. *"Nein,* Mr. Harrington, *nein.* Your science project is on magnets."

"No, Professor Mumbleby, no, it's not. It's on time travel."

"Mr. Harrington," Professor Mumbleby snapped, "you vill tell us about zhe magnets right now."

267

"NOOOOOOOOOOOOOOOOOOOO!!!!!!!!
Conrad yelled so loudly, and for so long, in a voice filled with so much primal rage, that it electrified every member of the classroom. Conrad hadn't planned on doing it. Indeed, when his mouth closed, it seemed as though it had come from some strange place inside.

Dead silence in the classroom. A shiver traveled up and down Professor Mumbleby's spine.

"My project is on time travel, Professor Mumbleby," Conrad quietly repeated in the silence. "But you won't have the privilege of hearing it because I'm leaving. Right now."

What!!?!? Conrad's fellow students could not have been more stunned. Eyes widened and jaws visibly hung open in shock.

Conrad spoke slowly, as though the words were coming to him just before he uttered them. "All of us need to get out. Right now." Conrad looked into the faces of his classmates. "Right now," he repeated.

Professor Mumbleby remembered himself. "Mr. Harrington, you vill calm yourself right now or I vill—"

"Or you'll what? Is that what you're going to do?" He pointed at Piper, who didn't appear to understand anything that was going on behind her vacant happy expression. "So what. You'll do it to us anyway, sooner or later. So I say, bring it on."

"You have taken leave of your senses, Mr. Harrington, and I vill get Dr. Hellion zhis instant to—"

Conrad blocked Professor Mumbleby's path to the door. "You'll do nothing unless I say so."

After forty years of teaching these children, Professor Mumbleby had prepared for everything but this. Students were spontaneously rising from their seats and forming a circle around him. He sensed something in his students that he'd never sensed in the classroom before, during all of his time as a teacher at I.N.S.A.N.E.—the absence of fear.

"Sit down now and no one vill be punished. I tell you this truly. Jasper, sit down. Violet, take your seat." Professor Mumbleby acted angry to cover his terror. "Conrad, I varn you."

"Then we can consider ourselves both warned." Conrad's eyes didn't flicker away.

Professor Mumbleby pushed Conrad aside and made for the door. He only managed to take two steps before he felt strong arms holding him in an iron grip.

"Sit," Daisy said.

Professor Mumbleby sat because he had no choice.

Everything happened at once. There was no forethought, but everyone seemed to know what they had to do all the same. Myrtle got a rope, and while Daisy held Professor Mumbleby, they tied him to a chair. When

Professor Mumbleby resisted, Kimber assisted in keeping him still with several thousand volts of electricity. Smitty went for the door and kept lookout. Conrad and the others gathered around the dry-erase board and quickly made a plan.

"We're getting out."

"How?"

"We haven't planned anything."

"True, but they aren't prepared either, and we have the element of surprise working in our favor." Conrad suddenly got an idea. "What time is it?"

"4:55 p.m."

"Good. At five, the freight elevator stops at every level to collect any specimens going to the experiment laboratory on the fourth floor. If we can get to the elevator shaft, we can use that to get to the surface." Conrad was already drawing floor schematics from memory on the dry-erase board.

"I could short out the main power to slow the agents down," Kimber offered.

"I'll take out the security cameras." Lily was chafing at the bit to be part of the action. As were they all. The energy in the classroom was electric.

Smitty suddenly jolted. "Conrad. Conrad, Nurse Tolle's leaving his desk. He's on his way to the classroom."

"What's his ETA?"

"Five minutes tops. Maybe less."

"Okay, so here's the plan—"

"Conrad?"

"Myrtle will go first." Conrad drew the plan as he spoke, showing them. "Kimber, you go here and short out the electricity in this grid. Lily, you take out this camera and this camera. Daisy, you'll run interference—"

"Conrad!"

"Once we get past this checkpoint, it'll be a straight shot down this corridor and then we'll crawl through this vent system to get to the eighth level and—"

"CONRAD!!"

Startled, Conrad turned to find Violet pale and shrunken. "What about Piper?"

Piper had managed to get to her feet and she was hobbling about aimlessly with a vacant expression on her face. Not only could she hardly walk, but she was almost completely out of touch with what was going on around her.

"She won't be able to do that, Conrad." Violet nodded to his plan.

Conrad knew immediately that Violet was right. It had taken Piper ten minutes just to walk to class, and it hadn't even been that far. There was no way they were going to be able to get her out in her condition.

"Nurse Tolle's walking up the stairs, Conrad," Smitty warned.

"What are we going to do?" Violet persisted.

Conrad hesitated. Logically, Piper should have been left behind. She was lost to them now anyway. But all the same, Conrad now knew that wasn't the right answer. But what was the right answer?

"Conrad, Nurse Tolle's two minutes away, tops. Maybe less."

Conrad began to pace back and forth. Should they leave her and he could come back for her? No, that would never work. What about trying to take her with them? No, even if Daisy carried her out, Piper, so thoroughly brainwashed by Dr. Hellion, was sure to resist or, worse, scream for help. What then? What was the right answer?

"Conrad? What do we do?" Nine pairs of eyes waited on his answer, but he didn't have the answer. Where could he find it?

"Nurse Tolle's ninety seconds out and counting."

He had no time. Conrad looked at Piper and suddenly the decision was easy. "Here's the plan. I'm staying behind with Piper. You guys will go without me. Lily, buy us some time with Nurse Tolle."

As simple as that, Conrad had finally done it. For the first time in his life he had the right answer. It wasn't the best decision and it certainly wasn't a logical one, but it was the right one.

Seeing the change in Conrad had a powerful effect on all of the kids. It was like Conrad had opened a door and stepped through it, and his actions somehow invited them all to do the same. It was frightening and new and none of them moved, except Lily, who roused herself to the hall, where she telekinetically stole the file right out of Nurse Tolle's hand and then tossed it in the air. Bits of paper were suddenly flying every which way down the corridor and Nurse Tolle was frantically waving his arms about, trying to collect them. Lily figured that they had a good ten minutes before he would be through collecting it all. She returned to the classroom to find Conrad trying to organize her stunned classmates.

"You need to get out now. All of you. We made a plan that will work. I'll take care of Nurse Tolle." Conrad pushed a few kids toward the door.

Still no one moved.

"I mean it. Go now!"

"N–n–no." The trembling voice belonged to Jasper. He was even more pale than usual and he stumbled as he came forward. "P–p–piper said we all h–h–have to go t–t–together."

"Jasper, there's no time to argue. You have to—"

Conrad began, but his words fell away as he saw what Jasper was doing.

Jasper was looking at his hands. Placing them together, he began to rub them up and down against each other. The contact created a light. It was dim at first, but as Jasper's hands moved faster and faster, the light grew until it was blinding. Then Jasper leaned forward and blew into his hands, which caused the light to change from red to bright white. It became so bright that none of the kids could look at it directly without blinding themselves.

"What's he doing?" Lily whispered.

"I dunno." Kimber was too stunned to even chew her gum.

Approaching Piper, Jasper knelt before her. He placed his glowing hands gently on Piper's legs and the light immediately jumped into her flesh.

"Ahhh," Piper gasped, inhaling sharply. The light took hold of her body, traveling up and down it in waves. The force of it was so strong that it rocked Piper back and forth. Suddenly, her canes went flying and the metal braces popped off of her legs.

At last the light began to fizzle and fade, and then it disappeared altogether. In its wake Piper stood straight and tall on two healthy legs.

"Jasper, you have the power to heal!" Conrad couldn't believe it. After all of this time the mystery was solved.

"I d–d–didn't remember but I do n–n–now." Jasper blushed, shyly. "Piper m–m–made me want to r–r–remember. And I know what I'm g–g–gonna do when I g–get out too!"

"What?"

"I'm gonna heal s–sick animals 'c–c–cause they can't t–talk too good just like m–me and I can m–make them well a–a–again."

Lily nodded her approval. "That's the best dream of all."

Conrad turned his attention to Piper. She still hadn't moved and her face remained blank. "Piper?" he asked cautiously.

"Piper, can you hear me?" Violet came closer.

"Piper, are you alright?"

THERE IS a place deep, deep inside every person that is hidden and hard to find. If things get bad enough and life gets too hard, though, some people will go to that place and never come back from it. Certainly, all outward appearances will suggest otherwise. They will look as they always did. They may even act somewhat like their old selves, but the truth is, the *real truth* is that they are hiding in this place deep inside where no one can touch or hurt them anymore.

After Sebastian was gone and the pain of the M.O.L.D.

got to be too much, Piper discovered her secret place, locked herself inside, and hid the key. She arranged herself nicely there, happy to be away from the pain and from the struggle of it all.

I plum can't fathom why I didn't come here sooner, Piper thought to herself. *I've got it made in the shade in this place.* And Piper could never think of a good enough reason to leave. Indeed, the longer she stayed the more the things of her life that she had cared so much about began to fade and disappear from her memory altogether. Soon it got so Piper couldn't have returned even if she had wanted to. She no longer knew her way back, and even if she had, she could never quite seem to recall what there was to go back to.

Unlike the many who had become lost in their secret places before her, a blinding white light came and found Piper. Uncovering her hiding place, it woke Piper with its sharp brightness. It wrenched her back to reality and exposed her to the fact that she was in a room full of strangers.

"Piper," the strangers said. "Piper, are you alright?"

Piper was shocked to suddenly find herself in such a strange place. She was even more surprised to be surrounded by so many other people. Piper had to admit that there was something very familiar about the strangers.

But where or when or how did she know them? And how had she gotten there?

Pins and needles tingled up and down her leg muscles as though they'd fallen asleep. Piper got up and carefully placed one foot in front of the other until her legs bore her weight, when suddenly memories began to bubble to the surface of her mind in quick flashes. The boy, that boy in front of her was Conrad! She remembered Conrad now. And over there was Violet. And Smitty and Kimber and all the rest of them.

"What's going on? Where am I?" Before anyone had the time to answer Piper's questions, she remembered everything all on her own.

It was immediately apparent to anyone looking at Piper that she had returned. Her shoulders straightened, her eyes filled with intelligence, and a smile took to her lips.

"Like I always said, Conrad," Piper quipped, "you just can't keep a good girl down."

The cheer that rose from the throats of the children was deafening.

"YESSSSS!!!"

"Piper's back!"

"We're gonna be free!"

Violet threw her arms around Piper and squeezed every bit of air out of her. Electrical sparks spontaneously flew off of Kimber, while the tears that clouded Smitty's vision prevented him from even catching a glimpse at Piper's underwear. As for all of the rest, there weren't enough hugs or sighs or joyful smiles to even begin to contain their gratitude and joy—except, of course, for Conrad.

Conrad's head hung low, his eyes stinging from the painful reminder of his deception, his heart so full of remorse and guilt, it had no harbor for the joy.

"Conrad?" Piper grabbed hold of Conrad, ecstatic to see him. Conrad crumpled and then regained a tentative control. He had thought he wanted Piper to tell him how to find answers, but standing before her, he knew that he'd made yet another mistake. He didn't want answers, he wanted forgiveness. Lifting his eyes, which were heavier than solar systems, he met Piper's gaze.

"Piper, it was me. I told Dr. Hellion. I betrayed you all."

CHAPTER NINETEEN

PIPER'S WATERY eyes crystallized to steely blue. Her face traveled from incomprehension to disbelief, and then finally settled into shock.

"You what?"

Conrad had spoken quietly, but it made no difference; everyone heard and was silenced by the revelation. Several children felt as though they had been sucker-punched in the gut.

"I told Dr. Hellion about the escape."

"*You* told Dr. Hellion about the escape?" The possibility that they'd been set up had never occurred to Piper.

"Yes, I told them everything. I'm sorry, Piper. I'm so sorry. . . ."

"You mean they were lying in wait for us that whole time?" Piper turned away; her mind wrapped itself around this surprising new information. "So we were caught 'cause you ratted us out?"

"Yes, that's what I'm trying to tell you. It was me."
Conrad felt mild frustration at Piper's repetition of the
facts. It was bad enough he did it, he didn't want it repeated over and over again.

"So the escape woulda worked if you hadn't told?"
Piper added it up like it was two plus two, and then went
over the calculation again.

"Like I said, it's all my fault. They caught us because
of me!!" He snapped, frustrated that Piper seemed to be
having such a difficult time understanding such a simple
concept. "I told them everything. And what I'm trying
to tell you is that I'm sorry."

"But what you're saying is that the escape would have
worked?"

"Alright, this isn't a difficult one. Let's go over it
again." Conrad had forgotten how frustrating Piper
could be. He spoke slowly so she'd understand. "I told
them how to catch us. They did. I'm sorry. End of
story."

Piper launched herself at Conrad, and he braced for
her blow. Instead, she threw her arms around him and ec-
statically squeezed him and laughed out loud.

"Yeeee-hawwwwww!!!!!!!!" Piper jiggled Conrad in
the embrace, and he wondered if the news had completely made her take leave of her senses.

"I thought I was wrong. I thought I couldn't trust my

heart, but I can. I can. There's not a thing wrong with my heart!!"

As Piper's laughter grew, Conrad became increasingly furious. It quickly got to the point where he couldn't take a second more of it.

"STOP IT!!! Stop it!" Conrad pulled Piper away from him. "What is wrong with you! Don't you understand anything? I—BETRAYED—YOU! That is bad. Get that? *I'm* BAD."

"Think you're the only fool who ever made a mistake?" Piper looked at Conrad as if he was crazy. "Phhhh! Talk about delusions of grandeur. One mistake isn't nothing. Heck, I've made more than that before I even get up in the morning. Can't learn nothing worth knowing without makin' a few mistakes first!"

Conrad wanted to argue, but then his face broke into a grin and his eyes grew strangely moist, and he didn't know whether to hug or slug Piper. He knew without a doubt, though, that she was the most infuriating person he'd ever met.

"Conrad, we gotta get out of here!" Smitty was dancing back and forth between his two feet. All at once everyone remembered what was at stake. "Nurse Tolle's almost got all those papers together."

"Yeah, let's go! Go now!" Myrtle was practically jumping out of her skin.

Piper saw the diagram on the board and the children's expectant faces. "We're getting out, Piper," Conrad explained. "All of us, just like you wanted. Right now!"

Piper silently walked up to the board, looking at the diagrams.

"We'll b–b–be out before s–s–s–sunset."

"And we'll do all our dreams, just like you told us we would."

"It's all 'cause of you, Piper. It was your idea in the first place."

Piper shook her head. "No. It won't work." Picking up a cloth, Piper erased the plans from the board. Throwing the cloth to the ground, Piper moved to the window overlooking the atrium. As precious seconds slipped by, Piper thought.

"Escape isn't the answer," Piper finally declared with finality. "I've got a better idea."

AT LONG last, Nurse Tolle collected the remaining stray papers belonging to Boris's file and put them all back in order. Anytime there was a new inmate, there was double the normal work and triple the worries. The first twenty-four hours were always the most dangerous too. He hoped for the hundredth time that Boris wasn't going to have a personality conflict with Kimber. They were both two tough cookies and could potentially do a lot of damage to each other. At the science room, Nurse Tolle checked the window on the door to the class.

Surprisingly, Professor Mumbleby was sitting at his desk in an entirely empty room. Nurse Tolle knocked smartly on the door. When he received no response, he opened it.

"Professor?" Nurse Tolle waited, but Professor Mumbleby didn't respond—didn't turn around. "Professor, you alright?" No response again. Nurse Tolle's internal warning system lit up like a Christmas tree, and he strode forward and rounded the desk to discover that Professor Mumbleby had been bound and gagged and was furiously fighting against his restraints.

"Vhhhet iiiis fffff meeee," Professor Mumbleby barked from beneath the gag, pointing at the door. Nurse Tolle's eyes went wide and he spun around to find Kimber, Lily, and Boris standing behind the door. Kimber closed the door with a bang.

"You all are in for a world of hurt when Dr. Hellion finds out about this," Nurse Tolle seethed.

"We don't think so." Even now, Lily was the picture of sweet innocence.

"Well, I know so." Nurse Tolle was furious. "You'll sit yourselves down now and wait right here."

"No."

"What did you say to me, Kimber?"

"I said no, and you don't get to tell us what to do anymore."

Nurse Tolle lunged forward, but Lily telekinetically lifted him into the air and kept him safely out of reach. As he dangled several feet above the ground, Nurse Tolle struggled to grab at the kids.

"You don't look so tough anymore, Nurse Tolle."

"You better put me down! I'll see to it you get what's coming to you!"

"And we'll see you get what's coming to you." Kimber sent approximately fifty thousand volts into Nurse Tolle's arm.

"Ahhhhh!"

"His shoes?" Boris asked. Not only had he been scooped out of Moscow earlier that day, and taken to a strange and hidden place, but now he was involved with these kids whom he'd never seen before. None of which mattered to Boris though, because he discovered his destiny the moment he set his eyes on Lily Yakimoto. She was the love of his life, he instantly decided, and he'd do anything her little, red button mouth told him to.

"Yes." Lily nodded, finding Boris's attention entirely appropriate. As far as Lily was concerned, everyone should be her willing servant. And that went double for boys.

Boris lumbered to Nurse Tolle's feet.

"What you doing back there, boy? You leave me be. Don't be doing that now." Nurse Tolle wiggled in the air, but Boris effortlessly got hold of his shoes. "Hey, hey!"

With one touch, the leather tightened and hardened and then turned to stone. The weight of the stone shoes dragged Nurse Tolle out of the air and to the ground with a *THUD*.

"Ummph." Nurse Tolle recovered. Once again he lunged forward at Kimber, who was standing closest to him. The stone shoes encasing his feet weighed more than fifty pounds per foot and held him firmly to the floor. Instead of reaching Kimber, Nurse Tolle fell flat on his face.

"I told you you were going to get what was coming to you." Kimber gave him a helping of her voltage.

"COME IN," Dr. Hellion responded absentmindedly to the knock on her door. Agent A. Agent was due to present the security reports, and as usual he was right on time. She'd had a hectic day, but the intake numbers were way down, which indicated that there was a growing trend of fewer and fewer incidences of abnormality. Little by little, Dr. Hellion's methods were proving themselves to be successful. The day was fast approaching when abnormality would be completely obliterated from the population.

"You can leave the report on my desk, Agent Agent."

285

Dr. Hellion didn't look up. "I'll also need your revised security protocols for level thirteen in respect to the new inmate."

"Dr. Hellion, it's time for you to leave." Piper stated it simply, as though it was obvious.

Dr. Hellion's head snapped up from her work to discover Piper McCloud and Conrad Harrington standing before her desk. Had Dr. Hellion been able to feel anything, she would have felt surprise and horror. As she wasn't bothered by such emotions, she calmly leaned back in her chair and selected her helpful expression, while taking everything in—the fact that Piper was completely healed and walking, that Piper and Conrad were together, and that Daisy was restraining Agent A. Agent in a chair in the adjoining waiting room.

"Is there something that I can help you with?"

"You're gonna havta leave now. We don't want you here anymore."

The smile broke on Dr. Hellion's face. She struggled to keep it in place. "Pardon me, Piper. What did you say?"

"Please leave."

Piper's words literally made no sense to Letitia Hellion, like she was speaking a strange foreign language. Dr. Hellion couched the situation in terms she could comprehend. "I suppose you are trying to escape again. It won't work, and even if it does, there is no place for you to go once you get out."

"Yeah, we figured that one out too. Fact is we're tired of hiding and we don't wanna run. So we're not going to escape. We're gonna stay right here. You'll havta leave instead."

"What?" Dr. Hellion's mind traveled over the idea like the fingers of a pianist on the keys of a piano. The notes started to form a song, and the song Letitia Hellion was hearing had the same effect as hearing nails on a chalkboard. *They weren't going to escape!!?!?! But, of course, they must want to escape!* All her preparation and planning and security had been geared toward preventing an escape. Never had it crossed her mind that they would— *"Revolt!!"* She breathed the words. "You're *revolting?!?*"

"That's a real fancy way of putting it. I didn't think of it like that, but now that you mention it—yup. That's exactly what we're doing."

Dr. Hellion held tightly to her self-control, unaware that she was pumping air in and out of her chest at an alarming rate. "You . . . it's not possible . . . I can't . . ." Dr. Hellion reached for the thoughts going through her head, but could not actually grasp any of them. "The thing is," she said finally, "there is something you should know." She was buying time. "You're so lucky and you don't even know it."

Conrad looked at Dr. Hellion like she was crazy. He was interested to see where she was going to take this thought.

"You probably don't know this but I had a brother. Johnny, my parents called him. He was much younger than my sister, Sarah, and I were, and there was something about him that was . . . different. Not like other babies. My parents said he was special," Letitia Hellion babbled. She hadn't thought about Johnny in years, and she didn't know why she spoke about him now, other than the fact that something inside her that she couldn't control was bubbling up, and she didn't like it. "You see, when he developed more and more of his specialness—when his abnormality grew—my parents encouraged it. Fools.

"After the accident I tried to tell them, tried to explain that Johnny had a problem and needed help, but they wouldn't listen to me. They told me that *I* didn't understand and that it was good. They said *he* was an example for *me*. So they encouraged him even more and this, of course, made the problem grow worse."

Piper watched as Dr. Hellion's face flushed and was genuinely moved by what the memory seemed to be doing inside of Dr. Hellion.

"Then one day I realized that if Johnny didn't get help his specialness was going to hurt someone. Like Sarah had been hurt. My parents, they didn't see things the way I did, and I knew they weren't going to stop him. So I was forced to. I called the authorities and later that day Johnny was taken away. My parents never thanked me but *I* was the only one who could see that Johnny needed help, and so I gave him what he needed. Just like *I* can help you to overcome this terrible affliction that you both have. Don't you know how much happier you will be without it? Do you want to hurt those you love? I can help you."

"But, Dr. Hellion, we don't want your help. We sure as heck didn't ask for it."

Dr. Hellion shook her head and a heavy silence hung in the room.

"Dr. Hellion, you can go quietly now or we'll call Daisy in. Those are the only two choices you have." Conrad battled Dr. Hellion with a firm gaze.

Letitia Hellion fished between Conrad and Piper and found that she had been completely unable to hook them. The most powerful weapon at her disposal was making the children feel helpless so they would reject their gifts. Without that, the residents of the thirteenth level were uncontainable and uncontrollable and, working together, there wasn't anything anyone could do to stop them. Had they been trying to escape, Dr. Hellion could have potentially managed a reasonable resistance, but ultimately even then they would likely prevail. But a revolt—that was a scenario that had never been considered. It was an idea outside of the box and it was her undoing.

Dr. Hellion stood up, but couldn't manage to select an expression off of her menu to wrap her face in. She had somehow shrunken in the course of the last few minutes and, gathering herself up, she started to shake as she left her office. Daisy met her at the door.

"This way." Daisy pointed down the hall and followed behind Dr. Hellion, watching her every move.

Conrad and Piper stood in Dr. Hellion's office and looked at each other, and Piper's face began to glow.

"We did it." She grinned.

"Almost," Conrad warned. He didn't want to get ahead of himself. There were still several key steps that had to be taken before the facility would be completely secured.

"I knew it." In Piper's mind, victory was already achieved.

"And you were right." Conrad smiled. Piper's optimism was infectious and he wasn't going to take away a moment of her happiness. Moving to sit at Dr. Hellion's desk, Conrad opened her top drawer and found exactly what he was looking for. He pulled out a blue ribbon, attached to which was a little wooden bird, and placed it in Piper's trembling hand. For Piper there were no words to express how she felt. She looked to Conrad, but he saved her from the effort of trying to speak. "Just put it back where it belongs."

Piper nodded and Conrad helped her place the ribbon around her neck. The little wooden bird fell across her chest, resting against her heart, and at once the words came to her lips.

"I'm as light as a cloud, as free as a bird. I'm part of the sky and I can fly."

Piper's body tingled and then her whole body ascended into the air. Conrad watched as she flew about the room, and then zipped out through the open window and into the atrium.

"I can fly!" Piper called up and down the large well. She had had a long absence from flying and wasn't exactly steady, but she made up for her wobbling with a blinding bliss. The air kissed her skin, her smile took over her face, and she flew faster and faster.

Conrad paused in his plans, appreciating the miracle and beauty of Piper's flight. She was turning and twisting through the large atrium and skimming across the sides of the building so that she was reflected in the glass.

Not taking his eyes off of the spectacle of Piper McCloud flying, he made himself comfortable at Letitia Hellion's desk and picked up the phone. "Yes, I'd like to speak to Senator Harrington, please." Conrad sat back and put his feet up on the desk.

"I'm sorry, but the senator is not taking calls right now. May I take a message?"

His father had yet another snotty assistant who was once again going to try to give him the runaround. Any other day, they would have been successful. But not today. "Please tell the senator that his son, *Conrad*, is calling. If he can't make time for me now, he will have the opportunity to see me on the six o'clock news, at which time I know he'll make the time to hear what I have to say."

Less than ten frenzied seconds later, Senator Harrington's careful voice was on the line. "Hey, sport. Great to hear from you. Uh . . . is Dr. Hellion there?"

"No, Father, she is not. Nor will Dr. Hellion ever be here again, because I'm now here. And from now on you'll be dealing with me."

Piper zoomed past the experimental laboratory, where she could see Jasper placing his hands on the bent and broken gray giraffe. Moments later a glow brighter than the sun streamed through the windows. Piper laughed out loud as she shielded her eyes from the blinding light.

The giraffe's wattage reached every part of the facility, and for the agents already captured it was yet another bizarre happening on this, their strangest day ever. The scientists and support staff followed the children's demands without resistance and peacefully left their workstations and reported to makeshift detention centers. Only a few agents put up a struggle, and those unlucky fellows were welcomed by Smitty, Kimber, Lily, Boris, Daisy, and Myrtle, itching to hand out a taste of what they'd had to endure over the years.

Much to Kimber's displeasure, by late evening there wasn't a single agent left to wrestle with and her fun was all over. In less than ninety minutes flat, and with remarkable ease, I.N.S.A.N.E. was officially under the control of the kids. Needless to say, their boundless joy was only slightly tempered with chagrin—why had they waited for so long and been so fearful when release had actually been accomplished so effortlessly?

"Making the decision was a whole lot harder than actually doing it." Smitty grinned, picking strawberry seeds out of his teeth. The kids were celebrating their victory in the kitchen with a generous snack. Staging a revolt worked up a healthy appetite. It was soon unanimously decided that their first course of action would be to reach the surface and feel the sun upon their faces.

Nalen and Ahmed immediately volunteered to clear the sky of clouds and they all excitedly boarded the elevator for the journey to the surface.

"Sure wish Bella was here." Piper sadly shook her

head. "She'd have made a rainbow that stretched from here to kingdom come."

The other kids nodded in agreement. There had been many casualties and things that just couldn't be put right, not even under Jasper's hands. Many creatures simply didn't have the strength, after the long weeks and months of torture, to reclaim their abilities. It tempered the triumph of the day with sadness and made the kids appreciate their good fortune all the more.

"Level eight," the computer voice reported, unperturbed by the goings-on of the day.

Despite themselves, the kids felt anxious as they rose to the top. What if something unexpected went wrong again?

"Level six."

"Piper? You think my parents will be happy to see me?" A nervous quiver played with Lily's voice.

Piper didn't want to lie. The truth was that some parents were going to be less than pleased and Lily's very well might fall into that category. "Will you be happy to see them?"

Lily thought before answering. "Yes," she said finally. "Very happy."

"Level five."

"I'm going to run and run and never stop." Myrtle's face shone with excitement. Her remark seemed to unleash the others.

"I'm gonna look right up at the man in the moon and wave to him."

"I'm going to brew up some thundershowers."

"And then some sun."

"And then some wind."

"I'm going to shrink so small that I'll ride on that wind like a leaf."

Giggles and laughter.

"Level three."

Piper looked at Conrad and he smiled. She smiled back. *It was worth it. It was all worth it. There isn't a thing I would change,* Piper thought.

"Level two."

No one moved.

"Level one."

Everyone held their breath.

"You are now exiting the facility. Have a nice day!"

"I programmed her to say that." Conrad shrugged. "It sounds more friendly, don't you think?"

CLICK. Slowly the doors retracted. The lobby was all steel walls and marble floors, as quiet and still as a church. Trembling, they moved forward to embrace their freedom. At the last and final door leading to their release, though, there was hesitation.

"You go first, Piper." Conrad stepped aside and reached for the door to give her first passage. "You deserve it. If it weren't for you, none of us would be here."

"Sure you would. I just told you what you already knew. There wasn't nothing to that."

"There was if we didn't know we knew it," Violet assured her.

"Here goes." Conrad swung the door open wide.

Standing before them, barring the way, and to the shock and horror of all, was none other than Letitia Hellion.

CHAPTER TWENTY

LETITIA HELLION was not poised and definitely not pretty. Clutching a military-grade stun baton in her scratched and bleeding hands, she swung it violently back and forth. Her hair wildly uncoiled out of rigid pins, her clothes were dirty and ripped from a to-the-death struggle to escape her cell, and she sported an insane look in her rolling eyes that was anything but practiced.

"You!!!" Dr. Hellion advanced on Piper menacingly, swinging the baton erratically. Piper instinctively flew several feet into the air and dodged back and forth to avoid the electricity of the baton.

"You will return to your room where you belong. None of you are going anywhere. Get back. Get back." Letitia aimed at Jasper and sent electrical voltage pumping through him. Jasper fell to the floor, out cold.

"Ahh," Lily yelped and jumped back.

Myrtle took advantage of an opening and easily

zipped past Letitia and out through the open doors. Ahmed and Nalen dodged, but Letitia was on a rampage, grabbing and hitting. Kids scattered like frightened mice. Kimber boldly charged forth to battle, but the electricity shooting from her fingers collided with the electricity from the baton and she was short-circuited. In a burst of electrical fireworks Kimber was thrown to the ground, singed and smoking. Conrad took advantage of the commotion to dart out. Daisy was grounded next, like a bull in a slaughterhouse. Piper dodged, but Letitia was supernaturally agile and seized hold of her ankle.

"You can't fly. Do you hear me? You are sick and you need help. I WILL HELP YOU." Letitia dug her feet into the ground to stop Piper from flying away. Piper fought back and propelled her way out of the shack, dragging Letitia's dead weight behind her.

"Please, Dr. Hellion, you gotta let me go." Piper lugged the fighting Dr. Hellion.

Letitia yanked her down with a vengeance.

"I will save you, Piper McCloud, if it's the last thing I do."

Piper pulled up. Letitia pulled down. Little by little, Piper towed Letitia Hellion off of the ground. And while the sky was the one place that Piper felt safe, it was also the only place where she would be unable to receive any help from the others, who remained land bound. Chasing after them in vain, Conrad, Myrtle, and Violet were rendered helpless spectators as Piper ascended out of reach.

"I won't ever let you go. I won't stop. *Ever*." With a failing grasp, Letitia Hellion doggedly held on for all she was worth.

"Ahhh." Piper was being pulled apart like taffy. Win or lose, she would be several inches taller by the time this was done. Piper reached six yards above the ground. Then seven. Then eight.

"Arrrrrrghhhhh." Letitia Hellion roared beneath her, a demon wrestling her back to the clutches of the dark underworld.

Letitia's little finger slipped away from Piper's ankle and she cursed it. The neighboring finger betrayed her next and she damned it. A moment later she could only count on the allegiance of her index finger and thumb to latch firmly around Piper's ankle. But then their loyalty was called into question.

Piper reached ever upward, her eyes only for the sky. Her heart welled with the words.

I'm as light as a cloud, as free as a bird.
I'm part of the sky and I can fly.

Nine yards up. They were quickly reaching the breaking point.

At ten yards the flagging resources of the exhausted index finger and thumb gave out.

Freed, Piper rocketed upward.

"NOOOOOOOO!" Letitia raged with the force of every emotion she'd ever repressed. Which, it must be noted, was a ridiculously large amount. Some might say it was even incalculable. Unleashed, the rejected and abandoned feelings chemically combusted in a cellular firestorm. It was so catastrophic that Letitia Hellion's mind and emotions, long distant strangers, were welded back together. The abrupt reintroduction after such a complete and rigid disassociation was brutal. Like a migraine of the DNA.

"NOOOOOOOOOOOOOOO!!!!!!!" Letitia Hellion directed her pain at Piper McCloud.

Smitty saw it first, as he usually did. "Conrad, are you seeing what I'm seeing?"

Conrad was indeed seeing. All of them were. It was shocking. It was terrible. It could almost not even be explained. And yet, Conrad was somehow not surprised. Everything now made sense.

"Piper, watch out!" Violet screamed.

Piper glanced over her shoulder and was so stunned, she did a double take. *I'll be! That's near about the prettiest thing I ever saw!* At last Piper had found what she'd always been looking for and her first instinct was to stop dead.

Dr. Letitia Hellion could fly.

At that moment Letitia was flying fast and with a burning fervor—it was a sight to behold.

The look of unadulterated rage splashed across Letitia Hellion's face woke Piper from her fantasy of an impromptu fliers reunion, and propelled her to beat a hasty getaway.

"Get back here!" Letitia Hellion stayed on Piper's tail, getting ever closer.

"Dr. Hellion, please. Just let me be." Piper twisted and turned. Their aerial acrobatics took them farther and farther due north, leaving the shack and watching children far behind.

Letitia Hellion flew like the wind—or a demon, depending upon your perspective. She was agile too. It was obvious to Piper that she wasn't going to be able to out-fly or outmaneuver her and that her only chance for escape was in the clouds. Unfortunately, flying through misty clouds is a dangerous proposition. With no visibility, a bird or an icy mountain could strike hard without warning. Not to mention the fact that Dr. Hellion would undoubtedly follow Piper into the white soup, where she would lurk, ready to pounce.

Piper took a sharp left and felt the mist of the cloud closing in around her. She changed her course several times and hovered a good long bit in what she hoped was the center of the cloud. Surrounded by white mist and quiet, Piper felt like she was suspended in a half-sleep state, waiting for a dream, or perhaps a nightmare, to hit her. Thankfully the nightmare was not materializing, and after waiting even longer, Piper tentatively dropped below the cloud, checking for any sign of Dr. Hellion.

What she discovered was an empty sky hanging over a vast expanse of icy cliffs far below. They had flown so far north that the terrain was both treacherous and beautiful. The sun shone off of the ice, making it sparkle like a million diamonds, and jagged cliffs proudly displayed opened jaws of razor-sharp teeth. The sight took Piper's breath away and distracted her for a moment from the imminent danger she was in.

"Don't move!" A wretched voice breathed in her ear. An iron grasp clamped down on her shoulder.

Piper braced for the worst as Dr. Hellion spun her so that they were face-to-face. Dr. Hellion's hair had been completely blown out during her flight and was strangely wild and beautiful.

Without thinking, Piper said the first thing that came into her mind. "Dr. Hellion, could you teach me to fly like that? I bet you're the best flier ever. Fastest too."

"You didn't practice enough," Dr. Hellion snapped. "Your turns are sloppy."

"Maybe if you showed me how—"

"You won't accomplish anything until you keep your

arms tightly in formation and your legs straight. Your left knee keeps bending out."

"Will you teach me to fly backward too?"

"Fly? Teach you to fly?" Suddenly concern knitted Letitia's brow. "You can't fly. It's not possible."

"But, Dr. Hellion . . . we're both flying. See?"

Jolted, Dr. Hellion looked around, and for the first time noticed that she was hovering several hundred feet in the air. What's more, she found she liked it up there. A lot.

"Yes, I can fly," she realized slowly. "And I'm good at it too. *Damn good.*"

Piper giggled and suddenly Dr. Hellion did too. The giggling grew.

"I don't know why I didn't remember before," Dr. Hellion said between her giggles. "It's fun, isn't it?"

"Most fun I ever had," Piper agreed.

"When I was a girl, I used to wake up in the middle of the night just so I could fly through the stars." The memory tickled Letitia. "But that was before Sarah and I . . ." A jumble of memories surfaced all at once—*pop, pop, pop.* "Sarah was my younger sister. She couldn't fly, but she used to love watching me." Letitia paused, remembering even more. "It was just so lonely in the sky. Do you know what I mean?"

Indeed, Piper knew exactly what Letitia meant. You yearn to share the joy of the sky when you are flying, because it's so awesomely beautiful.

"My parents told me not to, but Sarah and I didn't listen. She wanted to see the world from up high as much as I wanted to show it to her, and so we snuck off, the two of us, and did it one day." Letitia was no longer aware of Piper as her memories ran away with her. "Oh, what a day it was too! Glorious. Sunny, warm. There were only a few clouds in the sky, but it was like a picture postcard. Beautiful. I hadn't ever carried anyone, and Sarah was heavier than I thought. Much heavier. But we managed it and it was so . . . it was everything we both thought it was going to be. Sarah kept pointing at things and shouting, 'Look, Lettie, look at that cloud.' 'Lettie, go faster, go faster.' " Dr. Hellion smiled as though she were flying with Sarah that very moment. "It was like seeing the sky for the first time again too.

"I guess I had been distracted in all the excitement because we were already over the canyon before I noticed that a strong wind had blown in. And then I saw the clouds, dark clouds—thunderclouds. The storm started like that." She snapped her fingers sharply and Piper's eyes grew wide. "The rain was so heavy. And I was so high off the ground. Sarah started to slip and I grabbed her—tightly. She was screaming. She was so scared—we both were. I tried to fly down as fast as I could and I was holding her tightly. Really tightly."

Dr. Hellion held up her hand as though Sarah's hand

was still in it. "She was gone in an instant. Gone. She just slipped away." Dr. Hellion's hands clenched shut, empty.

Piper was aghast.

Letitia Hellion's chest heaved up and down from the terrible memories. Tears came to her eyes and she looked into Piper's face helplessly. "I can't," she whispered, and for the first time in as long as Letitia Hellion could remember, she showed someone her real face. What Piper saw there was fragile and vulnerable and scared. "Flying is wrong, Piper. I just can't do it."

Instantaneously, Letitia Hellion dropped like a stone and free-fell toward the earth.

"Dr. Hellion!" Piper swooped downward, grabbing Letitia's arms and trying to hold her up. "What are you doing? You have to fly."

"It's not possible. Flying is wrong. Abnormal. Humans can't fly." Letitia tried to pry Piper's arms away, fighting her. They descended rapidly.

"Please, Dr. Hellion. Please. You're gonna fall. You gotta fly." Piper was struggling to hold Dr. Hellion's weight, but she was too heavy and resisted any attempts Piper made.

"I won't be like you. I'm not like you. Let go of me. Don't touch me!" Dr. Hellion madly scratched and hit at Piper as they tumbled to the earth. In a last-ditch effort to hold Dr. Hellion up, Piper grabbed her right hand and pulled with all of her might. Dr. Hellion pulled away with an even greater might.

They stayed that way, suspended between the heavens and earth for a short while, Dr. Hellion insistently struggling to be released and Piper holding her. First Dr. Hellion's little finger slipped out of Piper's grasp—then the finger next to it.

"Dr. Hellion, please. Stay."

"Let go of me, Piper McCloud. I'm not like you. I can't fly."

"But you can. I just saw you."

"No. No." Dr. Hellion violently shook her head and her middle finger released itself from Piper's hold. "Let me go."

"But, Dr. Hellion, I don't wanna be alone up here. Just hold tight to me. Don't let go." Piper struggled to hold Dr. Hellion while she struggled to think of a way to convince her to fly. "Dr. Hellion, please—I need you . . . stay with me. Fly with me."

Piper prayed every word, but in the end there's no saving someone who won't be saved. When her two remaining fingers slid out of Piper's hand, Letitia Hellion fell without sound to the icy cliffs below, and Piper turned away, unable to watch.

Once again, Piper McCloud was alone in a blue sky—defeated and triumphant in equal measure.

CHAPTER TWENTY-ONE

ROW UPON row of freshly ploughed soil had been painstakingly planted already that day and it pleased Joe that all signs were pointing to a good crop. When the snows fell that year, he and Betty would have more than enough to last the winter. At the house, Betty stepped onto the porch and rang the old bell. Joe then obediently put down his tools and led the old mare back to the barn for lunch. Pausing in the yard to wipe the dust from his homespun shirt, something unusual in the distance caught Joe's eye, so much so that he stood there for a while, watching it grow larger and larger.

In the kitchen, Joe's transfixed form became a source of irritation to Betty, who had a ladies' auxiliary meeting that afternoon and a schedule that didn't allow for any dilly-dallying. In short order she bustled to the door. "Mr. McCloud, lunch is on."

Still Joe didn't move and Betty followed his gaze and

saw what he saw. Using her hand to shield the sun from her eyes, Betty shuffled next to Joe and watched with the same mute anticipation.

At first it appeared to be nothing but a black dot, and then it grew to what could possibly be a bird, and then it grew further until there was no mistaking the fact that their girl was returning home to them.

From up high in the sky, the sight of familiar trees, rivers, and farmlands was a welcome sight to Piper, filling her with gladness and peace. At last, she was back where she belonged. Everything was exactly as it had been before she left it, indeed as it always had been since her birth. It was as if no time at all had passed since Dr. Hellion had taken her away in the helicopter, and even her ma and pa were in exactly the same positions that she'd last seen them in.

Gently descending, Piper set her feet down in the dirt at the edge of the yard and suddenly felt nervous. Were her ma and pa going to be sore at her for flying? Was she going to get into trouble and sent to her room? Maybe they hadn't missed her and didn't want her back at all? The fact that Betty and Joe stood stock-still with expressionless faces did nothing to settle her ever-increasing nervousness.

"I'm home," Piper spoke finally, kicking her toe into the dirt.

Betty nodded. "I expect we can see that well enough."

It had been a very long journey back, and for most of it Piper had practiced what she was going to say next. Taking a deep breath for courage, she began quickly.

"You see, thing is that I fly and I like it and I'm not gonna stop. And I'm real sorry that it's not to your liking. Trouble is that there isn't anything else that makes sense to me like flying does." Piper paused before she got to the hard part and took another deep breath. "So I don't wanna hide it anymore and I don't wanna sneak off to the back field. Even if you won't like it, I'm not gonna lie about it anymore and I'm not gonna do it on the sly. And, well . . . that's all I have to say."

Betty sniffed. "Well, me and your pa ain't gonna lie to you none neither, we don't take to this flying much. It just ain't the way of things for youngens to be gadding about in the sky like that." Betty looked like she was on the verge of launching into another lecture on the evils of flying, and with only the greatest effort did she managed to rein herself in. Like Piper, she took a deep breath before continuing. "But we had a good spell to think things over and we figure as long as you do your chores and act as the good Lord would want, we'll just have to take you as you was made."

For Betty's and Joe's entire lives, and the lives of their

parents and grandparents and great-grandparents, and so on and so on for as long as anyone in Lowland County could remember, on those twenty acres of land, things had always been the same. Yet today Betty and Joe had taken their very first tentative step toward something different. It was nothing short of earth-shattering and no one could appreciate the incredible sacrifice more than Piper.

Rushing forward, Piper threw herself into her ma's and pa's arms. "Ma, I missed you so much. Pa, I still got my bird, look." Betty and Joe held their daughter tight.

"It weren't the same without you, child." Joe held Piper tightly. "We're powerful happy to have you back."

Betty didn't attend the ladies' auxiliary meeting that day, and after lunch Joe did not return to the fields. Instead Betty and Joe sat down, and Piper talked and told them all about her adventures. She told them almost everything and they listened with wonder and with fear, glad to have their girl back safe and sound. Not once did Betty reprimand Piper for talking too much, so grateful were they to have her lively voice fill the house once more. Piper talked into the night and Betty made her fried chicken and her prized apple pie for dinner, even though it wasn't Sunday.

"I always knew it. Them McClouds is flighty and un-reliable," Millie Mae Miller declared at the ladies' auxiliary that afternoon when Betty's absence was duly noted. It marked the only time in the thirty years since she first joined that Betty had failed to show up. "Can't say I didn't see it coming."

A week after Piper's return, a new member quietly arrived to join the community of Lowland County. It had always been Betty and Joe's plan to have a house full of youngens, not to mention the fact that a man can't help but long for a son, so they welcomed Conrad into their home with open arms. Conrad wasn't quite what Joe might have expected a son to be. However, both Joe and Betty had started to develop a taste for things not being as they had always been on the farm.

It had been at Piper's insistence that Conrad come and stay, and he had been extremely reticent. When he finally did arrive, Piper showed him around the place, overjoyed.

"This is your room." Piper pulled Conrad into a small, plain room next to the one she slept in. "See here, look." She threw open an old window overlooking green fields. "You've got a great view of the sunrise. And Ma put the new quilt on your bed and Pa made this desk for you 'cause I told him you like to sit and think up stuff."

The room was simple and humble, which was why Conrad found himself surprised by feelings of extreme gratitude and thankfulness. His parents had given him the best of everything and yet it had always struck him as meaningless junk. Betty and Joe had given him next to nothing but each item was bestowed with such care and consideration that it was almost painful for him to accept their generosity. From the moment he set foot on the farm, they opened their house and their arms to him, a virtual stranger, with full hearts. Until Piper, Conrad had never met people who gave with such simple kindness, expecting absolutely nothing in return. In contrast, it was only with threats of a public scandal that Conrad had been able to get his father on the phone at all. Even then, Senator Harrington had not been pleased.

"What is it, Conrad? I don't have time for this," he'd snapped when Conrad had called from Letitia Hellion's office.

"This call is a courtesy, Father. I'm happy to go to the press first," Conrad fired back.

Senator Harrington simmered down and found courtesy for his tone. "I'm listening."

"We've taken over the facility. Dr. Hellion is no longer in charge. I'm going to expose what is going on here, and I have documentation that proves that you were not only aware of it, but supported it. By my calculation, a conservative estimate of the laws being broken by Dr. Hellion numbers close to twenty. Including murder."

"Murder?" The senator's full attention was now focused on his son.

"And you have aided and abetted Dr. Hellion, which makes you an accessory to the crime." Conrad knew that this could easily take down his entire family. His father's icy silence on the other end of the line only confirmed the weight of his threats.

"What do you want?"

"You'll use your connections and influence to get approval today for the facility to be under your authority. As soon as you have the authority, you'll turn it over to me. We'll be running it from now on and you'll see to it that no one interferes with us or gets in our way."

"Connie, that's impossible. I'd need to get approval from the Joint Chiefs of Staff. I'll need—"

"Then do it. I'll expect confirmation by the end of the day." When his father had called back, Conrad didn't take his first call, or his second or third or even fourth. He waited until the messages became increasingly more urgent before finally picking up the phone.

"It's done." Senator Harrington had used every favor, every influence, every means available to him by dint of his family, his position, and his wealth to pull off the impossible, just as Conrad knew he would. Unfortunately, there was a caveat, and one Conrad had not been expecting. "But—" The Senator let the word hang in the air.

"But what?" Conrad prompted.

"The deal comes off the table unless you agree to one condition."

"You're in no position to negotiate with me, Father."

"This is nonnegotiable. You get everything you want on the condition that you never contact me or your mother again. We never want to hear from you or see you and you can no longer use the Harrington name. You are no longer our son."

"I see." Conrad's face crumpled and he bit his lip to keep from making a sound. This hurt, hurt so much. "Father . . . ?" Conrad stopped himself, taking a deep breath. How was he to beg his father to be his father? How was he to say all of the things he wanted to say before he no longer had a father and effectively became an orphan? In the end there were no words.

"I agree."

The minute the words were out of Conrad's mouth, the line went dead. The man who used to be his father had hung up and Conrad entered a new life where he was just plain Conrad and no longer Conrad Harrington III.

Tucked up in a tiny room in Lowland County, day by day, Conrad established himself in his new life, where he was expected to do chores every day and was served up three square meals of good country fare. He grew to like it.

It was a good thing that Joe and Betty had taken their

first tentative steps in accepting change, because Conrad pushed them to their limits and beyond.

"You don't say." Joe shook his head, his brow furrowed.

Conrad pointed to a detailed diagram of the twenty acres of land the McClouds owned. It included charts and graphs. "By planting an early wheat crop and then alternating with corn and barley you can get three crops in one season per field. In addition, I have engineered this hybrid seed that produces three times the bounty and twice the weight. You'll be able to harvest the same crops as a two-hundred-acre farm with no additional man power."

Joe shook his head in amazement. Holding up the seed that Conrad presented to him, he turned it over in his hand. "McClouds ain't never done that before." He considered Conrad's words, looking out over his fields, and shrugged. "Ain't no harm in trying it out, though, I guess."

Conrad smiled and Joe put his arm around him. Betty rang the bell for dinner and they walked together through the field and across the farmyard to the house. Since Conrad had the house wired for high-speed Internet and built a supercomputer in the kitchen, mealtimes had become an adventure. Conrad and Joe entered the kitchen to find that Betty had been busy downloading recipes, and Moroccan food was on the menu for the evening. Couscous and spiced lamb waited on the table, and Piper excitedly sipped mint tea.

"Wash your hands, Conrad. Sit yourself down, Joe, or the kebabs will get cold." Betty busily passed around a plate of exotically spiced carrots and lentils. "Wouldn't you know it but Piper's got some news to tell and I made her hold off so that we could all enjoy it."

"You'll never guess," Piper burst forth, unable to contain herself any longer. "Smitty cracked that big case. He caught the guys with the virus bomb holed up in an old bank vault in Times Square, so that virus can't hurt anyone now. They're making him a first-class detective, youngest one ever. Isn't that something?"

Betty sniffed and shook her head. "Don't know what the world is coming to when folks is running around with a bit of virus in a bottle and threatening to make folks sick with it. I'm sure glad we don't got any of 'em here in Lowland County."

"Smitty said that in New York, they got more criminals than anywhere else and he couldn't be happier about it. He says that there just aren't enough hours in the day for all he has to do." Like many of the kids, Smitty had the difficult task of balancing his schoolwork with his exciting new job. It wasn't easy, but he couldn't have been more fulfilled. Smitty was also one of the lucky ones whose parents welcomed him back with open arms.

"Smitty says that just the other night he went to Cirque du Soleil to see Kimber's show and it was sold out," Piper continued. "Folks can't get enough of her new act and he says she's got more voltage in her fingertips than ever."

"Did Smitty apologize?" Conrad asked between mouthfuls. As per usual, Smitty and Kimber were in the middle of one of their fights. This one started when Kimber caught Smitty, yet again, looking at her underwear, and she'd pumped thirty thousand volts into his left leg. Smitty, of course, pleaded his innocence, but Kimber didn't believe a word of it.

"Well, Kimber says that she won't forget but she'll forgive. Ahmed and Nalen got rid of that tropical storm that was turning into a hurricane off of Cape Canaveral too. They say that now they have the hang of it, there's nothing to it, and they can't wait to try their hands at a tsunami. Anyway, Lily landed easy as pie. She told me that after the third or fourth time up to the moon, it's no different than going to the corner store. She took more pictures for me just the same. Oh, and Myrtle and Daisy faxed that report you wanted, Conrad." Piper pointed to a stack of papers on the counter.

Conrad immediately rose from his seat, but Betty fixed a stern finger on him. "Not 'til you finished up your supper, young man. You knows better than that by now."

Smiling, Conrad sat down. He might be a supergenius, but he knew better than to cross Betty McCloud when she got that look in her eye.

"Daisy says that new alligator, the one Violet brought back from that tomb in Egypt, got stuck when he was metamorphizing between a snake and an alligator. He had the head of an alligator and the body of a snake, but was as mad as a hornet. Myrtle fetched Jasper at the Moscow Zoo, where he was healing a sick polar bear, and Jasper came right back and cured him. He said it was just a bad case of indigestion."

Ever since Daisy and Myrtle had taken over running the institute, things had changed drastically. It was decided that the institute would no longer imprison any life-form, but instead provide a safe haven only for those who required assistance or protection. It was also going to direct the vast equipment and research facilities at its disposal to the creation of scientific advances that would benefit all creatures, whether normal or not.

Unfortunately, very few of the inhabitants could be immediately released back to their original homes because they were simply too weak or damaged from Dr. Hellion's ministrations. Conrad devised a program to wean the drugs out of their systems while Daisy and Myrtle supervised the scientists, who were now tasked with rehabilitating the various creatures and retraining them in their talents. For many, the damage had been great and it was going to be a slow process. Myrtle and Daisy, who were overseeing every step and reporting back to Conrad, were relentless in their efforts to save each and every one.

Every time a rose reclaimed its bloom or a leaping turtle regained the spring in its step, it was a great cause for celebration. Myrtle was, more often than not, the one who ran across the globe to deliver the healed plant or animal back to its home. She was also the one to complete weekly, and then monthly, checkups to make sure that it was flourishing back in its natural habitat.

Conrad took a keen interest in every aspect of the daily reports and ensured that the true nature of the facility was being carefully concealed from the rest of the world. Before Conrad would even consider letting any of the kids leave I.N.S.A.N.E., he instructed them on the arts of discretion, much to Kimber's chagrin.

"I can do what I want. Who do you think you are, Dr. Hellion?" Kimber snapped.

"No, I think I'm the person who is trying to stop someone like Dr. Hellion from catching us again. The fact of the matter is, Kimber, that we scare a lot of people. They don't know what to do with us. So all I'm asking you to do is to give them an explanation that they can understand when you have to, and don't tell them about it when you don't. I'm not asking you to hide, I'm telling you not to flaunt it."

Conrad had finally won them over, and when newspaper reporters pressed Kimber for details on the amazing special effects she used in her circus act, she smiled tightly and said, "No comment." Conrad had negotiated ironclad employment agreements for the others that ensured their protection and privacy. It was an uneasy and potentially dangerous situation, and Conrad kept a close eye on them all to make sure that no one was suddenly going to find themselves on the front page of the *New York Times*, or the top story on the six o'clock news.

While much progress had been made, it was by no means a perfect solution and was potentially fraught with peril. Indeed, it weighed heavily on Conrad's mind, and a few months later, when the kids all gathered at the farm for a little rest and relaxation, he made a point of watching them closely to see what progress they had made. As it turned out, he wasn't the only one.

"There's something that ain't right about all them kids," Millie Mae Miller confidentially sniffed to the minister's wife. The Fourth of July picnic was in full swing and Millie Mae had cornered the poor woman under the trees. "Have you ever seen the likes of it?" She pointed her finger accusingly.

The minister's wife nervously cleared her throat.

"True, they ain't from around these parts but . . . they're just children all the same. Don'tcha think?"

Millie Mae was fit to be tied and squinted her eyes suspiciously. She couldn't put her finger on it, but something was definitely going on. Over a year ago those fancy suit-types from the institute had explained to the folks of Lowland County that Piper McCloud had played a trick on them and that she couldn't fly at all. They had called it an optical illusion and said they were going to take the naughty girl away for a while to teach her not to play such tricks. Millie Mae Miller wanted to make sure that Piper McCloud wasn't up to her old hijinks, because she, for one, wouldn't stand for it.

With no real evidence, Millie Mae resorted to grasping at straws. "Did I tell you that they wouldn't even give my Sally Sue the time of day?" She spat. "Sally Sue was standing next to 'em in line and they didn't say so much as 'howdy do.' Rude, is what that is. Bad manners. I'm telling you, I ain't never seen the likes of it." Millie Mae crossed her arms in front of her chest. "But they'll get what's coming to 'em. It's always the way."

Millie Mae waited all day for the strange group of youngens under Betty and Joe McCloud's care to get 'what was coming to 'em,' to no avail. When the baseball game was called to order, she licked her lips, certain that their just desserts would be quickly served up.

321

The shouting, pushing, and pulling had the normal result of producing two team leaders, but that year there was a strange name in the roster—Rory Ray Miller and *Conrad*. It wasn't because Conrad could outthink, out-argue, or out-anything that he scared the bejesus out of everyone in Lowland County. No, their fear was generated for reasons that they couldn't quite put their finger on, and which prompted them to cut the boy a wide berth. It was for that same reason that Conrad claimed the first draft pick and was quick to snap up the best player in the bunch.

"Piper McCloud."

Piper moved out of the waiting kids with her head held high and joined Conrad's team.

"Jimmie Joe," Rory Ray shouted.

"Lily Yakimoto."

"Junie Jane."

"Ahmed Mustafa."

"Billy Bob."

Like the rest of Lowland County, Betty and Joe enjoyed the baseball game on the side of the hill, and perhaps cheered louder than any of the other parents. It was a joy for them to see Piper so happy and to have such good friends. They'd watched her all day, laughing and playing. She'd taught Violet to do the jig, and then the two girls had laughed so hard under the trees that their stomachs hurt. Pretty much, they'd spent the whole day laughing, so much so that Violet had spilled strawberry ice cream down the front of her dress. This only made them laugh harder.

Betty could see how much Piper had changed in the last year. Just the week before, Betty had suggested that Piper might like to attend the local school. To her surprise, Piper didn't think on it long before solemnly telling Betty that she'd had enough schooling for the time being and wasn't much interested in going to school anymore. And that wasn't the only change. There were places and parts of Piper that she kept closed now, and things she didn't talk about. She was more thoughtful and there were periods when she became very silent, like she was deeply grieving something that Betty could only guess at. Betty knew that Piper hadn't told her everything that had gone on at the institute and Betty guessed that there was a good reason for that too. As a parent, she wanted to know everything, but some things are just too difficult to know. Betty was careful not to press Piper for information further than she was willing to volunteer, and took note of the fact that there was a knowledge and understanding that had grown in her child's eyes that spoke of wisdom.

But most of the time, like today, Piper was just like she'd always been, which is to say that Piper was full of life and bursting to meet the challenges before her.

"CATCH THE BALL, PIPER!"

Billy Bob hit a doozie. The ball climbed and climbed.

Piper shot Lily a meaningful glance and Lily responded with a mischievous smile. Piper then held her baseball glove calmly above her head and waited for the ball to drop into it. To the startled eyes of the spectators, not to mention the opposing team, it did.

"Awww, man!" Rory Ray sulked. His team threw their hats to the ground and Junie Jane used a few choice words.

Try as she might, Millie Mae couldn't actually point to a single thing that Piper or anyone else on her team was doing that was out of the ordinary. Sure, it was bad luck that every time someone on Rory Ray's team was up to bat they had blinding sunlight in their eyes or a suspicious wind roaring past. Not to mention the fact that there was one time that Piper McCloud seemed to linger in the air a bit longer than most kids might when she caught a ball. And even Millie Mae had to admit that the girl could jump amazingly high.

Of course, when Myrtle was running, Millie Mae did whisper that the girl was a "ringer." There were other things that just irritated her, like the fact that the big girl, Daisy, kept breaking both the bat and the ball, and that every time Kimber hit the ball it had a strange electrical charge on it that caused the unlucky person who caught it to immediately release it. And Conrad, well, even

Millie Mae Miller knew her limits and wasn't about to take him on.

As the sun began to set over Lowland County, Betty and Joe rose to their feet and cheered loudly for the winning baseball team. For Piper, Conrad, and all of the others, it was a victory, but not over the opposing team. It was the first time that they had played with other children and had not been ostracized or fled from in fear. It was the first time that they had been accepted by their friends for what they were, while being able to strike some sort of balance, however uneasy, with the outside world. A triumph indeed.

Betty and Joe packed the lot of them back to the farm after that. There was only so much scrutiny from Millie Mae that Betty's nerves could take. The rest of the day was spent away from all of the prying eyes, in the fields and pastures of the farm, where the games played were anything but normal.

That night Conrad found Piper quietly by herself on the roof of the house, enjoying a sky full of stars.

"It was fun today, huh?" For once Conrad actually sounded his age.

Piper smiled and nodded.

"You coming back inside? Violet said she could shrink smaller than a teacup and Smitty bet Kimber twenty bucks she couldn't."

"She can."

"I know. But Smitty and Kimber will get into a fight about it anyway and that'll be hysterical." Conrad laughed.

"True."

Sensing that there was something on Piper's mind, Conrad sat quietly next to her. Piper's eyes went back to the stars and Conrad noticed that she had been covering her stomach with her hands as though she wasn't feeling well. When her hands came down to her lap, he was surprised to see the linen handkerchief embroidered with small bluebirds clutched between her fingers.

"J. was here." Conrad was not asking a question.

"He just left." As he'd promised, J. had come back for Piper and had returned her handkerchief to her. He was exactly the way Piper had remembered him too: harried, with hair-trigger nerves and no time for small talk. "J. wants to take us away from here. He says that it's still not safe and he has some vital information to share with us."

"Safe from what, specifically? And what kind of information?" Conrad had read Letitia Hellion's file on J. It was extensive in specifics, but bereft of essentials, such as any psychological analysis or background information, which would indicate what was driving J. with such relentless and overwhelming passion. Until Conrad could learn more about this mysterious invisible man he was extremely wary of J.'s motives, regardless of the fact that all indications pointed to his benevolence. "Did he try to force you to leave with him?"

"No, of course not. He said something about a place that was hidden. It's far away and it's secret. He said we'd belong there. Do you think we should go?"

Conrad's mind raced in every direction at once, analyzing the information from all conceivable angles.

Piper was instantly sorry to see the carefree boyish quality vanish, after emerging on Conrad's face over the last few weeks on the farm. It was replaced by a deathly seriousness and slight anxiety, which she knew all too well. This was not what Piper wanted at all. After all that they'd been through, and all that they'd accomplished, surely they deserved a small respite to relax and appreciate their good fortune. And surely, there would be time— time for planning and understanding and for her to explain to him the many other things that J. had told her. But sitting on the roof under the stars, after such a delicious day, was definitely not that time, Piper decided.

"Conrad?"

"Um-hmmm."

"We did real good, huh?"

"Hmmmm?"

"Everything worked out. Everyone's real happy and . . . I mean, I know it's not perfect, but what's perfect? Right?"

"What are you trying to say?"

"Remember how mean you were when we first met?" Piper laughed and Conrad smiled and tentatively relaxed. "Boy, did you ever have everyone fooled 'cause you're about the nicest person I ever met." Conrad blushed. "That got me to thinking how Dr. Hellion seemed nice but was actually mean, but then it turned out she was just real sad. Ever wonder why there're so many sad and scared people out there? I always wanted to teach people to fly, but I don't wanna do that no more. Flying's alright but if I had the chance, I'd teach 'em to be happy instead. You know? You think you can teach someone to be happy?"

That was something Conrad had never thought about before. It relaxed him to consider the subject and he leaned back against the shingles and shrugged. "You got me there, Piper. I don't know."

"Bet you can."

"I wouldn't put anything past you, Piper McCloud."

Piper smiled at Conrad and let herself slide off of the roof. A moment later she took to the night air, gliding upward to the stars.

ACKNOWLEDGMENTS

There are so many people to thank. . . .

My dear husband, Wayne, who has stood by and watched me muddle through this process.

Roger Corman, who liked the idea in the first place, and Frances Doel, whose gentle hand first guided me through the craft of storytelling.

Dan Rabinow at ICM, for his nonstop enthusiasm and support, and Richard Abate, for fighting so hard.

Dean Georgaris and John Goldwyn, for asking me to take the story in new directions—it was a journey that served me well, even though it ultimately led me back home again.

Jean Feiwel, who deeply understood the story and gave it endless time and meticulous attention.

But mainly and mostly, I wish to thank Marta and Thomas, who were with me through the dark nights— reading, rereading, and then reading yet again everything I wrote. Without fail, you were understanding, encouraging, and enthusiastic, and there is no doubt in my mind that I couldn't have done it without you.